Sherlock Holmes

and the

Mysteries

of the

Chess World

Lenny Cavallaro

Foreword by Andy Soltis

2022
Russell Enterprises, Inc.
Portsmouth, NH USA

Sherlock Holmes and the Mysteries of the Chess World
by Lenny Cavallaro

ISBN: 978-1-949859-51-5 (print)
ISBN: 978-1-949859-52-2 (eBook)

Published by:
Russell Enterprises, Inc.
P.O. Box 332
Portsmouth, NH 03802 USA

http://www.russell-enterprises.com
info@russell-enterprises.com

Cover by Molly K. Scanlon

Photos: Page 128 courtesy Susan Polgar; page 158 reprinted with permission from the Historical Society of Pennsylvania; all others from the Russell Enterprises archives.

Printed in the United States of America

Table of Contents

Author's Preface

For a brief period in the late 1850s, Paul Morphy completely dominated the chess world, defeating every opponent he faced by an overwhelming margin. Among his matches was a convincing 8-3 (+7-2=2) triumph over Adolph Anderssen, who had won the first international chess tournament in London in 1851 and thereby (according to one of the event's organizers) garnered "the baton of World's Chess Champion." By virtue of his victory, Morphy thus deserves recognition as an "unofficial" world champion.

Of course, the Morphy saga did not end happily. Within a matter of months, he had returned to the United States, and he more or less abandoned chess shortly thereafter. His law career failed, and after the Civil War, his greatest battles were with mental health issues, rather than opponents either over the board or in a court of law. His death came at age forty-seven from an apparent stroke, almost surely precipitated by the cool bath he took after a walk in the mid-day sun during a heat wave.

Circumstances surrounding the death of Alexander Alekhine are indeed more controversial. He presumably strangled on a piece of meat that had become lodged in his throat. However, many have speculated that the world champion may in fact have been murdered, and we can indeed find plenty of evidence of a likely cover-up by Portuguese authorities.

In many ways the career (and decline) of Bobby Fischer, who had electrified the chess world by winning the championship in 1972, echoed that of Paul Morphy. Like Morphy, he withdrew from the game almost completely, although he did have a rather pathetic "revenge match" with Spassky twenty years later—an event that showed how much he had declined, and one that also left him with an outstanding arrest warrant for defying President Bush's Executive Order 12810 (in support of sanctions against anyone "engaging in economic activities" in the former Yugoslavia). His anti-Semitic diatribes and other political tirades can be heard on YouTube and warrant no further discussion. He died in Iceland in 2008, and his death was unequivocally attributed to renal failure.

The Lasker-Schlechter match of 1910 continues to provoke debate. Leading 5-4 in a ten-game match, the challenger—known as "the drawing master"—needed only a draw to wrest the title from Lasker. Nevertheless, he played rather aggressively, squandered a won position, failed to hold the draw, and had to settle for a 5-5 tie. Was this merely a case of "nerves," or was there perhaps more to the story?

The brilliant Harry Nelson Pillsbury shocked the chess world when he came out of nowhere to capture the 1895 chess tournament at Hastings, which was one the strongest of the nineteenth century. Later that year he played in an even stronger event in St. Petersburg (1895-96) and led the field midway through. However, he finished miserably, with three draws and six losses, and his career fizzled. His death ten years later was attributed to "general paresis" (i.e., syphilis), yet some believed his demise was caused by a penchant for simultaneous exhibitions (chess, blindfold chess, checkers, whist, and sometimes combinations thereof!) as well as a number of extraordinary memory stunts. No less a figure than former world champion Mikhail Botvinnik cautioned against overtaxing one's mental resources. Could blindfold chess, like boxing, present the risk of potential damage to the brain?

For nearly eight years (1985-93) Viktor Korchnoi engaged in a very unusual chess exhibition. His opponent was Géza Maróczy, the Hungarian grandmaster, who had died in 1951 but was now being "channeled" by Robert Rollans, a spiritual medium. Did this game indeed confirm the survival of consciousness beyond death?

The final entry does not involve an historical champion or leading challenger for the world title. The chess players are all totally fictitious. They include a brilliant woman grandmaster, poised to challenge for the world championship, until her life is tragically cut short by an automobile accident. Another is her fiancé, whom she has taught the game. After her death, the latter—a hopeless "patzer" rated in the 1200-1300 range—begins an unstoppable rise through the ranks. When he earns grandmaster norms in two tournaments, winning the second, FIDE (the international body that governs chess competition) becomes suspicious. Who better to unravel this mystery than the redoubtable Sherlock Holmes?

I should append that I use three generations of Holmeses (including Holmes Jr. and Holmes III). The original Watson appears, as do his son, grandson, two of his great-grandsons, and his great-great granddaughter.

The "conclusions" Holmes reaches are certainly reasonable, although the author must caution readers not to take any of these cases too seriously. Holmes's thoughts on the Lasker-Schlechter match are probably as good as anyone's, but unless and until further documentation materializes, we shall never know. The death of Alekhine was and remains highly suspicious, and the "official" story seems shaky, to say the least. The other tales, including the interpretation of the Korchnoi-Maróczy contest, are merely speculative.

With these preliminary words, the author can now start the clock and let the various incarnations of Sherlock Holmes make their moves!

Lenny Cavallaro
Methuen, Massachusetts
July 2022

Foreword

Chessplayers are not known for their love of fiction, even chess-themed fiction. But there are a few genres that have an enduring appeal to players. One is science fiction. There is a remarkable literature of chess-themed sci-fi novels, short stories and TV scripts. Much less explored is the nexus of chess and Sherlock Holmes.

Most of the small stock of Holmesian chess fiction relies on the detective's famous logic and personality. The actual chess content varies widely. There are diagrams in few of them. A notable exception is the retrograde analysis problems of Raymond Smullyan's *The Chess Mysteries of Sherlock Holmes*.

Another realm of Holmes/chess fiction touches on chess history. In *The Moriarty Gambit* the celebrated sci-fi writer Fritz Lieber has Holmes beat his arch-enemy during the great London 1883 tournament. Other writers have imagined Holmes posing as Harry Pillsbury in winning Hastings 1895 or the mysterious Colonel Moreau in his disastrous performance at Monte Carlo 1903. Holmes-the-player is either super-player or a patzer.

This book is different. It is a collection of Holmes mysteries in which he does what Arthur Conan Doyle had him do best: He solves murders and other deaths. He provides plausible—and more than plausible—explanations of events that have puzzled chess fans for well over a century.

Another novel aspect of this book: Holmers and his descendants are not limited to the Victorian era in which Conan Doyle placed him. Hollywood made Holmes more of a contemporary when he battled Nazis and other villains in the 1940s. Neither Holmes 2.0 nor 3.0 is a much greater a stretch when he solves mysteries in the late 20th century.

I look forward to new Holmes stories with a chess theme. There are many potential plots and subjects: Could he determine for certain how Leonid Stein died? It happened under suspect conditions, just before Stein was to travel to the West, amid speculation that he would defect and play a match with Bobby Fischer. Dr. Watson would, of course, provide invaluable medical insight.

And perhaps there is a serial chess killer for Holmes to catch. After all, isn't it strange that the great Hypermoderns – Gyula Breyer, Richard Réti and Aron Nimzovich – all died relatively young? Perhaps there was a disciple of Siegbert Tarrasch who wanted revenge for the assault on classical chess teaching.

I included Tarrasch as a character when I tried writing Holmes stories for my *Chess Life* columns many years ago. In one of them, I had Tarrasch explain why chess players make good, manic villains. "Chess, like love and music," he said, "has the power to make men crazy."

Andy Soltis
New York
July 2022

Dedication

To my son, Jacob Alan Wax Cavallaro.

Acknowledgments

First and foremost, I must mention my friend, the late Bob Long, who noticed the 62-year coincidence: the time gap between the deaths of the three champions (1884, 1946, 2008).

The late international master Danny Kopec strenuously urged me to write more about chess, and his encouragement also prompted me to update the Korchnoi saga, ultimately publishing *Superstition and Sabotage: Viktor Korchnoi's Quest for Immortality*, which includes the earlier *Persona Non Grata*.

Larry Tapper, a friend I have known since elementary school, found the anagram that helps Holmes solve the Bobby Fischer case.

When I was floundering for more "mysteries," Hanon Russell suggested Harry Nelson Pillsbury, whom I would otherwise have rejected out-of-hand.

Hanon also put me in touch with his brother, Reuven Russell, who provided some key information about the mission of the *ibbur*.

I shall also thank Al Lawrence, the marvelous editor who worked on this project.

Finally, I must express gratitude to my fiancée, Thuy Dang, who has listened so patiently to my ramblings about this and other literary ventures over the years.

Family Trees

The Watson Family

Dr. John Hamish Watson (the original) was born in 1852.

Dr. John Joseph Watson (his son) was born in 1886. He and his wife had two children:

Sandra Watson, who was born in 1923 and does not appear in any of these tales, and

Dr. John Michael Watson (the original's grandson), who was born in 1920. He and his wife, Martha, had two children:

Dr. John Simon Watson, who was born in 1952, and

Deborah Watson, who was born in 1954 and does not appear in any of these tales.

Rabbi Solomon Rosenbaum, son of Sandra Watson and Yehuda Rosenbaum, was born in 1953.

Dr. Joan Watson was born in 1983, the daughter of John Simon and his wife, Carol.

The Holmes Family

Sherlock Holmes (the original) was born in 1854.

Sherlock Holmes Jr. was born in 1892.

Sherlock Holmes III, who is sometimes called "Third," was born in 1926.

The Moriarty Family

Dr. James Moriarty was born in 1835 (according to some interpreters of the Conan Doyle canon).

Drs. James Moriarty Jr. and James Moriarty III do not appear in any of these tales.

Dr. James Moriarty IV was born in 1941.

Part I

Sherlock Holmes and the Sixty-two-year Chess Mysteries

Notes to Part I

The demise of Alexander Alekhine is legitimately and undeniably shrouded in mystery, and I discuss plausible culprits in greater detail in the notes to that episode. He may indeed have been murdered, and the resolution of the particulars would have made a suitable challenge even for a "real-life" Sherlock Holmes. However, readers may wonder how I came up with "mysteries" about Morphy and Fischer, given the consistent, official medical reports and lack of controversy.

In fairness, I do *not* believe Alekhine strangled on a piece of meat. I believe he was either the target of an assassin or else the victim of some inadvertent foul play. If "manslaughter in the second degree" is too much of a leap, we might posit a chimerical "manslaughter in the third degree," even though no such crime exists.

Some years ago, I engaged in correspondence with Canadian Grandmaster Kevin Spraggett, who has published extensively on this subject. Although he writes with passion, I was not convinced by his argument (i.e., that the Soviets killed Alekhine). In fact, I remain unconvinced that any particular group ever targeted the world champion. That is why Holmes (in this case, the 92-year-old grandson of the original Conan Doyle character) reaches his own extraordinary conclusion.

Sir Arthur Conan Doyle's character Sherlock Holmes has been a favorite of filmmakers for decades. Here we see Basil Rathbone as Holmes (l.) and Nigel Bruce as Watson in the 1943 film Sherlock Holmes and the Secret Weapon.

The case of Paul Morphy is in all ways the most tragic, and he is surely the most sympathetic of the three champions. Since the cause of death (a stroke) is absolutely irrefutable, it remains for Holmes (in this case, the original) to suggest an embellishment. Indeed, he presents a tolerably convincing elaboration, born of the lunacy that had completely overwhelmed Morphy by 1884.

If we can accept the notion that Alekhine may not have died in the manner originally reported, and if we can suspend disbelief and imagine that Morphy, in his madness, had become consumed by his anger at one particular opponent (who had declined to play him in such an ignoble, unsporting manner), we face a far greater challenge with the "murder" of Bobby Fischer. Even the "conspiracy theorists" amongst us may find this last conjecture too great for such a leap of faith. Nevertheless, I did stumble upon at least one internet post—"Doubts Raised About Bobby Fischer's Death," by Rev. Dr. Anthony G. Pike of the Cosmic Research Foundation— that supported this view.

Although I read almost everything I could find online and corresponded with as many significant people as possible (including Rev. Pike), I remain convinced that Bobby died of kidney failure: case closed. However, my medium is fiction, and along with Sherlock Holmes comes his arch-adversary, Dr. James Moriarty. In a flash I had found the vehicle I needed, and rather than trying to "prove" anything, I begin with the deathbed confession of Moriarty (the great-grandson), who claims *he* had poisoned Fischer. It now remains for Holmes (the grandson) to prove that he had not!

* * *

At the end of the day, we are left with the deaths of three world champions (one unofficial) and some baffling coincidences. However, the details Holmes and two Watsons unravel here are certainly not intended for any purposes other than entertainment. They do not present explanations about crimes real or imagined, but merely offer fictitious and certainly slightly "different" interpretations of the events that transpired. To this end I am reminded of Mark Twain's "Notice" in his Preface to *Huckleberry Finn*: "Persons attempting to find a motive in this narrative will be prosecuted; persons attempting to find a moral in it will be banished; persons attempting to find a plot in it will be shot." To this admonition I shall merely append that anyone who takes this author too seriously should report for an immediate mental health evaluation!

Sherlock Holmes and the Mystery of the Sinister Stroke

The 1884 Death of Paul Morphy

Notes on Paul Morphy

Most readers are probably familiar with Paul Morphy, who dominated the chess world from 1857 to 1859 even more completely than Bobby Fischer did 113 years later. Morphy also withdrew from chess after his greatest triumphs; he never played a serious game (i.e., match or tournament) after 1859. Instead, he adamantly insisted that he was an attorney by profession, not a chess player. However, his legal career was disrupted by the Civil War, and by the end of that conflict, the signs of mental instability were already apparent.

As Holmes and Watson learn, the historical Morphy did indeed challenge various people to duels, talk to himself, and give vent to unwarranted rage. His family attempted to have him committed, but he somehow talked his way out of institutionalization.

Death came at age forty-seven: a cerebral hemorrhage attributed to the effects of a cool bath after Morphy had taken a lengthy walk during a New Orleans heat wave. However, questions remained, as the original Holmes and Watson soon learn!

Chapter 1

A Journey to the United States of America

Having made the acquaintance of the redoubtable Sherlock Holmes more than four years earlier, I was certainly comfortable with both his genius and eccentricities by 1885. Suffice it to say that he never ceased to astound me, and in even the most obscure cases he would invariably find the "obvious" solution—obvious to a man like Sherlock, though not to the rest of us, I can assure you.

As a housemate, he was by no means a joyful fellow. Indeed, unless sufficiently stimulated by a challenging case, he tended toward an Achilles-like retreat, content to sulk and brood, careless in his personal appearance (though not his cleanliness), and utterly indifferent toward the tidiness of his personal quarters in London. It was only thanks to the good efforts of Mrs. Hudson that we contrived to confine the mess.

The year 1885 began uneventfully enough, but in late January I received an invitation to attend the wedding of my cousin, Harold, in the United States. We had been inseparable as young lads, more like brothers than cousins. However, while I had progressed toward the study of medicine and thence to the military (and the debacle in Afghanistan), he had gone into international finance and prospered wildly: so much so that he insisted not only on paying for my passage but on reimbursing me for time lost from my medical practice. There was but a single proviso: that I would stand as his "best man."

Naturally, I could not decline such a proposal. However, I was rather distressed by the apparent depression of Sherlock. Thus, in a moment of dubious lucidity I invited him to accompany me across the ocean, even volunteering to split the fare with him (since I was traveling at my cousin's expense). Of course, Sherlock declined my offer of assistance but pounced at the opportunity to "get away from this boring city."

I made the necessary arrangements for coverage in my surgery, and we departed. The journey was unremarkable; Holmes's behavior was generally quite good, and his mood improved immensely. We arrived in New Orleans, a prominent southern city, on Sunday morning, 12 April, and moved into a guesthouse on Harold's immense estate. The wedding was scheduled for the following Saturday.

On the 13th, Harold took us to what he said would be a "small, social gathering." Naturally, this proved a large event indeed, with not only a number of the area's leading citizens, but even the Fourth Estate.

I've generally had no dealings with the press whatsoever, but Sherlock was delighted when a reporter greeted him nervously. "Do I have the honor of addressing Mr. Holmes, the famous detective?" he asked.

"Sherlock, the same," replied my friend, smiling, "but you have the advantage over me, Mr. –"

"Oh, excuse me," replied the journalist, blushing. "Collins. Alexander Collins. But everyone calls me Alex, even my parents."

"Indeed!" exclaimed Holmes. "A younger son and probably the youngest child, recently engaged to be married, a writer of fiction who aspires to go far beyond his immediate position with the newspaper, and a left-handed dog-owner."

Needless to say, this barrage of unexpected information almost dropped the other man in his tracks. "Wh--, why, yes, everything you say is true, Mr. Holmes, but how could you tell?"

"Watson," said that gentleman, turning to me. "Could one not easily make the same deductions?"

I frowned, completely at a loss, and shook my head helplessly.

"A first-born son would be called Alexander, would he not? In my experience, the only ones called Alex were second- or third-borns!"

"You are right, Sir. My brother Edward is the eldest, and I also have two older sisters."

"Pray let me continue. Look closely, Watson! How could you have missed that long strand of blonde hair on this fellow's jacket? And yet you see no wedding band on his finger. Such telltale signs of intimacy would normally be covered up meticulously, would they not, unless…"

Alex blushed. "I suppose we haven't been trying too hard to hide anything," he confessed, almost giggling.

"Behold yet again, Watson. Although he has taken pains to wash his hands meticulously—would you guess forty-seven such ablutions per day, or somewhere in that range, Doctor?—he cannot wipe away the severe indentation of the writing instrument held against the third finger of his left hand."

By now, a crowd had gathered around us. I was, of course, rather indifferent to this latest development, whilst my friend continued to bask in the glory of a stunning performance.

"But the dog, Sir!" cried Alex. "He is short-haired and does not shed, and I have never been in contact with him while attired in formal wear!"

Sherlock looked around at those who stood within earshot and smiled. "Is it not obvious?" he asked. "You all look, but you do not see. Not even you, Watson?"

I shook my head.

"The dog did bite your right shoe at least once some weeks ago. You have polished it quite well, and the untrained eye may not easily pick up the indentation, but here"—he knelt down and pointed to the tiniest mark on the outer side of the leather—"we may indeed see proof of the pup's disobedience, may we not?"

The murmur of the crowd was doubtless magic to Sherlock's ears, and he seemed at once more animated and more relaxed than I had seen him in weeks.

"May I report on this to my readers, Mr. Holmes?" asked our newest admirer excitedly.

"Of course, you may!" replied the detective.

The rest of the evening passed uneventfully. Sherlock drank but a single glass of champagne and behaved very well. In truth, he can be altogether charming when he sets his mind to it, although such is not always his wont, as readers already know.

It was only while we were leaving that I perceived the melancholia returning. "What's wrong?" I inquired.

"Oh, it is nothing, Watson, nothing. It's just that I think I would feel quite splendid if I could get a nice, challenging case about now. Alas, this is the New World, and I doubt anyone will have use for my services in these parts."

He could not have been more wrong!

Chapter 2

The Chess Player's Sister

Tuesday passed by uneventfully, and then Wednesday. I did not realize that the article penned by Alex Collins had appeared in what passed for a "newspaper" that morning, but by the end of the day, half the city must have heard that Sherlock Holmes, the great British detective, was in New Orleans. Surely enough, we had already received a basketful of letters, addressed to Sherlock (c/o my cousin, of course) before dinner.

"Rubbish, Watson!" bellowed my friend. "Just look at this!" he snapped, handing me one of these missives.

I could hardly keep a straight face. "Dear Mr. Holmes," it began. "My dog disappeared four years ago, but I think he was stolen. Could you find him?"

"My horse died back in '81. I think somebody poisoned him. Can you help me figure out who did it?" responded Holmes, crumbling up another and throwing it into a pail. "Merciful Heavens, Watson! Doesn't anyone ever get murdered in this backward country?"

We were somewhat more favorably inclined toward a widow's invitation to tea, although I knew Sherlock's patience would run out rather quickly. However, the next moment he bolted out of his chair as though thunderstruck.

"Now this, Watson! *This* may be just what I've been waiting for!" He handed me the envelope, into which he had returned the letter.

"May I?" I inquired.

"Of course!" he replied.

I took out the document, which read as follows:

> *Dear Mr. Holmes,*
>
> *I write to you as the youngest sister of the late Paul Charles Morphy, an attorney by training, but better known for his exploits over the chessboard during a brief period before the unfortunate War Between the States. The circumstances of his demise appear clear, yet for personal reasons I would very much appreciate the assurances of someone skilled in these matters. My family, as you may know, do not lack for resources, and you will certainly be well compensated for your pains on our behalf.*
>
> *I am, Sir, yours truly, Helena Morphy*

"Paul Morphy. You have heard of him?" I asked.

"Of course, Watson. My old friend, Augustus Mongredian, mentioned having played a match against him back in 1859. He drew one game but met with inexorable defeat in the other seven. Augustus told me many a tale about the American's exploits. He must have been an absolute genius. Indeed, he had the good sense to abandon the game, which can be far too time-consuming for a creative intellect. However, rather than become a detective, he tried to practice law."

Although I push wood with passable skill, I was not altogether aware of Morphy's triumphs. Holmes proceeded to fire off all the details of every match, the overwhelming margins of victory, and even some anecdotes about the events themselves.

As it happened, there was a chessboard set up in the very room in which we talked. "Have you not seen this gem Morphy produced in the Italian Opera House in Paris? It was contested during a performance of Bellini's *Norma*! Here, let me show you," he insisted, and in short order he had played through the entire game.

I am not sure whether I was more impressed by my friend's memory or the Queen sacrifice by the American genius on the penultimate move.

"Oh, here's another Queen sacrifice by Morphy, this one against Louis Paulsen," Holmes continued. Yet again, he played through an entire game from memory. He even went back to the key position, sacrificed the Black Queen, and proceeded to find a yet faster path to victory than the one Morphy took.

"I must meet with this woman, Watson. Let us respond at once. Would your cousin mind if we received her here?"

"I'm sure it will be all right with Harold," I replied.

That evening we received a brief note from Miss Helena Morphy, promising to call upon us no later than 11 o'clock Thursday morning. For the first time in a while, my friend was in excellent spirits.

Chapter 3

Helena Morphy

Helena Morphy arrived promptly and was shown into our sitting room. Although she could not have been much beyond her mid-forties, she looked considerably older. Moreover—and I speak as a physician—she did not seem in particularly good health, although she appeared asymptomatic throughout our interview.

"Ah, Miss Helena Morphy," said Sherlock, greeting her cordially. "This is my friend and associate, Dr. Watson, whom I've shown a few of your late brother's masterpieces." He nodded in the direction of the chessboard. "But forgive me. I see that you are still in mourning, or should I say in mourning yet again. Moreover, I perceive that you are here despite some friction within the family."

The poor woman opened her mouth to say something but remained speechless for a moment. "Why, yes, I suppose my black dress and veil give away my most recent loss. My mother died on January 11th," she acknowledged at length. "But why do you think there is 'friction' within the family?"

"A quick deduction," replied my friend. "If I remember correctly, the late Paul Morphy had two sisters and a brother, am I not right?"

Helena nodded.

"Yet you, alone, have sought my advice—a fact that suggests your surviving siblings do not share your concerns, and which thereby opens the possibility that at least one of them may be somehow implicated or at least under suspicion. The fact that you have arrived with a small briefcase tells me that you have various documents therein, although these are more indicative of litigation than of murder—or am I going too far afield here?"

Amazement registered on the visitor's face, and for a time I thought she might engage in theatrics and faint. Thankfully, we were spared such a performance, as she soon recovered her composure.

"Where shall I begin, Mr. Holmes? Let me start at the end, and perhaps we can work backward."

"An excellent course of action!"

"My brother, as you may have heard, died on July 10th last year."

Having shared this information, she hesitated, so I thought to interject a medical question. "The cause of death?" I asked.

"They—the doctors—told us it was a stroke. You see, my brother had gone out for a walk in the heat of the day, and it was rather beastly that afternoon. He came back visibly overheated; moreover, he seemed extraordinarily upset, although he said nothing whatsoever about anything that might have provoked him. A short while later he went into a bath, which was considerably cooler, and they said that the contrast between the excessive heat outside and the relatively cold water caused the fatal stroke."

I shrugged my shoulders and turned to Sherlock. "I suppose that makes sense. Think about it, Holmes. The body first gets overheated, perhaps also dehydrated. Then comes the chill from the cool bath, vasoconstriction, and given the elevated blood pressure—exacerbated by the victim's bad mood, apparent irritation, and probable anger—it is not unreasonable to infer that the late Paul Morphy might indeed have suffered a hemorrhagic stroke."

My friend's face registered no emotion whatsoever. "Continue, Miss Morphy," he said, staring across the room at the chessboard.

"Paul lived with me and our mother in one of the family homes. If I could know for a fact that my brother simply died of a stroke, I would be perfectly satisfied. However, I have some fears and suspicions that someone may have deliberately antagonized him, thereby contributing at least indirectly to his demise." Turning to Sherlock, she added, "My surviving siblings do not share this concern, which is why I am here alone.

"As far as the medical profession is concerned, it's rather open-and-shut. He went out for a walk on a hot day. I saw him leave and return some considerable while later, quite flushed and sweaty. He took a bath to cool down, and that is where the body was found.

Sherlock grimaced. "Cases of this sort are rarely as simple as they sound, Miss Morphy. Knowing nothing of the particulars, I can raise a number of questions in quick succession. May I?"

He looked at our guest, who nodded affirmatively, and continued. "First, did he go out for walks every day? If he did not, perhaps the exertion was indeed too much for him, given the temperature outdoors. However, if he did, he was probably in decent physical condition, and the heat and humidity ought not have precipitated a medical crisis."

"He walked quite regularly, Mr. Holmes, almost every day, right around noon. And for a man in his late 40s he seemed in good health, at least physically."

My friend blinked twice as he processed the last comment. Then he continued, "You mentioned the heat, but was this city in the midst of a severe heat wave or merely normal temperatures for that time of the year—the peak of summer?"

"They said temperatures were a little warmer than usual that month. I remember it hit 95 degrees that day."

Without so much as blinking, Holmes turned to me and converted. "That's 35 degrees Celsius, if you require such information for your medical analysis, Doctor!" Then, turning to Helena, he said, "Pray continue. How was he attired?"

"He was dressed suitably for the heat, in long pants but in a light, short-sleeved shirt. He also wore a large straw hat to protect his head from the direct sunlight."

I felt compelled to interject something useful at this point. "The hat would surely not have trapped terribly much heat, so we should assume it was beneficial."

"Duly noted, Watson. Now, Miss Morphy, how long was he out of the house?"

"Not much more than an hour, and possibly slightly less," she replied. "That was about how long he was usually gone."

"Probably covering not more than three miles, given that heat. Next permit me to ask a more delicate question. Did your family's house have indoor plumbing, or was water brought in from a well outside?"

The woman blushed a little at this question. "We are among the more fortunate ones who have running water inside the house. We are also able to afford servants to attend to things like drawing the water for our baths."

"So, your brother did not exert himself at the pump or in carrying buckets of water to the bath itself?"

"Absolutely not."

Sherlock took a deep breath. "Fair enough, but there are still some loose ends here. If the late Mr. Morphy had come home, somewhat overheated and probably thirsty as well, it would still have taken some time for water to be drawn. This, in turn, begs the question of whether he might have had a sufficient number of minutes to have cooled off substantially, would it not, John?"

"Any critical hyperthermia should have been corrected within ten to fifteen minutes, particularly if he had had something to drink upon his return," I reported.

"Whereas, had the tub been filled and left for an hour, it would certainly have begun to approach ambient room temperature by the time Mr. Morphy returned, though it would still have been considerably cooler than the 95-degree temperature cited by our guest, would it not?"

"Indeed," I replied. "I should doubt it could possibly have topped the 65-to-70-degree range in so short a period of time, and this would have made it only slightly less likely to have precipitated the cerebral hemorrhage."

Holmes clasped his hands together with a big smile. "Fascinating, don't you think, John? We have at least sufficient reason to question whether the bath was cool enough to have caused the fatal stroke, even given the temperature outdoors. This, in turn, leads us to look for other possibilities. However…" He shook his head. "We have overlooked the obvious. If he was customarily gone from the house for around an hour, the servants might have drawn the water and filled the tub in anticipation of his return on or around one o'clock." He turned to his client. "Apologies for the oversight, and pray continue. I am quite sure you would not have sought my assistance if you did not have some reasonable suspicions. What other information can you impart?"

Our guest's jaw had dropped during this exchange, but she recovered her composure adequately to confirm that the bath waters had indeed been drawn prior to her brother's return from his walk. Helena Morphy now paused, opened her mouth as though to begin, and then stopped. She looked first at me, then at Sherlock, as though measuring her thoughts carefully. At length she asked, "How much do you know about my late brother, Mr. Holmes—and Dr. Watson?"

Before Holmes could reply, I mentioned that I was only minimally acquainted with his name. I knew that he had been a great chess player, and that was about as much as I could share. Sherlock, on the other hand, was somewhat more knowledgeable.

"As I recall, he had a very brief career, after which he distanced himself from the game with almost religious fervor. I know that he defeated everyone he faced by overwhelming margins, that plans for a match with our own Howard Staunton fell through—and I might append not without considerable acrimony—and that Morphy later offered odds to anyone who would accept them. Then he disappeared."

"What you say is true, Mr. Holmes. However, I should like to expand on what you already know, for it is only in that way that you may understand why I must wonder about possible foul play. Now, may I begin at the beginning?"

Holmes and I both nodded, and the Paul Morphy story commenced.

Chapter 4

The Sad History of Paul Charles Morphy

"My brother was brilliant, Mr. Holmes, and I think that if his career had not been blighted by both his success at chess and the terrible war, he would have had fared magnificently as a lawyer, possibly going all the way to the Supreme Court. However, that was not to be.

"Paul graduated from Spring Hill College shortly after he turned 17. He was admitted to the bar before he was 20 years old, and I should add that he could recite from memory the Civil Code of Louisiana in its entirety!

"He never studied chess, and as far as I can remember, he never possessed more than one or two books on the game. He played rarely and only in the area, though he soundly thrashed everyone he faced, including *Monsieur* Rousseau of France and *Herr* Löwenthal from the Austrian Empire, when those masters played in New Orleans."

"Ah, yes," nodded Sherlock. "Eugène Rousseau and Johann Löwenthal: noteworthy opponents in their day, particularly the latter."

"Still, we were somewhat surprised when he was invited to attend the American Chess Congress in New York in the fall of 1857—though certainly not at all surprised when he triumphed easily. In fact, after the tournament, he won a match against the former United States champion, Charles Stanley, in which he gave his opponent odds of a pawn."

"I believe the precise odds were pawn-and-move, meaning that he also took the Black pieces," my friend corrected.

Paul Morphy
The pride and sorrow of the
19th century chess world.

Miss Morphy hesitated but then continued. "He went to Europe, where your English champion, Mr. Staunton, indeed declined to face him. However, he played a number of matches against other noteworthy opponents, including *Herr* Anderssen, whom some considered champion of the world at that time. One after another, they crumbled.

"Paul even played some numbers of men without sight of the board. I think they call that blindfolded. His memory was such that even with this handicap he prevailed."

I was startled by the notion. "How could he play blindfolded? Surely, he would soon knock over all the pieces, would he not?"

Holmes laughed out loud. "My poor friend. What that means is that one plays with his back to the board. The moves are called out to him, and he holds the position in his memory. I can certainly keep a game or two in my head without difficulty, and I think it's a splendid cerebral exercise. For example, if I advance my King's pawn up two squares, and you do the same, I might then push the King's Bishop's pawn two squares and initiate a King's gambit. Do you follow?"

I shook my head. "For a move or two, yes, but some of these games go on for thirty, forty, or fifty moves. What then? And you say he played multiple opponents? This is incomprehensible, Holmes!"

However, my friend's attentions had by now returned to Miss Morphy. "Forgive our digression. Pray continue!"

Helena resumed. "Now, I should explain that my brother never really disliked chess, but he had contempt for those who sought to make a living from it. 'Mere hustlers,' he called them, along with some nastier terms in French that I shall not repeat.

"By May of 1859, my brother had returned to the United States, where he was feted and lauded in major cities of the north—New York and Boston. However, there was one interesting piece of unpleasantness, notwithstanding my late brother's extraordinarily proper behavior at all times.

Adolf Anderssen
One of the greatest attacking players of his era.

"At the University of New York, my brother received a set of gold and silver chess pieces and a board similarly crafted. Colonel Charles D. Mead, president of the American Chess Association, said something or other about chess as a "profession," and Paul took offense. It was clear even then, when he had beaten everyone he faced and might reasonably have been called champion of the world, that he considered chess no more than a pastime.

"Of course, I wasn't there, and Paul wasn't too forthcoming about the details. He did later mention, however, that Mr. Mead had simply 'vanished' after the incident. You see, my brother was always a perfect gentleman, and he worried that he had perhaps offended his host, notwithstanding the fact that his host had clearly offended him."

Sherlock's face registered no emotion, but his hands, with those long fingers, were certainly busy. Since he seemed disinclined to speak, I thought to interject a comment. "You present this episode in such a way as to suggest Colonel Mead may in fact have borne your brother some ill-will. Still, it seems inconceivable that he would have waited twenty-five years to seek revenge."

Miss Morphy shook her head. "And also quite impossible, Dr. Watson. The colonel died in 1876. But allow me to continue.

"Bear in mind that this was 1859, and that my brother would never play another serious chess match for the rest of his life. However, he was delighted to accept the opportunity to write about the game for *The New York Ledger*, which had recently decided to run a chess column. Paul wanted to analyze the games from a match some decades earlier between a French champion and his English counterpart."

Holmes sat up abruptly. "You must mean La Bourdonnais and McDonnell. Every educated chess player has heard of their eighty-five games."

"I don't remember," replied Helena. "However, I recall that he was quite pleased about the appointment and looked forward to writing a series of columns about the game. As for his own participation, he had offered to play anybody in the world at what I think you said was 'pawn and the move,' Mr. Holmes. When no one accepted the challenge, he declared his career finished. However, I know that he remained interested in chess, and he reviewed the matches of other masters most carefully. His good friend, Charles Maurian, engaged in casual games with him until around fifteen years ago, and while I don't believe they played after that, it is possible that they continued to review published chess scores from time to time."

"He defeated everyone, sometimes at material odds and sometimes blindfolded. However, he was a perfect gentleman, almost surely offended no one, and is effectively unlikely to have made any enemies as a result of chess—the more so, since he did not play anyone during the last fifteen years of his life. It would seem we have reached a dead end on this line, wouldn't you say, Sherlock?" I asked.

"A reasonable conclusion, John, though by no means a certainty," my friend replied. "However, I have one last question for Miss Morphy before we put this to rest." Turning to her, he asked, "Did he play *anyone else* during the last years of his life?"

"Oh, no, Mr. Holmes!" she exclaimed. "He wouldn't even consider it. When *Herr* Steinitz, whom some consider champion of the world today, came to New Orleans, Paul at first refused to speak with him, and when he

Paul Morphy's column in the March 3, 1860 edition of the New York Ledger.

finally agreed to an interview, it was only under the condition that chess could not be mentioned by either of them."

Holmes burst out laughing. "The greatest chess talent ever and the man some considered the best in the world agreed to meet, but neither could mention the game in any context. That's priceless!"

Our guest could not see the humor. "You don't understand, Mr. Holmes. My brother had beaten *Herr* Anderssen in 1858. *Herr* Steinitz

Wilhelm Steinitz, the first official world chess champion.

defeated *Herr* Anderssen in 1866, so some consider him the best in the world to the present day. There were even rumors that *Herr* Steinitz wished to play a match against Paul, but I'm sure my brother had no interest in such a contest. That was why he refused even to discuss chess during their meeting."

Sherlock nodded. "All right. It seems reasonable to conclude that if your brother did indeed succumb to some sort of foul play, chess probably had nothing to do with it. Nevertheless, I must assume there were other conflicts. Do continue."

Helena hesitated, took a sip of her tea, and looked fixedly at my friend. "It is somewhat embarrassing," she began. "I would feel more comfortable addressing this part of the conversation directly to Dr. Watson, if that's all right."

"Fair enough. Pay attention, Watson!"

The lady stared at the ground for a time before moving her gaze toward me. "My brother was not in good health," she began. "Oh, he was fine, physically, but…his mind did not always function properly."

She paused, and Sherlock broke the silence. "In what ways did these problems manifest?" he asked.

Helena hesitated. "I do not think," she began, "that it was so much chess that drove him mad, but rather that his life away from chess did not, shall we say, go as one might have hoped. My brother was a genius, Mr. Holmes, and he should have had a brilliant career as a lawyer. However, his aspirations were handicapped by two major problems: his fame as a chess player and the War between the States."

"That may give us the cause for his distress, Miss Morphy, but it does not tell us what actually occurred."

"Let me give you a single example. When my father died, my brother-in-law—my sister Malvina's husband, Johannes Sybrandt—was named executor of the estate."

"And that was when?"

"1856. Of course, Paul hadn't even completed his legal studies at the time, and he was too young to have served in the capacity of executor in any case. Johannes, whom we all called John, did a perfectly fine job, but some years after the fact, Paul got it into his head that he had been swindled out of his fair share of the estate.

"Nothing could have been further from the truth, of course. We pleaded with him to drop the madness, but he became obsessed. Things got so bad that he eventually took John to court, where my brother-in-law provided conclusive proof of his fairness and thoroughness with the tasks he had performed in fulfilling his obligations. The case was thrown out, and that produced even worse effects in Paul.

"He later came to the conclusion that John was trying to poison him. In order to avoid an unpleasant confrontation, my brother-in-law decided to stay away from the family house altogether, whereupon Paul declared that other people were also trying to poison him. This madness took various forms: some were in cahoots with Mr. Sybrandt, while others were acting independently. In sum, Paul had become...what is the clinical term, Doctor?"

"Paranoid," I exclaimed.

"That's it. Paranoid. Before long, Paul would eat no food unless my late mother or I prepared it; he trusted no one else. His anger at John subsided minimally, but he lashed out at several other individuals and even challenged some of them to duels."

"Can you provide us with their names, Miss Morphy?" asked Holmes. "If you suspect any sort of foul play, it might be an idea for us to interview all these gentlemen."

"I thought you might ask, Mr. Holmes, so I have listed them on this piece of paper," said Helena, passing a document across the table. "The first was in fact deceased before my brother's demise. The second suffered a crippling stroke in 1883, and although he is still alive, he has been unable either to walk or talk since that time. The names and addresses of the other four are as given, should you wish to speak with any of them. I can provide Paul's copies of some of the horrible letters he wrote, also," she added, pulling out another set of papers.

"Duly noted. Now, how far did these challenges go?"

"Naturally, no one took them seriously. Dueling has been illegal here for decades. Moreover, Paul never held a sword in his hands and didn't even own a pair of dueling pistols. The whole idea was madness, and these gentlemen were only too well aware of my brother's mental failures."

"What connections had they had to Mr. Morphy in earlier life?" I asked.

"All were members of the legal profession, and the deceased had known my father quite well. I believe that three or four of them may also have played at the New Orleans Chess Club. In fact, I think one had once toasted Paul as the greatest chess player in the world and thereby infuriated my brother no end."

Sherlock opened his mouth, as though to say something, but halted abruptly. A few seconds later he asked what was surely a very different question than the one he had originally intended. "You mentioned your brother's legal career which, from all I gather, did not generate anywhere near the success of his chess career. Surely a mind as brilliant as his could have done well in your courts of law. What happened?"

"As always, Mr. Holmes, it was chess. Initially most people would not retain his services, fearing that he was at best a chess player who 'also practiced law'—as, indeed, many considered him. It is possible that one or more of the people on that list referred to him in that manner. The horrible war broke out, and during the early days of the armed conflict, most of Paul's work involved writing simple wills. Then, in late April 1862, the Yankees came.

"I shall not bore you with the horrors of the invasion, Mr. Holmes. The Yankees had almost three times as many warships, and they were determined to capture our city in order to cut the Confederacy in two. Needless to say, the Northerners effectively *were* the law, such as it was, from that time until the end of the war. In October, Paul boarded a Spanish vessel and went first to Cuba, thence to Spain, and ultimately to France, where he stayed until 1865, when the war ended.

"Then came the dreadful period known as Reconstruction, in which we were for all intents an occupied nation. Paul's efforts to resume his practice of law were thwarted simply by the political realities he confronted. However, he later complained bitterly that his 'enemies'—and these included the gentleman on this list, who were almost surely innocent—had told the Yankees that Paul had gone to Paris as an agent of the Confederacy, hoping to procure French assistance in the war."

"Merciful Heavens!" cried Sherlock. "Your brother as a Confederate agent?"

"There was no truth to that whatsoever, which is why the Yankees never sought to punish or stifle my brother, and no one ever suggested that they do so. However, Paul was convinced that this was indeed the case, and he clung to this fantasy even after Reconstruction ended in 1877.

"We could see the inconsistencies in his thinking, Mr. Holmes. His enemies were at once accused of ruining Paul's legal career by telling the Yankees he was a spy, while at the same time telling everyone else that my brother was just a chess player who dabbled in the law."

"Delusions need not be consistent, Miss Morphy," I ventured.

"Perhaps I should mention one more thing," our visitor continued. "Paul played very little chess during and after the war, and as I mentioned, that was mostly with his good friend, Mr. Maurian. He may also have played with another friend in Paris, *Monsieur* de Riviere. However, I recall that someone in New Orleans was very anxious to play him and claimed he could hold his own at odds of a Rook."

"Given your brother's amazing strength, that would have been a tolerably good result indeed," nodded Sherlock.

"Of course, that person might have been any of the leading players at the local chess club, and not necessarily one of the lawyers who had supposedly ruined Paul's career. Paul never even identified him by name, whoever he may have been.

"Now, I don't know whether this is at all relevant, but once—I think it was early 1869, since I'm pretty sure Paul stopped playing altogether not long after that—it would seem someone may actually have played a game with Paul, both of them without sight of the board. Of course, there were several people who sometimes intercepted Paul in the streets during his walks. You see, his route often went right past a number of law offices, so these gentlemen, his colleagues, simply went out to greet him."

"And, of course, we don't even know for certain that the party in question was an attorney, do we?" asked Sherlock.

"No, we don't, Mr. Holmes. Let me just report that one individual—I have no idea which one, or whether he is even on that list I gave you—ended up walking with my brother for a while, and on that occasion Paul claimed he had been 'tricked' into playing a game.

"What had happened was this. That person had asked what move was best if White was giving odds of a Bishop plus a Knight, and Paul suggested some move. The other man then probably asked what could be done if Black answered in such-and-such a manner, and Paul replied, and soon they were effectively playing a game. The gentleman was evidently too strong for those odds, and by the time they parted company, he had a vastly superior position."

"I do not understand," said Holmes. "It is surely no disgrace to lose a game when giving such enormous odds!"

"True, but my brother was infuriated for two reasons. First, he felt he had not been challenged properly, *in the manner a gentleman would employ.* Second, it would seem that his opponent had subsequently declared that as a gentleman, Paul was now morally obligated to play him at odds of a Rook. Of course, that bizarre challenge drove him over the edge.

"A healthy person would simply have played—and probably trounced—his foe, but my brother soon stopped playing completely and would not play even with Mr. Maurian. A year passed, yet he continued to complain bitterly about the incident. Worse still, with his legal practice in limbo, Paul became more and more convinced that he had 'enemies,' chief among whom were my brother-in-law and those lawyers I have identified.

"He challenged someone to a duel in 1875, a full six years after the incident I mention. When that party did not respond, Paul's anger appeared to diminish, although I should add that he continued to heap vitriol on poor Mr. Sybrandt. Of course, I must also tell you for a fact that he had many lucid moments, and at times spoke quite warmly about his brother-in-law and even some of the people he often considered his enemies. However, his mood could change overnight.

"One day one of the six—Llewellyn Hamilton, an attorney on your list—called on us here. It was in 1882, shortly after Paul had convinced the sisters at the asylum that he should not be admitted therein."

"Apologies, Miss Morphy," I interrupted. "You tried to have your brother committed?"

"Yes, my mother, my brother Edward, and Mr. Maurian brought him to an institution called the Louisiana Retreat. However, he was having one of his better days, and he evidently presented a powerful legal case, arguing eloquently on why he ought not be detained within the walls. The medical authorities agreed, and he came back home. Some weeks later, Mr.

Hamilton dropped by, and Paul greeted him most civilly. They chatted for the better part of an hour and shook hands warmly when Mr. Hamilton departed.

"Of course, we had some hopes that my brother would slowly return to his right mind, but these were soon dashed. He became even more erratic, as bad periods interspersed with good ones. He might go months without mentioning a given individual and then lash out in an indescribable anger at the imaginary offenses that person had committed. A few weeks later he might speak most warmly about the same gentleman."

"This, again, is not inconsistent with what physicians have observed," I explained. "Paranoid people may indeed experience dynamic mood swings."

Holmes cast a glance in my direction. "Might such mood swings prove injurious to the heart and circulatory system?"

"Conceivably yes, though such an outcome is somewhat less likely if the victim of paranoia is in otherwise good health. Miss Morphy has indicated that her brother was indeed quite healthy for his age, but an apoplectic response of this sort could nevertheless have proven precipitously fatal."

"I have but a few more questions, Miss Morphy," declared Holmes. "First, are you quite sure that no one could have poisoned your brother?"

"It would have been completely impossible, Mr. Holmes. As I told you, he would eat nothing that had not been prepared by me or my late mother, and he would similarly drink nothing that did not come through us."

"Second, are you quite certain that on that hot July day, your brother was gone only about as long as usual, and certainly not noticeably longer?"

"Yes, Mr. Holmes. He was usually out for an hour or so, and I am certain he returned within roughly five minutes of that amount of time."

"Very well. I believe we have as much information as we can use for now. The only question that remains is whether someone, acting deliberately or inadvertently, provoked the late Paul Morphy to the point of blind rage, thereby elevating his blood pressure significantly and perhaps contributing to the fatal stroke. Permit us to call upon you as early as this evening and no later than tomorrow morning, and I'm sure we shall have tied up all the loose ends by that time."

Miss Morphy thanked us profusely, and the servant showed her out.

Chapter 5

Four Suspects, Four Short Interviews

Although it was by now early afternoon, Holmes was anxious to speak with the four lawyers on Miss Morphy's list. After a quick lunch, we ordered a carriage and proceeded to the center of New Orleans. Owing to his celebrity status, we were shown in immediately (save in one instance), even though two of the attorneys were meeting with clients when we arrived.

The first gentleman, one Amos Williams, spoke of the deceased with warmth and sadness. "Do you know, Mr. Holmes, the poor fellow challenged me to a duel on two occasions. Nevertheless, when I dropped by to visit him—I believe it was around a year and one-half or so before he died, during early 1883—he greeted me most warmly and begged me to call on him again when I departed. Regrettably, I never did so."

Holmes inquired as to whether Mr. Williams played chess. The attorney replied that he had indeed been a member of the New Orleans Chess Club in his younger days, although he had not played since the Civil War. "I served in the military and ended up in a prisoner-of-war camp, a true hellhole, Mr. Holmes. For diversion, one of the soldiers made 'pieces' by writing the names of the King, Queen, and others on some scraps of thick paper, and we then penciled a 'board' on a discarded piece of wood. On days when there was no wind, we could sometimes manage a few games, but the experience left such a horrible taste in my mouth that I haven't played since.

"Besides, New Orleans already had its chess hero. Paul was the greatest player in the world, as I had proudly proclaimed before the War broke out. Imagine my surprise when he took umbrage and said that I was not a gentleman. Then, several years later, he made other accusations about my character, and he finally challenged me to a duel. It was sad, Mr. Holmes, very sad.

"However, you probably cannot understand how much he felt the game had taken away from his life. His reputation as a chess player led many to doubt his competence as an attorney-at-law. Moreover, there was a woman by whom he was quite smitten. He had hoped to initiate formal courtship, but she declined to entertain the hopes of 'a mere chess player'—that's what she called him, Mr. Holmes."

Helena Morphy had made no mention of her brother's romantic interest. Sherlock immediately requested more information. Alas, it proved a dead end; Eleanor Mae Gibson died in early 1883, almost a year and one-half before the man she had rejected.

* * *

We took our leave of Mr. Williams and proceeded right across the street to the offices of Harold Brown, Esquire. An older man of perhaps sixty-five, he had heard of Paul's chess exploits, but he professed not to know the game at all. His testimony proved interesting to me, though Holmes appeared to register no emotion.

"The truth is that I observed him in court early on, and he seemed bored by the laborious pace of the proceeding. During recess I made some glib comment to him along the lines of how this must have felt like waiting an hour for his opponent to make a move. His face flushed, as though I had insulted him. He clenched his fists, and for a moment I thought he was going to assault me. Then he calmed down, grabbed his briefcase, and walked out without a word.

"Such a loss of control in the courtroom is unacceptable. I suspect that he had patience over the chessboard but not with the law. Given his volatile disposition, I'm afraid that what others said—that he was a chess player who also dabbled in jurisprudence—was probably not inaccurate."

"And did you ever express that opinion yourself?" inquired Holmes.

"I surely said something of the sort a few times. This was twenty-five years ago, Mr. Holmes, and I was not the only one who felt that way. I was merely one of the unlucky ones whom he decided to challenge to a duel.

"Morphy was said to be quite brilliant, yet he clearly seems to have failed miserably as an attorney. If you'll excuse my use of legal idiom here, I think we can rest our case."

"And when did you last see the deceased?"

"I doubt I saw him more than a handful of times after that courtroom debacle, and certainly not in the past decade. Why would I wish to socialize with someone who had effectively threatened to kill me?"

"An excellent question, Mr. Brown. Thank you so much," replied Sherlock, and we departed.

* * *

The offices of Reginald Jones were on the other side of the block. Our reception was far chillier there.

"I know who you are, Mr. Holmes, and if you want to talk about the late Paul Morphy—rest his soul, if any—you are barking up the wrong tree. He died of a stroke, and I had nothing to do with it. The man was a lunatic, and if you had come by a couple of years earlier, you could have dragged him back to England with you and thrown him into Bedlam."

"I would not have presumed," replied Holmes dryly.

"Well, not much more could have been done with him. He was a chess genius but an inept lawyer, and his record on both counts speaks for itself. He made scurrilous attacks on my character, attributed comments to me that I never uttered, and challenged me to a duel on more than one occasion."

Sherlock nodded and stroked his chin. "Do you, perhaps, play a little chess yourself?" he asked.

"I used to play regularly, and I still manage rather well over the board, if I say so myself. Who knows? Maybe that's why Mr. Morphy hated me so much. I wouldn't worship him as the 'god-of-chess,' because quite frankly, chess is just a game. I'm sure he was better than I ever was. In fact, from what I read, he was better than everyone on God's green earth. However, when I challenged him to give me Rook odds, he simply turned his back and walked away. Is that a gentleman, I ask you?"

"I am a foreigner, Mr. Jones, and thus unfamiliar with your social mores."

"Well, he was no gentleman, and that's for certain. I never did him any harm whatsoever, so why did he repeatedly challenge me to a duel? I still have the papers, written in his own hand, if you'd like to see them. In fact, come back tomorrow at this time, and I'll be happy to show them to you. He, as an officer of the Court, challenged me, his colleague-officer of the Court, to a duel, despite knowing that dueling is illegal in the State of Louisiana! Is that a 'genius' for you, or is it a damned lunatic?"

Holmes smiled wryly. "As I am neither a barrister nor a physician, I fear I am not qualified to pass judgment. Still, I must cheerfully concede that the late Paul Morphy did not treat you particularly kindly. One last question, though. When did you last see him, and in what context?"

Mr. Jones hesitated a moment, as though trying to recall. "Let me think. I know it was in the early summer, around the time he died. It was hot as Hades, and I saw him walking right past this window. His lips were moving, as though he was talking to someone, but no one was there. He never looked up in my direction, and as soon as I saw who he was, I pulled back into the interior of the room. I was honestly a little frightened when I saw him, since he looked like an absolute madman. You're not suggesting I *should* have hailed him, are you?"

"No, indeed I am not. We thank you very much for your time, Mr. Jones," answered Holmes, and we departed.

* * *

Mr. Llewellyn Hamilton, Esquire, was with a client and could not be disturbed. We were asked to sit in the waiting room. Some half-hour or so later—it was almost dinnertime—the gentleman greeted us and showed us into his office. A tall, balding man with a graying beard, he seemed delighted to receive the famous Sherlock Holmes despite his obvious fatigue.

"May I inquire, Mr. Holmes, how I warrant the honor of becoming your host?" he began, with a broad smile.

"Indeed, the honor is mine, Sir. I trust you are also familiar with the name of my inestimable colleague, Dr. John Watson."

"I believe the doctor and I shook hands just three nights ago," replied the lawyer. "How may I be of assistance?"

Holmes studied the other man's face for just a moment. "I wish I could request your help for a case, but we are merely trying to learn more about the famous chess player, Paul Morphy, who died last year. As you may or may not know, there is tremendous controversy in England about the proposed match between that gentleman and our own Howard Staunton, so anything you can tell us would be helpful."

The older man smiled again. "I am relieved, Mr. Holmes, since for a while I wondered whether I was a suspect in some crime. After all, you are a famous detective! But I'll be happy to answer all your questions and then some.

"First, let me tell you that I did not always enjoy a cordial relationship with the deceased. Should the truth be known, he made horrible accusations about me and challenged me to a duel no less than three times."

"We have heard that others received similar invitations," responded Holmes.

"Oh, indeed. May I speak bluntly? The poor fellow was mad as a hatter! I think playing chess for all those hours—sitting on his posterior and waiting forever for the other man to move—may have caused his mind to snap. Moreover, he was always angry and bitter."

"Why was that?" I asked.

"Because he was frustrated. You see, he achieved fame as a chess player, but never as a lawyer. This was hard for him to accept, because his father had been a judge. However, the sad truth is that the younger Morphy never had the right disposition to practice law. He was bright enough, mind you, probably a genius, but he was just wrong for this noble profession. No wonder people began to say something along the lines of how he was a chess player who merely dabbled with the law.

"On top of that, he had horrible judgment. When the Yankees occupied our city, he fled to Europe. This made more than a few people suspicious, and some opined that he was an agent working for the Confederate government. I never thought so, of course, but the point is that it was a terrible move on his part politically. The repercussions upon his return were inevitable. I had warned him against leaving a few weeks before that Spanish ship sailed. Unfortunately, when he started to go insane, he concluded that I was conspiring against him with the Northern army during Reconstruction. It was a despicable notion, and I resented it profoundly.

"Well, can you imagine my indignation when he added insult to injury? After all, I was the aggrieved party here, yet *he* challenged *me* to a duel! This was back in 1867, when his legal practice was failing miserably.

"I ignored the challenge, of course, and after a few months things calmed down. In fact, he greeted me civilly in church one Sunday, so I assumed all was forgotten."

"Did you ever play chess with Mr. Morphy?" Sherlock asked.

Our host smiled. "As you can probably tell, I'm a few years older. I beat him a couple of times when we were lads, but he quickly became much stronger. However, I got rather good at the game during the War. You see, there wasn't much work for lawyers in those days, since the Yankee military controlled virtually everything in the city. I got a couple of books, studied, and began to play at the New Orleans Chess Club. I came within half a point of winning the championship one year. On top of that, I could even play without sight of the board. They call that 'blindfolded,' Mr. Holmes."

"Yes, I have heard of it," replied my friend.

"So, one day I looked out my window, and you'd never guess who was coming down the street! As it happened, I had no pressing business, so I stepped outside and caught up with him.

"It was a cool afternoon, and we chatted aimlessly for a while. Then I asked him, perfectly innocently, about the best move for White if he was giving odds of Queen's Bishop and Queen's Knight. Morphy always preferred to advance the King's pawn two squares, as I knew. I then asked what to do if Black replied with the same move.

"Now, bear in mind that the King's Gambit opening, advancing the King's Bishop's pawn, is a little trickier with the Queen's Bishop off the board. In addition, the Black King's Knight will soon attack White's pawn by moving to King's Bishop's file, third rank. Thus, things were a little harder than they might have seemed.

"Well, Morphy developed his King's Bishop three squares, and when I suggested that Black could now move the King's Knight, he said White's best move was to defend with the Queen's pawn. We kept talking, and soon we had a game in progress. I should add that with the handicap I had received, I quickly achieved a superior position, and once I forced an exchange of Queens, an easy victory was within my grasp.

"At this point, Morphy realized what had happened. He snarled something about how I was not a gentleman and departed without so much as a handshake. Three days later, he again challenged me to a duel!

"Of course, I had experienced this madness before, so I thought to deflect it. I wrote back that since he had challenged me, I was entitled to my choice of weapons. I insisted on the Black pieces plus odds of a Rook."

"And I shall guess that this witty riposte was not well received!" noted Holmes.

"No, indeed it was not. He challenged me yet again, alluding vaguely to dueling pistols. This time I did not reply at all."

"And when did this occur?" asked Sherlock.

"I would guess at some point in the fall of 1869; I am not sure."

"And thereafter you kept your distance?"

"As a rule, yes, although I was in regular contact with John Sybrandt, Morphy's brother-in-law. Through John's wife, I kept abreast with news about Paul's mental state. When he was raving like a lunatic, I thought it best to stay away. However, while he was more lucid, I sought to rekindle our long friendship. After all, I had known him most of my life.

"I will say this much: Paul Morphy could be extremely courteous and gracious. Shortly before Christmas, 1882 I had occasion to be near his family home. On a whim, I called on him, and he greeted me most warmly. From that time on, although I saw little of him, we remained on good terms."

"Do you recall when you saw him last?" asked Holmes.

Hamilton nodded. "Yes, sadly. It was quite literally the day he died, and I have wondered ever since whether I should have foreseen his premature demise."

At this point, I thought it reasonable to interject a question of my own. "How could you possibly have done so?" I inquired. "What did you observe?"

Hamilton sighed and shook his head. "One of my clerks had just come in. He told me that 'the famous chess player' was walking in our direction and 'looked very angry about something.' Despite the heat, I dashed outside to see him.

"Paul was dressed sharply, as always, in a short-sleeved shirt, freshly pressed pants, bootblack-shined shoes, and a straw hat to keep the sun out of his face. As I approached, I could see that his lips were moving, and once within earshot I could hear his voice. As I drew nearer, I heard him say something along the lines of 'King's Bishop to Queen's file, third rank,' or words to that effect. I hailed him, but he did not even seem to hear me. Then he said, 'devilish bad games,' shook his head, and added, 'If I must sacrifice my Queen, so be it.' I followed for another block or so and heard him grow steadily more agitated. He would cry out, 'You are not a gentleman, Sir,' even as he called out moves of the game.

"At length he turned on his heels, looked right at me with fury and sheer hatred in his eyes, and shouted in an unearthly voice: 'The evil son of a Knight hides on his stony farm, but *he will not escape me*!' If I live to be one hundred, I shall never forget those words. I stopped in my tracks, very confused and more than a little afraid, while Morphy pivoted around and marched off. I fled back to my office, a nervous wreck for the rest of the afternoon. The next day I learned that he had died."

Holmes, inscrutable as always, stretched his fingers. "What did you fear, Sir?"

"As I have explained, Mr. Holmes, Paul Morphy had technically challenged me to a duel on three occasions. Moreover, he seemed extremely distraught; angrier than I have ever seen any man. Though he was incoherent, I could sense a clear threat. Here is why:

"He had once beaten me three times in a row at odds of a Knight. In one game, after I made a terrible oversight, he quipped good-naturedly, 'I should not have expected such a move from your son'—who was only three years old at the time—and graciously let me take back the blunder. He knew that I live in a stone house on a small farm—clearly, that was what he meant in his madness by the 'stony farm.' Naturally, I feared he once again intended me, or perhaps my son, some violence. Yet perhaps if I had stayed with him, I might have calmed him down and prevented the fatal stroke."

I now thought it best to venture a medical opinion. For the poor fellow's peace of mind, I assured him that he had no way to know what was about to transpire. Moreover, I told him, it sounded to me that anyone so fully enraged in the heat of the sun was imminently likely to have suffered a cerebral hemorrhage, whether that day, the next, or the one after.

Having brought some measure of closure to this last attorney, we took our leave.

* * *

I was totally confused after this last interview, though Holmes seemed quite cheerful, as he usually was when he had reached his conclusion. "Now see here, Holmes," I began. "We've heard a number of interesting fragments that fit Miss Morphy's narrative, but nothing substantive.

"Let's start with Mr. Williams. He seemed most charitably inclined toward Morphy, and he appears to have visited the deceased shortly after they decided not to institutionalize him. He had also hailed Morphy as the greatest chess player in the world—a comment that drew the latter's wrath, yet one that was sincerely intended."

"And his mention of the romantic interest?" asked my friend.

"The late Miss Gibson predeceased Paul Morphy, so she could not in any way be of major consideration. Thus, all in all, I don't find Mr. Williams remotely suspicious.

"Mr. Brown was notably less kindly disposed. Moreover, he effectively admitted that he deemed Morphy a chess player who also dabbled in jurisprudence, to the latter's consternation. However, he denied that he played chess and clearly seems to have been rather afraid of Morphy because of the challenge to a duel.

"And what do you conclude about the others, Watson?"

"Well, in Jones we have a man who was clearly antagonistic to Morphy. He considered him an inept attorney and even denigrated his accomplishments over the chessboard. Moreover, it seems he *does* play the game and had challenged Morphy to a match at Rook odds. Finally, he admits having seen Morphy in July of 1884 on a very hot day, when the ill-fated man walked past his office, although he did not give us a precise date. However, he, too, seemed somewhat afraid of Morphy's madness, and while we appear to get another piece or two of your client's story, we still see no evidence of a personal argument that might have precipitated a cerebral hemorrhage.

"That brings us to Mr. Hamilton. He admits that things between him and the deceased were not always cordial and says that poor fellow was 'mad as a hatter,' which does not seem far from the truth. He had wisely counseled him against leaving for Europe during the occupation of New Orleans. As a result, Morphy later made baseless accusations against him. What did Hamilton call it—'a despicable notion' and one he profoundly resented? That might give us some kind of motivation, but for what?

"Of perhaps greater interest, the gentleman has also identified himself as the person who had 'swindled' Morphy into a blindfolded game at some point in 1869, and when challenged to a duel, he requested the Black pieces and the now-familiar odds of a Rook. Thus, he, too, appears to have tried to provoke Morphy into some kind of match, and he seems slightly more suspect than Mr. Jones.

"Furthermore, Mr. Hamilton appears to have visited Morphy at his home, a detail that once again fits nicely with Miss Helena Morphy's account. Finally, he saw Morphy walking on that fateful day, followed him, and heard him calling out chess moves to some unknown opponent. Hamilton ultimately cited bizarre comments he reasonably construed as a clear threat, whereupon he presumably stopped dead in his tracks and abandoned Morphy to his madness."

Holmes clapped his hands. "Bravo, Watson! Your record of the testimonies is excellent. And your conclusion is what?"

I shook my head. "I'm flummoxed, Sherlock. All I can conclude is that Helena Morphy related facts as they actually occurred. In fact, some are corroborated by more than one of these attorneys. Both Williams and Hamilton appear to have visited Morphy at his home, though perhaps his sister was out of the house on one of the occasions. Both Brown and Jones openly stated he was an attorney of dubious skills. Both Jones and Hamilton seem to have challenged him to a match receiving Rook odds, and both saw him talking to himself as he walked nearby during the heat wave.

"Hamilton offered the more compelling testimony. He is clearly the one who 'swindled' Morphy into a game without sight of the board. He also claims Morphy was talking to himself, calling out chess moves and thinly veiled threats as he walked through New Orleans for the last time."

"Again, you give me a synopsis, John. I want your deduction."

I shook my head. "We have nothing, Holmes. Speaking as a physician, I don't see how any of this information could possibly alter the earlier medical conclusion. Paul Morphy died from a cerebral hemorrhage precipitated when he immersed himself in a cool bath after taking a long walk during a heat wave. True, he appears to have been infuriated by someone, and such rage doubtless triggered the stroke. However, we have absolutely no idea who it was who might thus have provoked him."

Holmes fixed me with his penetrating stare. Then he uttered a single word: "Rubbish!"

I was a little taken aback. "One of us is a physician, Sherlock," I reminded him.

This observation brought forth a big smile. "John, John, John! You look, but you do not see; you listen, but you do not hear. Behold: here comes our carriage. As we drive to the home of Miss Helena Morphy, I shall explain what you missed, and precisely what so infuriated her late brother. Then I shall ask whether such immense anger might indeed have contributed to his demise, and you will dutifully agree with me. Let me begin with a question."

Chapter 6

Conclusion – and Afterword

"Miss Helena Morphy gave us a list of six people whom her brother had challenged to a duel. You and I have spent an afternoon hearing testimony from how many men in all?"

I always hated it when Holmes asked me questions an imbecile could answer. "One attorney is deceased; one is severely incapacitated. Therefore, we heard from Williams, Brown, Jones, and Hamilton: four men in all."

"However, we heard about Morphy's exchanges *with five men*, John. Mr. Jones told us he had seen Morphy walking about and moving his lips, as though engaged in conversation. Mr. Hamilton not only saw him thus engaged but overheard some of Morphy's actual words. And these, my friend, explain precisely why he was truly so over-heated when he returned home and took the fatal bath."

My face surely registered my confusion. "Why, he mentioned some chess moves, and then he threatened Mr. Hamilton in some vague manner. I don't see—"

And now Sherlock burst into laughter. "Indeed! But it's all so obvious, John! Yes, Morphy was playing chess in his deluded state. Do you know whom he was playing?"

I shook my head. "No. I'm not even sure it matters."

"Ah, but it *does* matter. What was probably Morphy's greatest—and only—frustration over the chessboard?"

"From what you and Miss Morphy have told me, it was his inability to secure a match with Howard Staunton."

"Precisely! You also recall that Mr. Williams said he overheard Morphy punctuate his moves with the comment, 'devilish bad games'—the same phrase he had used as a teenager! Morphy handed a certain gentleman, one James McConnell, a copy of the book of the London tournament of 1851, which Staunton had edited. On the title page, Morphy alluded to Mr. Staunton as 'author of *The Handbook of Chess, Chess-player's Companion,* etc. (and some devilish bad games).' Thus, those words clearly alluded to Howard Staunton!

"And who were the Staunton families of England? Their name had at least two meanings in Old English: 'Stan's farm' or 'the stony farm,' since 'Stan' also meant 'stone.' Are you with me?"

I nodded.

"At this point our story gets even better, John. After the Anglo-Norman invasion of Ireland during the 12th century, some of the Stauntons began to use the name, MacEvilly—which means 'the son of the knight'!"

"My God!" I gasped. "So in his madness, Morphy was playing chess against Howard Staunton. He took the 'evil' from MacEvilly and got 'the evil son of a Knight'; from the name of his nemesis he got 'the stony farm.' What else did I miss, Holmes?"

"He eventually realized that his pursuit of Staunton had ultimately obliged him to 'sacrifice his Queen'—in this case the late Miss Gibson. The rest falls into place neatly, does it not, John? He had been consumed by bitterness ever since 1858, when plans for the match fell through. He felt that chess had deprived him of both career and marriage, yet it had also denied him the one victory he so desperately desired. As he sank more and more deeply into the lunacy, he created one last, final contest against Howard Staunton."

"And the outcome?" I inquired.

"Elementary, my dear Watson! Unless you choose to believe he was indeed playing against Staunton's ghost—our former champion had died ten years earlier—we may safely infer that in his madness Paul Morphy was somehow playing both sides of a game he *imagined* was against Howard Staunton. Now, if Morphy played against Morphy, White and Black were perfectly evenly matched, and the outcome, rather than a crushing victory against the despised opponent, would far more likely have been a mere draw! Meanwhile, even as the poor

English master Howard Staunton, widely regarded as the world's best player around the middle of the 19th century, just before Morphy.

man continued to dwell on Staunton, his already high blood pressure began to escalate, and his failure to win—despite the promise that the 'evil son of a Knight' would not escape him—must have left his blood close to the boiling point!

"And *now* tell me, Doctor. Might that indeed have been enough to have induced the fatal stroke after he reclined in a cool or even lukewarm bath?"

I nodded affirmatively. "As you have explained to me so many times, once we eliminate the impossible, whatever remains, no matter how improbable, must be the truth. Your encyclopedic knowledge and pure genius have cracked yet another bizarre case!" I conceded. Then I paused. "But what will you now tell your client?"

"The truth: that we have investigated all the leads she provided, and we have concluded that Paul Morphy did indeed suffer a fatal stroke in his bath, exactly as she had been told. Moreover, she may rest assured that *none* of the gentlemen on her list engaged in hostilities with Morphy that fatal day. In fact, the incident that appears to have provoked him so immensely had, for all intents, occurred more than twenty-five years earlier, and the target of his wrath, Mr. Staunton, had been dead for ten years."

...and that is exactly what Holmes explained that evening.

Now, I must append a few final footnotes to my narrative. First, I should report that he truly did give Helena Morphy some peace of mind, which was surely a positive development. Alas, the poor woman was in ill health herself, and I later learned from Harold that she died the following year, on 8 September 1886.

The next pertains more to Sherlock Holmes. He graciously declined to accept any fee whatsoever from Miss Morphy, and thereafter rarely accepted payment, although he generally sought reimbursement for any expenses he incurred.

Finally, I should mention yet another event that occurred in 1886. Wilhelm Steinitz, who had been unable even to discuss chess with Paul Morphy during their brief encounter, trounced Johannes Zukertort, whom Morphy had also met briefly, by a score of ten games to five, with five draws, thereby becoming the first official world chess champion.

I have no doubt that Mr. Steinitz deserves the title. Still, I wonder how far Holmes might have gone had he chosen to pursue chess as a profession.

Sherlock Holmes and the Mystery of the Meddlesome Meat

The 1946 Death of Alexander Alekhine

Notes on Alexander Alekhine

At some time after 11 p.m. on the evening of March 23, 1946, Alexander Alekhine, the world chess champion, died under rather mysterious circumstances. The "official" cause of death was asphyxiation; presumably a large piece of meat had become trapped in his throat, and he was unable to dislodge it. The photographs showed him resting peacefully on his armchair. In front of him were the empty plates used during his last meal and, off to his right, a chessboard.

Everything about this picture appears staged. Moreover, the "official" story inevitably spawned various rumors, all of which reached the same conclusion: that Alekhine had in fact been murdered.

If someone did indeed kill the champion—and like many others I share this suspicion—one question remains: who? Books have been written on the subject, and various writers, including Kevin Spraggett and Edward Winter, have uploaded considerable copy, based on immense research.

Of course, I should have been delighted to solve the mystery, but I must confess that every hypothesis I explored—and a number of them arose—appeared to have one or more major flaws. Thus, I deemed it appropriate to retire the serious efforts and turned instead to fiction, summoning up no less than Sherlock Holmes for the hero of my tale.

I do not for a moment take the deductive reasoning of Mr. Holmes (who in this incarnation is the 92-year-old grandson of Doyle's protagonist; the year, after all, is 2018) with anything more than a grain of salt. The text that follows is intended as little more than an exercise for the reader's enjoyment. I do hope, however, that this novelette can serve as a vehicle to prompt further interest in the untimely demise of Alekhine.

Chapter 1

The Visitor

The old man rarely had visitors. Thus, Francisco Aguilar took the staff somewhat by surprise when he arrived at Kensington Village, the gated community in London, clutching an attaché case in one hand and the printout of an e-mail from Mr. Holmes (inviting him to discuss his situation) in the other. The supervisor hastily had someone call to confirm that Mr. Holmes was indeed willing to entertain anyone that day. To everyone's surprise, the old man seemed if anything most anxious to receive the stranger, who was dutifully led into his flat.

The violin lay on the coffee table. It was unclear to Francisco whether it had been played at all recently, although a closer inspection led him to believe it had. The presence of the nearby music stand seemed to support that conclusion. *How strange!* he thought. *I walk into the home of Sherlock Holmes, and almost instantly I, too, begin to think like a detective!*

The spry nonagenarian Sherlock—technically Sherlock Holmes III— motioned him to sit down.

"Mr. Holmes," the visitor began. "As I explained in my e-mail, I am reaching out to you in desperation. You see, I need...ah...assistance." He took a seat and placed the attaché case by his right leg.

His host smiled, as though trying to reassure him. "Of course, my friend, and I shall be delighted to be of service. And that said, I begin to see a considerable trail of information at once."

"Indeed, Mr. Holmes?"

"Yes, yes. You are here because of something involving a murder, a large sum of money, and your family, perhaps going back a generation or two."

The visitor's jaw dropped. "Why, this is true. How can you tell all that?"

"Elementary, my dear Mr. Aguilar. First, you have asked for my professional services. This, at once, indicates that the issue is most grave indeed, possibly involving blackmail or embezzlement, but far more likely involving murder.

"Second, out of all the people practicing this craft, you have chosen me, perhaps the most expensive one available on those rare occasions when I charge a fee—and, I might add, doubtless one of the very best who ever lived, and grandson of the most famous private investigator ever. Yet from your attire, it is clear you are not wealthy enough to afford my services. This, in turn, suggests that you stand to come into funds sufficient for the task at hand, and the most obvious way to effect such a change of financial status is through inheritance."

"Why, that is true, Mr. Holmes, I—"

"However, the benefactor in question obviously needs to know the answer far more desperately than you do, which suggests that it concerns an ancestor of his. Hence, a logical deduction, and if I may be so bold as to hazard a guess: your grandfather?"

Francisco's eyes were nearly popping out of his head.

"But please continue. Wherein lies the problem?"

It took the visitor a moment to recover, but to his credit, he did not back down. "Do you perhaps play chess, Mr. Holmes?"

"I did long ago, although I rapidly concluded that it would take far too much of my time and energy to master the game. Alas, I determined that it was probably not worth all the study and practice, so I put my pretensions aside for more worthwhile pursuits. Of course, I still enjoy chess and follow the big tournaments online."

"Then you have surely heard of Alexander Alekhine." He pronounced the name quite deliberately: Al—yekh (guttural kh, and accented)—in. Holmes, of course, had heard a number of other pronunciations, some more Anglicized than others, but he had long ago concluded that the stress belongs on the second syllable.

"Of course! The fourth world champion! I played against him once when I was only twelve years old—in Margate, after some or other tournament. I was fortunate enough to defeat him, although he was doubtless somewhat distracted by playing nineteen of us simultaneously, and blindfolded at that! Moreover, because of my tender years, he insisted on giving me odds of pawn-and-move. Still, I was the only one to prevail. He drew three games and won all the rest."

Francisco, increasingly overwhelmed, stared at the floor and seemed reluctant to speak. At length he replied, "Have you ever heard rumors that Alekhine might have been murdered?"

"Of course, I am no stranger to this conjecture, although as with so many other alleged crimes, no one has yet found any substantive proof." He studied his guest somewhat more carefully. The man before him did not appear much more than fifty years of age, if that, with generally youthful features that stood in sharp contrast to his apparent fatigue. The fellow surely needed a good night's sleep; that much was certain.

"In fact, it seems more likely than not, if only because the list of plausible suspects is so long. Perhaps he knew his assailant; perhaps he was unaware that he was about to die. We do know he expressed fears that he was being followed," Francisco continued somewhat excitedly.

"All right," Holmes replied, seeking to calm him. "Why don't you begin by telling me what this is all about? I no longer go abroad, of course, so I am not at all certain whether my services can in fact benefit you. Besides, what is so important about Alekhine?"

Francisco looked again at his watch. "I have very little time to solve this problem, Mr. Holmes. Surely, as one who follows chess and plays a little, you are familiar with 'time pressure'! I have at most only a matter of days."

"But the murder—if it was indeed murder—occurred more than seventy years ago. I doubt severely that the assassin is still alive. Please: you must explain what this is all about. But no! Let me guess. Somehow it involves you, or more accurately, your family."

Holmes's client drew a deep breath and exhaled slowly. "Yet again you are correct, and doubtless you are as good as your grandfather was reputed to be. But perhaps we should discuss your terms," he began.

The detective nodded. "You surely know that I usually waive my fee, although I am otherwise beastly expensive."

"Oh, you will be paid, you will!" Francisco promised. "It's just that I am a little compromised right now. You see, I have had enormous expenses, having traveled all over Europe—Portugal, France, Germany, and Russia. And after that I had to go to the United States."

The old man rolled his eyes. This, as one can imagine, was a tale he had heard before, in one variant or another, and he had already made up his mind not to charge his visitor.

"However, as you yourself deduced, I shall be coming into a considerable sum of money soon."

"Oh?" Holmes asked. "Please explain, then."

Aguilar seemed almost too nervous to continue. Nevertheless, he somehow recovered his composure. "All right. I shall."

Holmes offered him a hand gesture, sufficiently intrigued to hear him out.

"My grandfather, Miguel, was a friend of Alekhine after the war."

"In Portugal?"

"Why, yes; in Estoril. They played cards and chess together. He was better at poker, but reasonably strong at chess as well. My father told me that when Alekhine gave my grandfather Rook odds and two-to-one time odds they were 'just about even.' And then one day—24 March 1946—my grandfather went to visit Dr.

The fourth world chess champion, Alexander Alekhine.

Alekhine in his hotel room but found there were police everywhere. 'What has happened?' he asked, and someone explained that Alexander Alekhine had died."

"And could your grandfather offer any information—useful or otherwise—to the police?"

"Why...no; he simply turned around. One of the detectives called out to him and asked him why he had come to the room, and my grandfather explained that he had wanted to play chess with Dr. Alekhine. They asked a couple of other questions, took his name and address, and told him he could leave. Of course, most people would have been terrified. The police needed little excuse to arrest anyone in Portugal in those days. However, my grandfather...uh...shall we say, he had access to some 'higher-ups' within the secret police, the *PIDE*."

Holmes winced with mild disgust at this last information. He could also already anticipate where his potential client was leading him. "And let me guess again: When he saw the photograph in the newspaper and read the official report, he didn't think it was altogether accurate?"

"This we do not know, since he never talked about it. However, something must have bothered him, because on his deathbed, he called my father over to him. 'Rodrigo, Alekhine…killed. Some day, you have to…' Just those eight words, and then he died."

Sherlock Holmes shook his head. "Okay. This is ridiculous. You expect me to help you solve a seventy-two-year-old mystery? Why, who do you think I am? True, I am Professor Emeritus Sherlock Holmes III, the master of deductive reasoning, grandson of one legend and son of another. However, I am also ninety-two years of age and unable to travel out of the UK. Unless you have already done all the detective work—and at that, I must hope you've done a vastly superior job than poor Detective Lestrade was ever able to perform!—I do not see how I can help you."

Francisco Aguilar stood up, excited. "Yes, yes you can! You are exactly the person I need! Only someone with your extraordinary skills can put all the pieces together, figure out what I am missing, and solve this murder case!"

There was a moment of silence, during which Aguilar sat down. At length Holmes replied. "I devoutly wish you had come to me ten years ago, when I was still able to move about freely. However, even if my body has begun to betray me, my mind is still sharp. The Holmes men all retain their remarkable intellectual powers to the very end. In fact, my grandfather, the original Sherlock Holmes, was born on 6 January 1854. That means he would be 164 years old if he were alive today, yet I can guarantee you he would be as keen and insightful as ever!"

The visitor nodded. "Of course, he would, Mr. Holmes."

"Even so, I must ask you two questions. First, are you sure you have done adequate research? Can you present all the evidence I shall need?"

"Oh, absolutely, Mr. Holmes. I've taken copious notes, and I have some documents for your perusal in my briefcase. Moreover, everything is up here," he declared, pointing to his head. "It's just that I lack your deductive powers, Mr. Holmes. But I'm sure all you will need to do is sift through the information I can provide and show me what I am missing."

Holmes was forced to admit that the sheer conceit of the proposal intrigued him. It was a seventy-two-year-old mystery with the clock ticking away. "I shall need the details, Mr. Aguilar, all the details. My second question—and please do not concern yourself about my fee—involves your actual circumstances. Pray enlighten me!"

"It is as I have told you. If I can solve this case in the allotted time, I stand to come into a large sum of money, and I shall gladly pay you everything you might normally charge for such a service."

Holmes realized that his visitor might in fact be stark, raving mad, but something about the man told him otherwise. The latter's response caught his attention.

"Let me explain, Mr. Holmes. As I told you, my grandfather instructed my father to tell the world how Alekhine was murdered, but he died before he could say anything more. That was January 1965. However, my father soon had many other things to worry about. You see, while my grandfather had been on excellent terms with various individuals within the Salazar regime, Rodrigo was of a different political persuasion and had become friendly with some of the people involved in the campaign of Humberto Delgado. Do you know who he was, Mr. Holmes?"

"Of course: the ill-fated presidential candidate—the man who vowed that he would dismiss the prime minister, the same Antonio de Oliveira Salazar! However, Salazar took care of him."

Francisco was by this time completely in awe of the old detective. "You are truly most well informed, Mr. Holmes. Yes, Delgado had been exiled for a while, but he was coming back. He got as close as Olivenza—which is really Portuguese, not Spanish, by the way. Anyway, that February he was attempting to cross the border when he was shot and killed by the *PIDE*."

"Yes, yes; I know all about them. They were Salazar's secret police, a gang of thugs who murdered with impunity. And in Delgado's case, if I remember correctly, they explained that he and his secretary were killed in a shoot-out after they had precipitated an exchange of gunfire—all of which would seem perfectly reasonable, except that Delgado was unarmed, and the secretary was garroted, strangled to death! So much for Portuguese 'justice' in those days!"

Francisco's jaw dropped yet again. "Why...yes...that is correct, exactly as you tell it, Mr. Holmes. So, my father felt it would be safest if he fled, because he knew they would soon start to round up Delgado sympathizers. Fortunately, he had occasion to go to London on business, and once there he met my mother, whom he married just two weeks later. I was born the following year, 1966, slightly more than 20 years after the death of Alekhine."

"Ah, excellent! We can certainly rule *you* out. You clearly had nothing to do with it!" quipped Holmes with a wry chuckle.

Francisco smiled and nodded his head. "But now, Mr. Holmes, my father is dying. He has prospered in the United Kingdom and is a very wealthy man. Unfortunately, he and I have been estranged for some years. However, when I heard about the cancer, I immediately went to see him, and we have effected some sort of...shall we say—"

"Reconciliation?"

"Yes, that is the word, Mr. Holmes. Still, it turned out that he had disinherited me in favor of my cousins—his wife's sister's children. However, he has drawn up an alternative will, contingent upon one last task. If I can figure out what my grandfather was getting at and determine who killed Alekhine, I shall inherit half of my father's fortune—three million pounds! And that is why I have spent almost everything I had, traveling all over Europe and the United States, interviewing men in their 80s and 90s, reading through official and unofficial documents, and trying to make sense of it all."

"And your conclusions—such as they are, for had you reached a firm conclusion, you would surely not have sought my services, would you?"

"Unlike you, Mr. Holmes, I am not a great detective. In fact, my skills are those of an amateur. However, I have found my suspects."

"Suspects? Plural? Do continue!"

"Yes. After ruling out natural causes and suicide, I have narrowed it down to five groups of people, any or all of whom might have murdered Alekhine, and most of whom had the motive to do so."

Holmes nodded. "And you want *me* merely to listen to your catalogue and tell you which ones are the legitimate suspects?"

Francisco Aguilar hesitated. "Well, yes, Mr. Holmes. Either that, or tell me they are all hopelessly wrong, and—unless you can solve this seventy-two-year-old mystery in the next week or so—send me back empty-handed and destitute."

To Francisco's surprise, the old man let out a whoop of joy. "By Jove, I like it! I need an exercise of this sort. Pray begin, and please spare me no detail, for nothing is insignificant in a tale of this sort!"

Chapter 2

The Death – or Murder – of Alekhine

Francisco now eagerly began his narrative. Although quite in awe of his host, he wanted the old man to appreciate the immensely thorough work he had done on his own.

"Alekhine defeated his bitter rival, Jose Raoul Capablanca, and won the championship in 1927. Many felt that Capablanca had not trained seriously, and the popular consensus was that the Cuban would win the rematch. This, however, would never take place, for whatever reasons.

"Nevertheless, the new champion soon established his domination, and during the early 1930s stood head and shoulders above his colleagues. Surprisingly, he proceeded to lose the title to Max Euwe in 1935, due at least in part to his heavy drinking. He regained the title two years later, but certainly faded somewhat thereafter, finishing tied for fourth to sixth place in the AVRO tournament. Then came World War II.

"It was at this juncture that a controversy arose. With the outbreak of hostilities, Alekhine returned to France in time for the Germans to overrun the country. The Nazis offered to permit him to play tournaments in occupied Europe and effectively left the considerable estate of Alekhine's fourth wife—who may have been part-Jewish—at least somewhat intact, but in all likelihood not without a quid-pro-quo.

"Alekhine wrote, or was at least credited as author of, a series of articles on the subject of 'Jewish and Aryan Chess.' These were designed to conform to prevailing Nazi theories about the Jewish character and were full of vicious attacks on a number of prominent Jewish players, including Steinitz, Lasker, Rubinstein, Reshevsky, and Fine. The champion actually spoke proudly about these articles in an interview with a Spanish newspaper in 1941, but after the liberation of France insisted that the texts had been rewritten by the German editor and repudiated them altogether.

"Alekhine died in March 1946. He had been in ill health for a number of years, and some speculated that he had succumbed to a heart attack. The official autopsy report claimed he died when a piece of meat he had been eating became lodged in his throat.

"Others, however, insisted that he had been murdered. This is apparently what my grandfather implied, also, and I must determine by whom."

There was no response from Sherlock Holmes, and for a brief while Francisco wondered whether his host might have "nodded off." At length, however, the detective replied.

"You suggested a heart attack. Why? What was the physical condition of Dr. Alekhine at the time?"

Aguilar hesitated. "He was quite ill. You see, he had already had two heart attacks. Moreover, he had drunk heavily for many years, reportedly up to three and one-half pints of brandy per day."

"That's more than enough to damage one's liver," noted Holmes.

"Indeed, he was known to have suffered from cirrhosis of the liver, and he also got scarlet fever during the War. The post-mortem confirmed arteriosclerosis, duodenitis, and gastritis. And, of course, the cigarettes didn't help, either—with all due respect to your grandfather's famous pipe, Mr. Holmes."

"Apologies are unnecessary," replied the other. "But what of his finances?"

"Why, he was impoverished, or painfully close thereunto. In fact, just fifteen days before his death, he had asked his friend, Francisco Lupi, to help him write a book about the Hastings tournament, adding that he was completely without funds and needed some money to buy cigarettes."

"Ah…and what came of the project?"

Aguilar had already researched that question and answered immediately. "Why, as far as I have been able to discern, absolutely nothing."

"And why not?"

"Well, perhaps Alekhine had come into some much-needed funds."

"How much money did he have on his person at the time of death."

Now this question *did* surprise Francisco. "None whatsoever, unless the *PIDE* walked off with it. In fact, the only item of value—probably more sentimental than material—he yet retained had been shattered. It was a Sevres vase that had been given him by the Czar, which Alekhine valued very much."

"So, he went from dire poverty to a condition at least minimally comfortable, yet at the time of his death he seemed once again penniless. Interesting, don't you think?"

Aguilar nodded. "In fact, two nights before he died, on the 22nd, he went off to Lisbon, probably to enjoy the bars and spend some money he did not have thirteen days earlier!"

"And there was an autopsy?"

"Yes, yes, indeed. However, a doctor who witnessed it is later rumored to have admitted that the official story—how he choked on a piece of meat—was a complete fabrication. You see, the *PIDE*—"

"Ah, those villains! Let me guess. They didn't want any sort of investigation, since that would call international attention to their country, where far greater crimes were committed by the regime every day. Am I close?"

"Why…yes, that is so, Mr. Holmes, and as you noted, they couldn't really allow too much attention from the rest of the world. A sick man had died. He was fifty-three, which is only a shade older than I am, but he was in very poor health, so they preferred to keep the matter quiet. The fact that the person in question had also expressed fears that he was being followed was completely ignored during the ensuing investigation."

"And the police—those incompetents who are paid so well in every country across the globe to bungle up any investigation? Did *they* not at least take a large number of photographs of the death scene, which your grandfather insists was also a crime scene? But please—perhaps I am rushing you. Start at the beginning, or where you feel most comfortable."

Francisco took a deep breath. "The official story derives from a letter to the Associated Press by one Luis Lupi—ironically, the stepfather of that same Francisco Lupi, who was a close friend of the world champion—and also from the autopsy report dated 27 March. Lupi's letter included photographs of the deceased, but only two have been published," he explained. "Now, what we are told is that at 10:40 p.m. on the 23rd, Alekhine had ordered dinner, which was delivered to his hotel room. Lupi also noted the calm appearance of the man and concluded that he 'must have died suddenly just when he was beginning to eat'—his exact words."

"And the food," noted Holmes "was delivered by someone who might be said to have functioned in the capacity of a butler. Surely, you've heard the old stories about how the butler did it, haven't you?"

Francisco stared at his host, confused. At length the latter explained, with a slight smile, "That was a joke."

"Oh," said the other, obviously relieved. "Well, a death certificate was signed by Dr. Antonio Ferreira, who apparently also witnessed the autopsy, and that procedure was performed by one Dr. Asdrubal d'Aguiar."

Holmes opened his mouth, as if to speak, but apparently thought better of it and motioned to his client to continue.

"You were about to say, Mr. Holmes?"

"Oh, nothing, really; it's just a coincidence, don't you think? Your given name is Francisco, like that of Alekhine's last friend, whose stepfather just mysteriously arrived at the scene in some or other journalistic capacity. Then one Dr. d'Aguiar—whose name is rather frightfully close to yours, Mr. Aguilar—did the autopsy. But pray continue!"

The other swallowed, paused long enough to process what he had been told, and resumed his discussion. "You make an interesting observation, Mr. Holmes. In fact, Dr. d'Aguiar was a second cousin of my grandfather. For some unknown reason, my father added the 'L' when he came to the United Kingdom. But please let me continue:

"As I was saying, the autopsy report attributed the death to asphyxia and effectively claimed the deceased had choked on a piece of meat. It mentioned arteriosclerosis, gastritis, and duodenitis, but *not* cirrhosis of the liver. It also—conclusively—ruled out foul play."

"Wait!" cried Holmes. "You mentioned photographs. Do you have copies with you?"

"Of course! Here they are. I've been very thorough with my research, Mr. Holmes, and I have come to you prepared." He reached into his attaché case, pulled out copies of the pictures in question, and handed them to the detective, who studied them carefully with his magnifying glass and then put them aside as the other continued. "What was stranger still was that Ferreira later wrote a letter to Alekhine's son, in which he repeated the assertions from the autopsy report—i.e., that there was no evidence of either suicide or homicide. In fact, he even went so far as to append that the late champion showed no evidence of *any* other diseases that might have caused his precipitous demise."

"Well, he was certainly at least a witness to the autopsy. The photos you gave me look as though Alekhine died rather peacefully." Holmes paused long enough to sit forward in his chair. Then he shook his head.

The famous photograph of the deceased Alekhine. He allegedly choked on a piece of meat. But one would think that the immediate area around him would have shown signs of a violent albeit natural reaction to, as well as an attempt to clear the blockage of his air passage. However, there does not appear to be anything "out of order." Did he pass peacefully or was there something more sinister going on?

"Rubbish!"

"That's what I have concluded, also, Mr. Holmes. It all sounds too sanitized, as if it were what the *PIDE* wanted everyone to believe. Nevertheless, even in heavily censored Portugal, rumors began to spread. One such report claimed that Ferreira later repudiated the official autopsy and swore that Alekhine's body had been found in the street. Of course, this was only a rumor."

Holmes shook his head. "Perhaps we should begin with the photographs. What do you make of them?" he asked.

"They were staged—set up, Mr. Holmes. I know, because I once got something lodged in my throat. I struggled desperately, jumping, stomping my feet. Surely, if nothing else, the chessboard and make-shift table would have been knocked over!"

"Precisely, Mr. Aguilar. We'll make a detective of you yet!"

"Moreover, this Luis Lupi was also a 'higher-up' within the *PIDE*, and if there were a cover-up, it would probably have been his job to contrive it, beginning with the photos."

Holmes returned to the copies and handed them back to Francisco. "Look at that thing that looks somewhat like a binder—the dark object. Do you see a difference in the two pictures?"

This caught the younger man by surprise, and it took him little time to see the point. "Why, of course. In the second shot there are some papers on top of it!" he cried.

"Does this not suggest that someone was altering the crime scene?"

"Indeed, and there is more. Francisco Lupi later admitted that just as they were about to shoot the pictures, his stepfather added the chessboard to the background. I suppose it was a nice touch, but clearly an inaccuracy, and certainly unconscionable for police investigating a possible homicide."

Holmes smiled broadly. "Unless they were instead manipulating it! And look at the dinner table itself. How does it strike you?"

Francisco scowled and looked closely. "Why, I don't see any food whatsoever!" he exclaimed.

"Correct! Yet people generally do not conclude their meal with meat, do they?"

"Why, no. And Lupi's letter to the Associated Press referred to how Alekhine had another piece of meat in his hand, yet I cannot see it in either picture."

"So, then, what do we conclude, Mr. Aguilar?"

"That Mr. Lupi clearly did not photograph the crime scene as it was first discovered. But here's another discrepancy, Mr. Holmes. Presumably, the body of Alekhine was found at 11 A.M. the following morning, the 24th. However, Francisco Lupi later wrote an article—the title translates, 'The Broken King'—in which he related how he was awakened at 10:30

A.M. and told to get to the Parque Hotel because something had happened to his friend, Alekhine."

"By whom?" Holmes asked. "Who awakened him?"

Francisco shook his head. "He didn't say, but I suspect that it was by Luis Lupi, his stepfather."

Holmes merely smiled; his client continued.

"Luis Lupi, of course, operated under the cover of a different profession. He presumably worked as a journalist. But let us continue with the report. Alekhine had died—most peacefully, it would seem—as he was beginning to eat his meal. Beginning to eat his meal, yet the plates were already clean! Now, even if the official story were correct—even if he had choked on a piece of meat lodged in his throat, could that not possibly have provoked a heart attack? And yet a cardiac arrest was ruled out."

Holmes smiled. "We all know he drank excessively, and he had been diagnosed with cirrhosis. Do you not find it strange that the inestimable physician performing the autopsy neglected to mention that disorder?"

"Indeed. And I can tell you something even stranger, Mr. Holmes. From all I have been able to glean—and I read Portuguese quite well—the witness to the autopsy, Dr. Ferreira, was not a medical doctor, but a veterinarian. Of course, that didn't matter, since he had another qualification that was far more significant. He, too, was involved with the *PIDE.*" And with that statement, Francisco pulled two more sheets out of his attaché case. "Look at the first two names I have highlighted."

"Curiouser and curiouser," said Holmes, softly. "Ferreira and Luis Lupi. I suspect that Lupi was the one in charge. Ferreira was his underling, and his presence—a veterinarian's presence—at an official autopsy was probably designed for one purpose: to ensure that d'Aguiar's report presented all the information exactly as the *PIDE* wanted it."

Francisco nodded. "Yes, I agree. And this raises an intriguing question. Why was the *PIDE* so extensively involved in an apparent cover-up?"

Holmes took a deep breath. "Something else bothers me here. You alluded to a Sevres vase, which was somehow damaged. Now I—"

"Oh, yes, Mr. Holmes. Here! I have a picture of it." Once more, Francisco reached into his briefcase.

Holmes looked carefully. "Yet there is no mention of this?"

"None."

"Give me more discrepancies, if you would."

"One Artur Portela reported in a published article that Alekhine had lost his overcoat on 22nd March—in other words, the night before he died—in Lisbon, and yet what do you think he was wearing in the photographs?"

Holmes's eyebrows shot up. "Strange, indeed, and it raises the question of why he was wearing a coat inside his room. Now, you said he was in Lisbon. Were there any witnesses?"

Francisco smiled. "Oh, yes, Mr. Holmes. Two. The first was his friend, Francisco Lupi. The other was another chess player, one Jose da Costa Moreira. If you go to page two of that print-out listing the cast of the *PIDE* characters, guess whom else you will find."

Holmes flipped back the first page. "Jose da Costa Moreira! That is well and good, but please fill in the gaps, Mr. Aguilar. Who was this Artur Portela, and why should we deem him a reputable source?"

"Because he had earned international renown as a journalist, Mr. Holmes. In fact, he wrote a noteworthy interview of Winston Churchill. He also received the *Ordem da Liberdade*, the Portuguese Order of Liberty Award, but that was some decades after Alekhine's murder."

The older man reflected for a moment and seemed once again lost in thought. However, he soon snapped back to attention with yet another line of inquiry. "We see the fingerprints of the *PIDE* all over the place, effectively escorting him to Lisbon, clearly taking custody of his overcoat, and indisputably masterminding a cover-up, most notably taking pains to stage the photographs and present an autopsy that defied medical reason.

I must now make a logical deduction: Since Alekhine had complained that he was being followed, and since we know of the *PIDE*'s involvement in the cover-up, you briefly considered those thugs as possible assassins, but you quickly rejected the notion."

Francisco opened his mouth, but before he could get out a single syllable, Holmes interrupted him. "Of course, you did well to consider them! However, you ruled them out completely, as have I, simply because they had no motive. On to the next suspects, Mr. Aguilar."

The latter was clearly taken aback, and it took him a few seconds to regain his composure. "You are right, Mr. Holmes. I did consider them, and it is clear they covered up whatever actually *did* occur. However, the world champion was warmly received by the Salazar regime, which had recently declared chess a sport for the intellect. Moreover, Alekhine's earlier visits—during the war, in particular—had raised interest in the game. And as you may or may not realize, he had effectively been granted asylum in Portugal. In late 1945 he was apparently wanted for 'questioning' in France—you know, about the alleged collaboration with the Germans. He was living in Spain at the time, but when word filtered out that the Franco regime planned to hand him over to French authorities, he fled to Portugal, where he was welcomed with open arms."

"So why do you think the *PIDE* was invariably in the picture?"

"Well, you must remember that he was staying in Estoril. It was rumored that the Nazis had hidden large amounts of gold in Portugal, including a fair quantity right in that city. Thus, the *PIDE* had to keep things clean and tidy. The Salazar government, corrupt as it was, did not want an international inquiry, which the assassination of a world chess champion might have provoked. No, it was safer by far to keep things quiet."

"Of course! And in this way, they could also keep foreign intelligence from finding some excuse to search more thoroughly for the alleged deposits of gold."

"Exactly!"

"Very well, then Mr. Aguilar. We have ruled *you* out, since you weren't born until twenty years or so later. We have ruled out the *PIDE*, though we acknowledge that they covered up the details of what had happened. If the Portuguese weren't the assassins, who were? First, as my grandfather always explained to Dr. Watson, we should seek those who had some motive. I believe you mentioned no fewer than five possible suspects, and we're now down to four.

"Let us pick up the thread. According to one rumor, Dr. Ferreira, this enigmatic veterinarian, may have told someone—a friend with a loose tongue, perhaps?—that Alekhine's body had been found in the street. We may safely surmise that if this is indeed what happened, it was easy enough for his *PIDE* colleagues to bring the body back to the hotel, move some furniture around to stage the photographs, and even stick a piece of meat down the deceased champion's throat.

"However, it is also possible that the rumor is completely false, and that Ferreira never told anyone anything of the sort. Whatever the case, I suspect such speculation is not germane to your investigation, so we should now return to what we *do* know.

"For some reason, the *PIDE* felt strongly motivated to keep everything quiet; such orders probably came directly from Salazar's office. Thus, they were covering up, but for whom?"

Francisco Aguilar drew out one last sheet of paper. "What do you make of this, Mr. Holmes?"

The latter read and scowled. "It seems that immediately after the *PIDE* had finished the 'investigation,' every last piece of furniture was removed from the room, and even the door number was changed! Fascinating! Now, on to your suspects, Mr. Aguilar."

Chapter 3

"But None of Them Works, Mr. Holmes!"

Francisco Aguilar paused and then asked if he might have some water. Holmes led him into the kitchen and offered his guest a seat at the table. He pulled out two crystal glasses from a cabinet and a pitcher of ice water from the refrigerator. After filling both vessels, he sat down opposite Francisco and bade him continue.

"The most popular suspects—and arguably the most villainous—are the Soviets. Whether we refer to the NKVD or KGB, their intelligence *apparatchiks* were certainly ruthless. Also, the Soviet chess czar, Boris Veinshtein was a known NKVD officer, and he adamantly opposed the idea of a match between Mikhail Botvinnik and Alekhine. Nevertheless, orders from 'above'—from the Communist Party, and perhaps even from Stalin—paved the way for the challenge."

Holmes nodded. "And given the amount of blood on Stalin's hands, there was no way for Veinshtein to interfere with the dictates from on high."

"Precisely, Mr. Holmes. In fact, the Soviets viewed the world chess championship as a title that would lend prestige to their system of government—and indeed they held the crown until the breakup of the USSR, save for those three years after Fischer defeated Spassky."

"I agree," replied the detective. "From all you have told me, Alekhine was in terrible shape physically—cirrhosis, diverticulitis, scarlet fever, two heart attacks, and the cumulative effects of alcohol and tobacco. You have

The "Patriarch of Russian Chess," the sixth world champion Mikhail Botvinnik.

perhaps heard the saying, 'one foot in the grave and the other on life support'? It would seem to apply here."

"Right! There is no way Botvinnik would have lost a match to Alekhine in 1946. Moreover, another consideration reared its head at this point, namely that Alekhine might die. In that case, FIDE would probably allow the title to revert to Euwe, who might then accept a challenge from either of the top Americans, Fine or Reshevsky. Euwe was also well past his prime and would almost surely have lost. To the Soviets, it was imperative to prevent the crown from falling into American hands. Thus, they truly *wanted* the match pitting their superstar against the shell of Alekhine."

Holmes nodded. "It is safe to rule them out, then. Next?"

Francisco hesitated. "Well, I am almost embarrassed to suggest this, but I wanted to leave no stone unturned. I had already ventured as far as Russia, where I met a number of people who understood the Soviet mentality, even if they were not involved with the decisions that were made. I would later journey in the opposite direction, to the United States."

Again, the thick, gray eyebrows shot up. "You didn't think the Americans could possibly have been involved, did you?"

"No, of course not. But let me tell you what I *was* thinking. Alekhine had certainly been acknowledged as author of some articles that disparaged the Jewish people, particularly chess players. In fact, at one point he suggested that no Jew would ever again hold the title, which was a remarkable statement, given that Reuben Fine, who had tied with Keres for first place in the AVRO tournament, had defeated Alekhine in both of

Alexander Alekhine playing Max Euwe in their 1935 title match. Although considered a distinct underdog, Euwe defeated Alekhine to become the fifth world chess champion. He would lose the rematch to Alekhine in 1937.

their games. Reshevsky had tied with the world champion, and Botvinnik had finished half a point ahead, and they were all Jewish.

"Now, this was completely preposterous, but I was trying to think like you, Mr. Holmes, and thus I sought a motive. Was it even remotely possible that some Jewish extremists, perhaps veterans of a partisan band, might have targeted him?"

The detective merely shook his head.

"I know; you feel this was foolish, but I had vowed to leave no stone unturned. In New York, I met one Chaim Orlowski, a Polish Jew who had somehow escaped from occupied Lida. He apparently joined the Bielski brothers, survived, and then ran afoul of the NKVD—which later became the KGB—after the Red Army moved into the area. He was put on a train destined for some or other *gulag* but escaped yet again. Most implausibly, he got all the way across Europe to France, where he lived for a while until he immigrated to the United States in 1951. He was the only member of his family to have survived. All the rest had been butchered by the Nazis.

"Orlowski was eighty-eight when I interviewed him. He dismissed me as though I were an imbecile. "We had so many more important things to do—to survive; to create the State of Israel," he began. "And there were so many truly important Nazis to bring to justice, like Alois Brunner, Adolf Eichmann, Dr. Josef Mengele, and Heinrich Müller. Do you really think anyone cared about an intoxicated chess player who may or may not even have written the articles attributed to him?"

Holmes smiled. "Of course not! Moreover, there is really scant evidence that Alekhine was actually anti-Semitic. Charles Jaffe's analyses had helped him in the match against Capablanca; Salo Landau had seconded him in the first match against Euwe. He was very generous to Arnold Denker and had the highest praise for Isaac Kashdan. Now add to the above the possibility that his fourth and last wife was at least part Jewish. Let us bury this group as well. Proceed; there are still two others."

Once more Francisco hesitated, as though reluctant to continue. "The next suspects cannot be taken seriously, either. Indeed, they are as implausible as the Jews, if not more so. Nevertheless, I wanted to consider every possibility, so I investigated the Germans."

The old man could not suppress his laughter. "Well, I suppose there were plenty of Nazis walking the streets of both Spain and Portugal, but—" He motioned to his guest to continue.

"The articles attributed to Alekhine were obviously a political necessity, and he had repudiated them as early as 1944, after the liberation of Paris. *However, the repudiation was also a political necessity*! It is extremely unlikely that Nazi agents who fled to Spain and/or Portugal would have sought to murder him for that. Nevertheless, I spoke with three individuals, two of whom had hunted Nazi war criminals; the other was the son of a Nazi-hunter. All three dismissed this possibility out-of-hand. And that's not all.

"During this part of my investigation, I made—shall we say?—some 'contacts' who knew people. Through them, I was also able to speak with someone who will remain nameless—the son of a much-wanted man. He, too, echoed prevailing sentiment. Those Germans in Spain and Portugal were, like his father, consumed with one objective: to escape to Argentina or some other South American destination. They were far more interested in saving their hides than in the plight of a pathetic chess champion who had opposed them, later been coerced into working with them, and finally repudiated what he may or may not have written at their direction."

Holmes held up one finger. "This leaves us with exactly one group. Let me guess: the French? Of course, I doubt the killers could possibly have been official government agents, so I'll bet your interest arose from the Underground. Could certain rogue elements who had served within the French Resistance have sent someone to kill Alekhine?"

"The French were indeed my prime suspects, since I had already ruled out suicide, the *PIDE,* and the last three we've discussed. A Portuguese news report stated that Alekhine had beside him at the time of his death *Chosen Races*, by Margaret Sothern, an anti-Nazi novel. Could that have been a calling-card left behind by Underground hitmen?"

"If so, why did they take such pains to hide their identities?" countered the detective.

"Of course," replied Francisco. "Moreover, far more evidence suggests that Alekhine was in fact *not* a traitor to France in any way. Let us start at the beginning.

"First and foremost, he had absolutely no connection whatsoever to the Vichy Regime. Quite the contrary: In 1939, Alekhine played on first board at the Olympiad in Buenos Aires. However, when hostilities broke out, he immediately refused to allow his team to play Germany. In addition, although he could have remained in Argentina—or more comfortably still, he could have gone to the United States with his American-born wife, he instead decided to return to France to join the French Army. Does this sound like a Nazi-sympathizer, or perhaps more like someone who might later have been coerced?"

"A good question, Mr. Aguilar. You are developing a logical mind."

The younger man smiled. "Thank you, Mr. Holmes. I appreciate that, coming from you! But let me continue:

"Alekhine enlisted in the French army, where he served in intelligence as some sort of interpreter. He was, after all, quite skillful with foreign languages. However, the Germans soon overwhelmed the French, and as history records, they set up a puppet regime to administer the country, based in Vichy."

"Ah, yes; old Marshall Philippe Pétain."

"...who would later face justice. He was sentenced to life in prison and died in Ile de Yeu at age 95. Now officially—if we are to believe the French—perhaps 10,000 or so collaborators were executed without trials shortly after France was liberated. Some think as many as ten times that number may have been lynched or shot. Once the legal system had been restored, over 100,000 were charged with collaboration, though fewer than 2,000 received the death penalty."

Holmes shook his head. "I don't know how accurate your numbers are, and they are irrelevant. I'm more concerned with the 'hit-lists' allegedly set up by the Resistance. If I remember correctly—and I invariably do, of course—they were even said to have had a list specifically devoted to those who had fled France to escape justice."

"Indeed, Mr. Holmes. That is exactly my point! You see, while the French officials deny to this day that such groups ever existed, many believe that they killed 100,000 people, and I have heard even higher figures. Could they not have had Alekhine in their crosshairs? I thought it worthwhile to investigate."

"And your conclusion?"

"First, I tried to determine exactly what crimes Alekhine had committed. Precisely how did he service the Nazis, with whom he allegedly 'collaborated'? Well, by 1943 and 44, with the tides of war distinctly turning against the Germans, Alekhine spent most of his time in Portugal and Spain, presumably representing the Third Reich at a number of rather weak tournaments. And that was that. Did he give away state secrets? No. Did he betray people to the Nazis and get them shipped to Auschwitz? No. Did he in fact have anything more to do with them than support himself—barely—through chess tournaments? No. Moreover, he had declined to join the Nazi Party, even though the Germans offered him a prestigious rank and considerable financial incentives."

"That is well and good, Mr. Aguilar, but remember another old adage: 'Violence has no mind.' If he had somehow been placed on such a hit-list, the killer or killers would scarcely have taken the time to review the situation as carefully as you have."

"True, but why Alekhine? They might as well have murdered anyone who had been coerced into working within the Nazi system. Did they assassinate schoolteachers in Alsace for holding classes in the German language? Did they condemn the music teachers in Lorraine whose school bands performed *Deutschland über alles*? Of course, not, Mr. Holmes. I have researched this issue very carefully—far more diligently than the others, since it was the most plausible. I have spoken with a few former Resistance fighters and several of their children. All were proud of what had been done, *both during and after the War*, yet they spoke of meting out justice to people who had betrayed the Underground, exposed other French citizens to the mercies of the Gestapo, or caused Jews to be sent to Auschwitz and elsewhere. They also mentioned Frenchmen who had joined the Waffen SS, the so-called 'Charlemagne Division,' as well as various 'war profiteers.' *Those* were their targets. However, when I suggested Alekhine, every single one of them dismissed the idea as preposterous."

The two men stared at one another from across the kitchen table. The thoughtful eyes of the well-preserved, sprightly ninety-two-year-old studied the exhausted eyes of the fifty-two-year-old. At length Holmes spoke.

"So, what do you conclude, Mr. Aguilar?"

"After ruling out suicide and the *PIDE,* I found four groups of people who might have had motivation, but none of these solutions—not even the French—works, Mr. Holmes."

The old man smiled. "No, of course not, and for one simple reason. They're all incorrect!"

"Yes, that is what I feared," replied the other with resignation. "Thus, it seems as though my quest must end in failure."

"Not at all, Mr. Aguilar. The answer is obvious. You look, but you do not see. Pray let me explain."

And the redoubtable Sherlock Holmes now put the riddle to rest.

Chapter 4

"Elementary, My Dear Aguilar!"

Holmes smiled. "How often have my grandfather, father, and I all said that when you have eliminated the impossible, whatever remains, however improbable, must be the truth?"

The bewildered look on the face of his client confirmed that the latter had no comprehension whatsoever. "Why, yes, Mr. Holmes," he stammered. "I have read that before."

"And when you put the pieces together, what do you find?"

"I am sorry, Mr. Holmes, but I have found nothing thus far. Someone killed Alekhine, so he did not commit suicide. The *PIDE* did not do it. The Soviets certainly did not do it. It is ridiculous to imagine isolated Jewish partisans or Nazi war criminals arranging the assassination, particularly given their circumstances. The French are a slightly better set of suspects than the others, but it requires an enormous leap to 'like them' for the crime. I am at a total loss."

The old man smiled a smile that comes only with age and is the privilege of only the select few blessed with abilities far beyond those of their fellow mortals. "Why, it is quite simple, isn't it? It was your grandfather who killed Alekhine, although it was *not* murder!"

This last evoked a gasp from poor Francisco. "What!?" he cried, almost choking.

Holmes pointed to the glass, and his client dutifully took a few sips of water. When the younger man appeared to have recovered, Holmes resumed.

"Simply look at what you have told me. First and foremost, your grandfather had obvious ties to the *PIDE*. His distant cousin, d'Aguiar—without the "L"—may have been a mere physician, but he doubtless had access to and the sympathies of Luis Lupi, who appears to have been the person in charge. For that reason, d'Aguiar would naturally have been the physician called upon to do the post-mortem.

"Now, bear in mind that the *PIDE* effectively ran Portugal at the time. They answered only to Salazar, and Salazar had absolute power.

"Something seemed out of place in your narrative from early on. Alekhine must have been 'completely out of money,' since he needed some just to buy cigarettes. Nevertheless, a mere thirteen days later, he had enough to go out for a night in the city. He had not played in a tournament; he had given no simuls; he had taught no lessons: yet mysteriously, money had returned to his pockets. Did that not strike you as strange?"

"Yes, of course."

"You told me that your grandfather played cards and chess with Alekhine, apparently accepting odds on the clock as well as material odds over the board. Does it not seem likely that they played for money from time to time?"

"I realize that many chess players to this day gamble when they play speed chess, and card games, particularly poker, lend themselves to gambling, also."

"Good! Now, behold: Alekhine was out of money because he had lost it gambling, but he must have made it all back and then some at your grandfather's expense, perhaps with the cards, perhaps over the chessboard, and perhaps via some other means of diversion.

"The world champion had complained that he was being followed, and he was. The *PIDE* had strict orders to protect him, and it was they who monitored his comings and goings—and, more pointedly, kept track of anyone who might have visited him. And even though Francisco Lupi was arguably Alekhine's closest friend at the time, it was necessary for Jose da Costa Moreira to tag along when the two went off to Lisbon on the night of the 22nd. However, that was only because Alekhine was removed from the safety and shelter of his hotel room. Do you see where this is leading?"

The other hesitated. "I begin to, Mr. Holmes. The *PIDE* would not have had to worry about my grandfather, since he had obvious connections through his cousin, and also because they were meeting in the champion's room."

"Excellent! Now are you ready to put the pieces together?"

"I should very much like to!"

Holmes moistened his lips. "Behold: Your grandfather, Miguel, had lost a large amount of money to Alekhine at some point between the 8th and 22nd of March. He came back to visit late on the 23rd—perhaps to gamble some more, but with no intentions of murder whatsoever. And if we look at the clues, we begin to see a far more plausible pattern emerge.

"In all likelihood, Mr. Costa Moreira had retrieved the coat and brought it to his superior, Luis Lupi. Item: one overcoat, its reappearance explained. Please hold that thought.

"Next, permit me to remind you of your grandfather's dying words as you conveyed them to me: 'Alekhine...killed.' Note that he used 'killed,' and not 'murdered.' That was very deliberate, as we shall see. Please hold that thought, also.

"I suspect that by the time Miguel arrived at the hotel, Alekhine had indeed finished his dinner—and washed it down with copious amounts of some alcoholic beverage. Thus, he was by no means at his best when the two men sat down to gamble. Soon, his recent gains turned to losses, and before long—bearing in mind he was also perhaps somewhat impaired—he followed in the shoes of so many other gamblers and placed large wagers beyond the limits of his wallet. Miguel, in short, 'cleaned him out,' but probably realized that he had no convenient way to collect his ill-gotten earnings.

"Picture if you can the final position. Miguel is owed a considerable amount of money, and he looks about the room, desperately seeking some tangible asset. At length, he espies something of legitimate value—the Sevres vase. After all, this had been donated by the Czar, and was the one item Alekhine valued above all others. I once read that Alekhine intended to surrender it to the person who ultimately conquered him over the board.

"Miguel grabs the vase. This gesture prompts a sudden response by Alekhine, who tries to snatch it away. They struggle, probably knocking over various items. The sudden exertion puts a strain on the champion's severely damaged heart, and when the vase drops to the ground and shatters, he suffers a third heart attack, which proves fatal. He slumps to the floor, and Miguel quickly realizes that it is indeed checkmate.

"Your grandfather is, of course, smitten with guilt, but at the same time, he intends to escape the gallows at all costs. He is no murderer, and Alekhine had attacked him! Miguel departs, probably unnoticed, and dashes off to his cousin, a physician, who in turn telephones his *PIDE* contact, Louis Lupi, and begs a favor. By early the next morning, Lupi has already begun to sanitize the crime scene. The broken vase remains, but no other signs of struggle can be observed, and the overcoat has been returned to its rightful owner, who will don it for the photographs.

"Now here is where the rest of the pieces fall into place. Dr. d'Aguiar, as a conscientious physician, is somewhat troubled; it is almost certain that the deceased succumbed to a heart attack precipitated by the struggle with his cousin. 'What can I possibly say?' he asks Lupi. Lupi seeks advice from his veterinarian colleague, Dr. Ferreira, and in all likelihood it is the latter who conjures the story of a piece of meat stuck in Alekhine's throat. Ferreira's reward? He gets to oversee the key remaining issues: the death certificate and the autopsy. And Lupi is absolutely adamant that this fiction must be preserved, with no hint of cardiac arrest anywhere to be seen."

At last Francisco was beginning to understand. "Of course!" he exclaimed. "This explains why Ferreira would later write Alekhine's son and assure him that the late champion's body showed no evidence of *any* other diseases that might have caused his precipitous demise. He simply wanted to whitewash my grandfather's role in precipitating the fatal heart attack!"

"Correct!"

Francisco shook his head, knowingly. "Well, Mr. Holmes, this is positively brilliant. I only hope I can convince my father with your explanation."

"Just tell him it came directly from me, Sherlock Holmes."

"Oh, I shall, believe me. But one last question, if I may. When did you begin to suspect my grandfather?"

Holmes smiled. "Almost from the beginning."

"But how? Why?"

"Elementary, my dear Mr. Aguilar. Did you not tell me that he showed up late the next morning?"

The other man hesitated. "Why…yes."

"And have you never heard that the criminal always returns to the scene of the crime? It was almost too simple. He came back the next day, just to make sure he had left nothing behind and also to clear his name from the police lists as quickly as possible—not that he actually had anything to fear, given his connections. Meanwhile, everything worked out smoothly. The *PIDE* would no longer be responsible for protecting Alekhine, the cover-up ensured that no one would think the world champion had been murdered, and the Salazar regime had found a simple expedient through which to announce a death by natural causes, thereby diverting international speculation about the various criminals it was harboring, including a number of Nazis—and, of course, about the rumors of Nazi gold in its banks!"

The two men stood up, and Francisco extended his hand. "Your reputation is surely well deserved, Mr. Holmes. You are truly remarkable! Now, as for your fee—"

The nonagenarian smiled. "None, whatsoever! Thank you, Mr. Aguilar, for both your kind words and for entertaining me with this wonderful exercise."

The visitor stammered as he expressed his deepest gratitude, adding, "I am certain that you can figure out anything, Mr. Holmes!"

"I hope you are right," replied the other. "You see, this was my easy case. Next week I must solve a far more challenging murder mystery."

"Oh? Whose?"

"That of another chess player. You've already mentioned him this afternoon: an American by the name of Bobby Fischer!"

Sherlock Holmes and the Mystery of the Eccentric Icon

The 2008 Death of Bobby Fischer

Notes on Bobby Fischer

The career of Bobby Fischer presents chilling parallels to that of Paul Morphy. In 1958 Fischer qualified for the Candidates tournament as a fifteen-year-old, and he won the Stockholm Interzonal in 1962. However, he did not capture the world championship until 1972, and during the 1960s he twice "retired" from the game.

After winning the title, Fischer all but disappeared from view, and signs of mental instability were blatantly apparent during rare "Fischer-sightings." He refused to defend his championship, which was awarded to Anatoly Karpov by default. Rumors abounded that he would play a match against a worthy challenger on his own terms, and various prominent grandmasters were suggested as possible foes.

Sadly, no such match materialized, and Fischer's downward spiral continued. His weight nearly doubled; he had his dental fillings removed; he was arrested by the Los Angeles police.

Fischer resurfaced in 1992 to play a rematch against Boris Spassky, but the quality of play was disappointing. Thereafter came more rumors of various sorts: a "man vs. woman" match against Judit Polgar, a Fischer Random Chess contest against Viswanathan Anand, and even a match against Anatoly Karpov (of all people) at Gothic Chess (now called Trice's chess, after the inventor, Edward Trice). Alas, these ultimately proved as unsubstantial as the earlier hearsay.

Death came in Iceland in early 2008, while Fischer was still sixty-four years of age. The cause of the champion's demise was also unequivocal: renal failure.

Or was it? The deathbed confession of Dr. James Moriarty IV presents an interesting challenge for Sherlock Holmes III, who is assisted by Dr. Joan Watson, great-great-granddaughter of the original.

Chapter 1

An "Urgent" Request

I come from a long line of doctors, although I am the first female to have pursued this field. My great-great-grandfather, John Hamish Watson, is surely the best known of us all, having collaborated so often with the immortal Sherlock Holmes. My great-grandfather advised the son of that famous detective on more than one occasion, while the third (though not necessarily last) Sherlock Holmes consulted with both my grandfather and father, as well as a cousin. [The latter is a rabbi, not a physician.]

Of course, both the son and grandson of the original Sherlock Holmes kept much lower profiles, having also been deprived of the literary services of a man like Watson *Primus*. Indeed, I had assumed the grandson had expired some years ago.

The reader can scarcely imagine my surprise when I received both an email and a fax, scarcely a minute apart, from someone purporting to be Sherlock Holmes! Had he not alluded to a family secret—something carefully guarded and kept within the family for these five generations—I would simply have deleted the email and tossed the fax into the waste basket. Obviously, I do not feel at liberty to share that portion of the mysterious communication. However, I present the most relevant excerpts below:

Dear Dr. Joan Watson:

Of course, you are familiar with my name and are well aware of the long family ties we share, going back to the 1800s. Your grandfather, John Michael, was of immense assistance to me on two occasions, while your father, John Simon, also helped me crack a difficult case when you were a teenager.

Somehow, alas, I never met you, but I have followed your career from a distance. I know that you graduated medical school in 2008, did a combined residency in neurology and psychiatry, and are currently an assistant professor at Harvard Medical School and attending physician at Mass General Hospital. More pointedly, I understand that you have done considerable research into neurotoxins and were recently lead author (with an impressive cast of colleagues) of an article that appeared in the prestigious Journal of Neurology, Neurosurgery, and Psychiatry.

Let me come right to the point. Less than a week ago I received a communication from Her Majesty's Prison Wakefield, which (as you may not know) is the largest high-security prison in Western Europe. It seems a prisoner has made what some might call a "deathbed confession." The fellow is in hospital and not expected to last more than another fortnight, and he has had the effrontery to challenge me to disprove his claim to yet further ignominy (having already earned a vile and most unsavory reputation, by dint of which he was eventually consigned to the very facility in which he will die).

Due to those few details that have been shared with me—to say nothing of my rather advanced age—I shall require the services of a consulting physician, and I think you will serve admirably in that capacity. Suffice it to say that this case has attracted the attention of an unnamed gentleman of great wealth, and that you will be most generously compensated for your first-class transportation, normal fees (plus considerable supplement thereunto), and any and all peripheral expenses. I must append that I consider this a most urgent matter and request your immediate response, hopefully affirmative.

Thank you very much for your consideration.

Respectfully, Sherlock Holmes III

Sherlock Holmes? The grandson of *that* Sherlock Holmes? Why, if he were in fact alive, he would probably be close to 100, wouldn't he? "That's surely a little old for detective work," I thought. Moreover, I did not understand how a deathbed confession—to a murder, I assumed—could possibly be "urgent."

Anyone reading such a communication would assume it had been written by the same "Nigerian prince" who has been soliciting people over the Internet for decades. However, the author also interpolated a phrase that led me to believe he absolutely *was* connected to the Holmes family, since this was something the original Sherlock and my great-great-grandfather had devised.

I hit "reply" and sent back a short message: "Please call me at 617-555-6465." Less than one minute later my telephone rang.

Chapter 2

An Awkward Introduction; the Holmes-Watson Team Reunited

"This is Sherlock Holmes calling. Have I the honor of addressing Dr. Joan Watson?"

I must have gasped. Despite his advanced age, the man certainly spoke with a firm voice! "Yes, indeed! And the honor is mine, Professor Holmes, all mine!" I stammered.

"Thank you so much. And now that we have the formalities out of the way, perhaps you will be kind enough to address me as Sherlock."

"Certainly, Sherlock, though I must in turn request that you call me Joan."

"Joan it is!" he replied. "Well, Joan, I wonder whether I might have the pleasure of your company for a few days. You see, I shall require the services of someone more knowledgeable about neurophysiology than I. Moreover, this will almost certainly close a chapter in the Sherlock Holmes saga, and it may well be my final case. Thus, I seek the most trusted name in medicine: Watson. Can you extricate yourself from your other professional obligations?"

As it happened, I was slated for a week off. Still, I was somewhat confused by the old man's request. "I am supposed to work tomorrow— Friday—but after that I shall be free for the weekend and the following full week, nine days in all."

"Can you make it ten and fly out tonight?"

I was more than a little taken aback. "I suppose I can, but may I first inquire as to the details of the case. How can a deathbed confession possibly be as 'urgent' as you insist it is?"

A brief silence was punctuated by a forceful sigh. "I am ninety-two years old, Joan. I believe you are a mere thirty-five. Now, that makes you far too young to recall the exploits of the brilliant world chess champion, Bobby Fischer, yet if memory serves me correctly, you showed considerable promise at the game yourself at one time, and you are surely familiar with his career."

Bobby Fischer? Of course, I recognized the name! He had died during my last year of medical school. I had practically cut my teeth on *My Memorable 60 Games* and *Bobby Fischer Teaches Chess*, and I could vividly remember sitting with my father and playing through the moves of his 1992 "revenge match" against Boris Spassky, although in fairness, I was not quite nine years old at the time.

Chess came rather easily to me, although I probably lacked the talent to have gone particularly far with it. During my sophomore year of college my rating hit 2150, but it plateaued and then dropped a little. By the end of my junior year it had slipped back a little below 2100, and while I continued to play blitz from time to time, my interest had begun to wane. I never played a USCF-rated classical game again, and I'm sure my strength today is considerably weaker than the solid expert's rating I still hold.

"Yes, Sherlock," I replied. "I am certainly familiar with both Bobby Fischers: the brilliant genius who won the world championship and the rather odious wretch into which he devolved. But what does Bobby have to do with your case?"

"Do you know how Fischer died?"

"If I remember correctly, the cause of death was given as kidney failure, which probably led to congestive heart failure, pericarditis, or something similar. Why do you ask?"

Fischer's My 60 Memorable Games *is one of the classics of chess literature.*

"Suppose I told you that the gentleman in question has confessed to the murder of Bobby Fischer, or at least to having played a vital role in his demise!"

I did not even hesitate. "I would ask whether the man was insane."

Holmes chuckled. "Insane? Certainly not, Joan! He is brilliant, yes, but certainly not insane. And that is why the prison authorities have contacted me."

"Why you? I don't understand."

"I am the only intellect sufficiently attuned to the criminal mind, and thus the only person who can possibly be adequate for the task at hand."

"But who on earth can this person be, and why does anyone care, given his imminent demise?"

"Ah, so you *are* interested, aren't you?"

I had to concede that I was, and in short order Holmes had given me the flight information. Even while we were speaking, the boarding pass came through as a pdf file. I made the necessary phone calls and got coverage at Mass General. Then I hastily threw a few changes of clothes and some cosmetics into a traveling case, grabbed my computer and cell phone, and summoned a cab to Logan Airport.

* * *

I was fortunate enough to be able to sleep on the plane. All during the ride to Logan and throughout the security checks and inevitable delays before takeoff, I had been silently fuming about the lunacy of this venture. *What was I thinking?* I was certainly convinced that the gentleman who had contacted me was indeed Sherlock Holmes, and he sounded lucid enough. Still, at 92, perhaps he was failing somewhat.

Or perhaps it was I who was failing! I would soon depart for Heathrow Airport to lend my medical expertise to the grandson of my great-great-grandfather's close friend and colleague. That much made sense. However, the case involved an unnamed party's deathbed confession involving the alleged "murder" of Bobby Fischer. That made absolutely no sense whatsoever.

Bobby Fischer Teaches Chess is one of the best-selling chess books of all time.

I woke up shortly before we began our descent. My bags were quickly rushed through customs, and I was greeted by none other than Sherlock Holmes. The old man looked remarkably fit for ninety-two, although he clearly suffered from some sort of knee injury and walked with a slight limp. His skin suggested the complexion of a man perhaps twenty years younger, and his eyes had the sparkle of someone perhaps half a century younger still.

We had little time for niceties, as he quickly hustled me onto a flight to Robin Hood Airport—and no, I'm not making that up!—in Doncaster. Once there, we were picked up by a chauffeur, who led us silently to his limousine. All the while, Sherlock respectfully declined to provide any details about the case, although he generously shared anecdotes about my father and grandfather.

"Why do you hold your cards so close to your vest?" I inquired. "Surely you intend to let me know the gentleman's name at some point, don't you?"

Holmes responded with a dry chuckle. "I had given that notion considerable thought, but at length I decided against doing so."

"Why?" I demanded.

"Your great-great-grandfather was a splendid physician, but he was also a skillful man of letters. I should prefer to let you make the discovery yourself, simply because this will provide a far greater dramatic impact to your experience, and that may in turn assist you in the literary account of a case you will almost surely put to paper."

I realized that little purpose would be served by continuing the argument. If Holmes wanted me to learn the identity of the self-declared murderer from someone else or on my own, he would never budge from that position. I knew my pleas would fall on deaf ears, and I recalled the words Shakespeare gave to Julius Caesar: "But I am constant as the northern star, / Of whose true-fixed and resting quality / There is no fellow in the firmament."

I suppose I might comment on the food we ate along the way. The British reputation for breakfasts is still well deserved, and I certainly could not complain about either quality or quantity. Alas, their coffee is another matter.

Security at the prison was considerably more stringent than at airports. Wakefield is, after all, a maximum-security facility, and they would take no chances. I was led aside by a prison matron, and I trust the reader will not be offended if I respectfully decline to share all the details. I assumed Sherlock had fared comparably, and I was rather chagrined to learn that he had been checked through without incident. My status as a foreigner apparently aroused more suspicion, although I later received a handsome apology from the warden.

At length two guards escorted us to the hospital, a setting with which I am certainly all too familiar. We were led down a hallway to a door guarded by yet another pair of well-armed men.

Holmes turned to me, smiling. "And now, Joan, you will discover the identity of the person whom I have so steadfastly declined to name. Behold: the door."

My jaw dropped. There, in bold letters, I read the name that sent chills down my spine: Dr. James Moriarty IV.

Chapter 3

A Chilly Reception; Bobby Fischer's Health

As a medical practitioner I have certainly observed any number of patients at Death's door. Dr. Moriarty seemed better off than most, notwithstanding his emaciated appearance, pallor, the attached electrocardiogram, and two tubular insertions: the IV drip connected to his left arm and what was surely a catheter through which he excreted urine. Both hands and arms showed numerous hematomas, and it was clear that his circulatory system was failing. Nevertheless, he continued to breathe on his own, and his voice, though somewhat frail, projected his contempt for the world, an acerbic—if not mildewed—wit, and a tempered resignation to the inevitable.

We had overheard a nurse ask whether the patient cared to receive visitors. Our names were announced.

"Sherlock Holmes and Joan Watson? It will be like old times for the end of times. Sure! Show them in."

Sherlock, ever the gentleman, insisted on letting me through the doorway first. Moriarty ignored me altogether and cast a gelid stare at the figure who limped in behind me. Sherlock, in turn, locked his eyes upon those of his nemesis, a dying man some fifteen years his junior. I saw quite clearly that no love was lost between them.

"Well, Sherlock. Here we are, then! You have tried for so many years, yet invariably failed to have me put away. Given your ineptitude and my terminal condition, I have kindly taken the job off your hands. I very recently turned myself in for a host of egregious crimes against humanity, simply so that I might taunt you with my deathbed confession."

Holmes gave him a condescending smile. "If I may borrow from the Bard—"

"...which you might as well do, since you've never had an original thought!"

"I believe it is Horatio who says, 'So I have heard and do in part believe it,' or words to that effect."

"Bravo, Holmes! It seems you've even read a little Shakespeare. Fair enough! Now let me send a passage back to you, though I shall treat it more *originally*: 'I think thy horse will sooner con an oration than thou'...solve a real crime."

The thinnest of smiles forced its way upon Sherlock's face. "In fairness, I must perhaps suggest that my same horse is far more likely to commit a criminal act than you are at the moment."

"Oh, very good! 'I pray you do not mock me,' Holmes. 'He jests at scars that never felt a wound,' yet you are surely not that far behind me in the race to the grave!"

Holmes clapped his hands three times. "Do you know, Moriarty, you and I could have become good friends had we merely matched wits at quoting Shakespeare. I'll wager you've read all thirty-eight of the plays."

"I have *memorized* all thirty-eight. I have also read *Edward III*, at least one act of which has been attributed to Shakespeare, plus—of course—all the sonnets. And I hope you haven't forgotten about *Cardenio*."

"A work attributed to Shakespeare, yet we have no manuscript. If it ever existed, it is truly a 'lost' play."

Moriarty snorted. "Lost? Even a man with your cerebral limitations should have known I long ago located and stole it. That should have been obvious to you from the very fact that I mentioned the drama."

Holmes seemed genuinely surprised by this announcement. "Well, if you do indeed possess such a treasure, I hope you will consider sharing it with the rest of the world," he ventured timidly.

The patient responded with a feeble chuckle. "I wish I could applaud you, Holmes, but as you can see..." and his eyes darted toward the intravenous line. "Yes, what a capital idea. I suppose you would also like the *St. Mark Passion* of Bach, which is similarly hidden from the multitude. Nonsense! If you truly want them, go search for them after I am dead. And if you succeed, you'll be rewarded with a set of precise coordinates that pinpoint Captain Kidd's treasure."

At this the poor man began to laugh, but his hollow laughter soon gave way to a fit of coughing. The nurse rushed in to give him something to drink, but it still took a few moments before he could speak again.

"Now, where were we, Holmes?" he asked, taking one last sip from the straw and nodding to the nurse to place it on the table.

"I'll be right outside the door if you need me, Dr. Moriarty," she said, exiting as abruptly as she had entered.

"Suppose you tell me," replied Holmes. "It appears as though you are holding court today, not I."

Moriarty smiled. "Your humility amuses us, Holmes. But pray be seated, so that you and Miss Watson can pay better attention."

We pulled up chairs as the man continued.

"I confessed to nothing whatsoever, and I have not been officially charged with any offense. Thus, your best efforts went for naught, Holmes. Nevertheless, on the strength of your unproven allegations, most of which are surely actionable, I have been a hunted man for several decades. When the illness reached critical levels, I faced a dilemma. Wherever I went, my name would immediately surface on Interpol, and I would probably be consigned to a prison. Therefore, I thought to make the best of a hopeless situation. I returned to my native England and turned myself in, thus gaining access to this place, better known as Monster Mansion, where I receive adequate care to keep me comfortable for the last few weeks, or even days, of my life. Still, I have confessed to nothing and continue to maintain my innocence with respect to all the criminal charges of which your thuggish friends at Scotland Yard accuse me. After all, what do they really have? Nothing, except a handful of imbecilic allegations masquerading as 'deductive reasoning' and pieced together by an old fool in his near dotage: a man who had the audacity to consider himself my intellectual equal."

I could almost feel Sherlock wince under the lashes of Moriarty's tongue. I don't think he was bothered by "old fool in his near dotage," but the notion that he was somehow intellectually inferior to *anyone* must surely have hurt.

"Well, since you are innocent, why don't we pack you off to some other facility—perhaps a nice, very costly hospital like Mass General in the United States, where Dr. Watson is employed. That would surely relieve you of some of your ill-gotten wealth," snapped Holmes.

"*Doctor* Watson! Oh, this is good!" replied the other, smiling. "You have followed in the footsteps of your great-grandfather?"

"Actually," I replied, "the John Watson to whom you allude was my great-great-grandfather. I am the fifth generation."

"I stand corrected. Five generations of Watson, four of Moriarty, and only three of Holmes. However, Sherlock's clan all seemed to have longevity on their side."

Patience is a virtue, and Holmes had an abundance of it. "Would you like to hear about my own family?" he asked.

"No, they are of no concern. What matters is my confession. Are you interested?"

"Indeed."

"Well, then: I have formally confessed to the murder of the late Bobby Fischer. Your challenge—should you be man enough to accept it—will be to prove I am innocent!'"

Holmes pretended to yawn. "Yes, we had heard about this earlier, and I have already perused the official autopsy report from hospital. Unless the Icelandic translators failed miserably at their task, the official cause of death was renal failure."

"Rubbish!"

Holmes—perhaps somewhat startled to hear anyone use *his* favorite interjection—looked at me, clearly indicating that he wanted my input. "We know that Bobby Fischer was in excellent physical condition prior to the 1972 match with Boris Spassky," I began. "In fact, various periodicals published pictures of him training at Grossinger's, where so many famous boxers and other athletes worked out. He stood six-feet-one or so, and some or other journalist referred to him as a "light heavyweight," meaning somewhere near 175 pounds."

Sherlock interrupted. "Would you like me to convert those figures to meters and kilograms?"

"That won't be necessary," replied the other. "They're already up here," he quipped, pointing to his head.

I continued, "But what happened to this marvelously fit Bobby Fischer in short order? By the late 1970s and early 80s he was frightfully obese. Several people who had seen him said that he had apparently stopped counting his calories, and one claimed he weighed 'three bills and change,' while another guessed at least 325 pounds. He was clearly not packing on muscle from weightlifting and steroids but was instead indulging in 'all-you-can-eat' orgies and cultivating a sweet tooth."

At this point Holmes interrupted. "Admittedly he did get himself into slightly better shape for the dreadful match against Spassky in 1992. However, Vlastimil Hort, a grandmaster and friend, reported that when he saw Bobby in 1993, the former champion tipped the scales at 'about 130 kilograms,' which is to say somewhere in the 285-to-290-pound range, hardly svelte by any twist of the imagination. But please continue, Dr. Watson," he added, and I resumed.

"We know that Fischer ate far more than he should have, and we know that he also ate many foods that make most physicians cringe these days. Moreover, he began to drink fairly heavily during his later years.

"Any of these factors might have caused serious trauma to the kidneys, and taken as an ensemble, they were, and still are, potentially lethal. Moreover, one must also consider the extent of *external* stressors, of which there seemed no shortage in Bobby's life. He was a Type-A personality before he was in his teens. Indeed, he found no end to the factors that fueled his bitterness.

"Consider the assaults he took in 1961: loss by forfeit in the match against Reshevsky, then his mediocre score at the 1962 Candidates Tournament in Curaçao, a result he attributed to 'collusion' amongst the top three Soviet players and 'thrown games,' particularly by Viktor Korchnoi. Next, only months later, he could not find the win against Botvinnik after their game at the Olympiad was adjourned.

"How much stress must a player have felt to have walked out of the Interzonal in 1967 while leading the field with a remarkable eight and one-half points through the first ten rounds? How great was the stress Bobby was under during the 1960s, given that he felt compelled to go into a virtual retirement twice during that decade?

"That brings us to the remarkable run-up to his championship match, which almost fell through several times over. He also blundered miserably in Game 1 and then forfeited Game 2.

"And all of these things pale miserably when weighted against the stress that followed, beginning with the forfeiture of his title in 1975. I have read about his subsequent rants, in which he repeatedly accused the Soviets—Karpov and Kasparov, and even Soviet defector Korchnoi—of playing rigged, pre-arranged matches. His rematch with Spassky included 'the spit heard around the world,' but at the end of the day he was *persona non grata* in the USA and would have faced arrest had he stepped on

American soil. This fact, in turn, prevented him from attending the funerals of his mother and sister.

"Do you need more, Dr. Moriarty? I could also mention the entanglements with at least two women, one of whom he considered his lawfully wedded wife, and the other of whom was the mother of a child he thought was his own, even though she wasn't.

"I must append that he was also clinically paranoid. The CIA, FBI, KGB, Mossad, and various other entities were all out to get him—or so he believed. It is well known that at one point he felt compelled to have all the fillings removed from his teeth for a variety of reasons, but primarily because his 'enemies' were using them to poison him with radiation. Needless to say, Bobby held both the dental and medical professions in low esteem and certainly did not get the help he required."

At this point Holmes took over. "Kidney failure, with or without resultant uremia, endocarditis, pericarditis, or heart failure, would seem a logical outcome, and the confirmation from hospital appears to put an end to your assertions about poison. Quite bluntly, Dr. Moriarty, even if you had been able to sneak into the Reykjavik hospital where he was a patient and inject some toxin into an IV drip, you would probably at most have hastened the outcome only minimally."

For perhaps thirty long seconds all three of us remained silent. At length the patient spoke. "Are you both finished?"

Holmes grunted, while I nodded in response.

Chapter 4

Moriarty's Confession

"I am not disappointed in you, Miss—er, Dr. Watson. You are still relatively young. Your colleague, however, has reached a new depth, even by the Holmesian standards. Tell me, Sherlock: Have you never searched for the *reason* behind any turn of events? Both of you have probably seen the YouTube video of a Bob Hope 'special' with Fischer, shortly after he had vanquished Spassky for the title. He was absolutely charming and witty."

"Quite true," replied Holmes, "although I enjoyed the earlier interview with Dick Cavett even more."

"At which Fischer was also quite the gentleman, wouldn't you say?"

"Indeed."

"Then, tell me this, Holmes: What could have caused such a dramatic metamorphosis? How could a man at the peak of his powers degenerate into the pathetic wreck who got his sorry tail hauled into jail by the Los Angeles Police Department? What caused him to snap so completely?"

Holmes smiled. "As I clearly do not know, and I assume Dr. Watson is similarly without an answer, we humbly entreat you to enlighten us!"

"I shall indeed do so," responded Moriarty with a leer. "Now, let me begin with an American television program from the 1980s, recently re-booted to mediocre reviews. I refer to *Dynasty*. Do you remember it?"

A King of Comedy and a King of Chess, Bob Hope and Bobby Fischer.

"Indeed," replied Holmes calmly. "I was in Germany during some of that time and watched it as *Der Denver-Clan.*"

"Do you perhaps remember the episodes in which Jeff Colby began to lose his mental capabilities after his brother-in-law, the evil Adam Carrington, added a neurotoxin to the paint while Jeff's office was redecorated?"

"I do."

"And do you perhaps remember how Spassky's seconds asserted that U. S. agents had used some sort of "mind control," ostensibly via electromagnetic fields, to disrupt Spassky's mind?"

"Pure rubbish, of course," snorted Holmes. "They took the chairs apart, but all they could find were two dead flies. Of course, Iivo Nei, one of Spassky's advisors, then suggested that they do post-mortems on the flies! He was sent packing and returned to Estonia shortly thereafter."

"For once I agree with you, Sherlock," answered Moriarty in a low voice. "I also read your rebuttal of Viktor Korchnoi's claim that the Soviets were using such machinery against him in Merano. I think Karpov was simply far stronger than the aging Korchnoi by 1981, even if his superiority had been far more dubious a mere three years earlier.

"However, you miss the point, as usual. The question was not whether mind control was effected via electromagnetic devices hitherto unknown, but whether someone had somehow contrived to work a neurotoxin into the match. I, alone, know what was done."

The white, 92-year-old eyebrows of Sherlock Holmes shot up at this claim. "Really?"

"Yes! You see, I was truly the master of disguises in those days, and I easily passed myself off as hotel staff. While no one was around, I managed to work my way into the room in which Fischer stayed. It required but the smallest amount of a chemical I, alone, had developed in my laboratories. I carefully applied it beneath the future champion's bed. In time, I knew it would unhinge him just enough to let his innate paranoia take over. The rest, as they say, was history. Oh, he was fine on Bob Hope's program, yet within months afterward he had all but vanished, and his epic descent had begun."

Sherlock turned to me, clearly somewhat agitated by this outlandish claim. "Your opinion, Doctor Watson?"

I hesitated. "You are talking about the introduction of some sort of agent powerful enough to induce mild to severe psychosis. Of course, rumors of such drugs have existed for many years, and it was at one time widely believed that both the CIA and KGB were developing rather large arsenals of such psychological weaponry. However, these were but unconfirmed rumors. Neurotoxicity is itself a very broad topic and goes back at least 2,000 years. Various scholars have posited that lead from the plumbing systems in ancient Rome contributed to the bizarre behaviors of some of the Empire's rulers and the general decline of the civilization."

Moriarty, clearly fatigued by this point, was struggling to keep his eyes open. "You, too, miss the point. Such drugs *are* possible, and I developed one. However, it was merely an improvement on a cruder toxin developed by my grandfather, Dr. James Moriarty Jr. On a whim, he slipped such an agent into a beverage that was consumed shortly thereafter by Akiba Rubinstein. Slowly but inevitably, that genius spiraled down the path toward madness, and in short order he was no longer among the world's elite."

"Rubbish!" snapped Holmes. "Rubinstein peaked during the period between 1912 and 1914, while he was somewhere between thirty-two and thirty-four years old. It was long held that chess players peaked around age thirty-six. World War One broke out, destroying all hopes of a match against Lasker, and given the upheavals, relative inactivity, and inevitable decline as he aged, it was only natural that his results were less consistent. Nevertheless, he sparkled as late as the 1930 Olympiad, winning a gold medal with thirteen wins and four draws just months before he turned fifty."

"Sherlock, Sherlock!" cried Moriarty. "The issue is not his chess, but his insanity. Have you forgotten about the enchanted princess who haunted his hotel rooms? You surely know that he became schizophrenic and spent the last twenty-nine years of his life in a desperate battle with reality. By 1932 he had effectively been forced to retire from tournament chess, and that was the handiwork of my grandfather!"

Holmes shrugged and feigned boredom. "Whatever you say, James. Far be it from me to take your delusions away from you."

"Delusions! You only wish they were. The truth is that these agents *do* exist, and that I have tested mine on Bobby Fischer. All I require is that the target is slightly off-center to begin with, as Fischer certainly was. Thereafter, the agent will work its toxicity, and the victim's behavior will modify to his detriment.

"Just think what a weapon this could be!" he rasped. "So many of the world's leaders manifest signs of mental instability already. A judicious dosage of the Moriarty solution could drive them over the edge and perhaps even provide the impetus to start a nuclear war. Now wouldn't that be precious!"

The excitement was clearly too much for the patient, who began coughing again. The EKG registered considerable cardiac stress as well, and nurses and physicians rushed into the room. "You'll have to leave now," someone ordered, and we joined our escort on the other side of the door.

Chapter 5

"But Could This Be True?"

We were both hungry, so our guards brought us to the dining hall, where the food was adequate though hardly distinguished. I waited for Holmes to speak, but he would say nothing while the guards were within earshot. Fortunately, we were soon escorted to a small office, which we had to ourselves. Better still, we were given clearance to use a computer.

I was pleasantly surprised by Sherlock's apparent comfort with technology. "Of course, Joan, it's really quite simple. One merely puts together a typewriter keyboard, a filing cabinet, and a television set."

"Well and good, Sherlock, but there were no televisions during your childhood."

"True enough," he replied, "yet we had the other two items, and I had a TV by the mid-1950s. But enough on computers! Tell me what you think."

I opened my mouth, but no words came out. I wanted to dismiss Moriarty's claims, yet I wasn't 100 percent certain. At length I replied. "It all sounds much too far-fetched. In fact, I'm inclined to believe his motivation is the most obvious one. His sole purpose is to upset you, or at least to try to make you believe that he created such a chemical. If he did, he might also have sold it to any number of dangerous organizations, governmental or otherwise. His parting shot spoke volumes. Just imagine what the American CIA, the Russian SVR-RF, the Chinese MSS, or even your own MI6 might do with such an agent, assuming one existed."

Drawing of Spassky and Fischer doing battle in Reykjavik 1972

"Ah, but my question, Doctor, is the obvious one: could such an agent possibly exist, and could it work in airborne fashion?"

I paused before answering. "In other words, *could* Moriarty actually have stuck something under Fischer's bed that would have caused so drastic a change of character?"

"Exactly! I want to know what caused him to abandon the game so precipitously. Think about it for a moment. With a string of late-round wins, he swept to an overwhelming victory in the Interzonal tournament at Palma de Mallorca, topping the field by three and one-half points. He then clobbered Mark Taimanov by 6-0 in the first candidates match. Bent Larsen had defeated Bobby brilliantly during the Interzonal, but Fischer trounced him by the same 6-0 score in the semifinals. Former champion Petrosian managed to snap Bobby's win streak at twenty but lost the match by a convincing 6½ to 2½ margin. Then don't forget the 19-3 score in the speed tournament before the Interzonal, a mere 4½ points ahead of runner-up Tal, and the 21½-½ result in the blitz event at the Manhattan Chess Club. Following all that, he overwhelmed Spassky and won the world title.

"People have speculated that after a three-year layoff, Bobby might have had difficulty against Anatoly Karpov in 1975, but Karpov had barely eked out a win over Korchnoi in the finals of the candidates tournament, and Korchnoi was certainly way below Fischer's level in 1972. Thus, had the new champion kept playing, he would surely have retained the title for some years. And yet, he dropped out of the chess circuit for two decades. Why, Joan, why?"

I shook my head. "He was always erratic, and he was always rather paranoid. If you're asking me whether some toxic substance might have given him a push over the edge, I shall have to answer in the affirmative, though I am still unaware of any such agent, much less one in airborne form, as Moriarty claims. Moreover, as many have observed, there is only a thin line between genius and insanity to begin with, so in answer to the broader question, I am afraid I must reluctantly concede that it is not altogether impossible."

Holmes nodded. "I suppose you are familiar with an old adage my grandfather used to tell your great-great-grandfather: once you have eliminated the impossible, whatever remains, however improbable, must be the truth." He shook his head. "I have been challenged to prove that something could not have happened. In other words, Moriarty wants me to disprove his far-fetched claim. All we have is our own ignorance. The fact that so prominent a neurologist as yourself is unaware of such a neurotoxin does not mean that it does not exist, or more pointedly that a brilliant man like Moriarty might not have invented it."

"Well, I'm afraid I cannot offer you anything more at this point, Sherlock. Still, one thing continues to bother me."

Holmes took a deep breath, as though to contain his excitement. "Out with it, Joan!"

"What was his motivation? What prompted him to destroy Fischer, assuming he did indeed do so?"

"A good question, Joan. Perhaps we shall have the opportunity to ask him tomorrow. At the moment, however, I'm afraid we have driven down a dead end. Let us hope that Dr. Moriarty survives."

Chapter 6

Moriarty's Motive

We took a cab into town, checked into our respective rooms in a small hotel, dined at a miserable dive of a place, and turned in for the night. Holmes expressed a wish to be alone for a while, so I took advantage of the opportunity to check my emails and cruise the web for a while.

Quite inadvertently I stumbled upon Mary Jo Maestri's article entitled "The Curse of the Oval Office," which ran in *The National Gazette*, an ill-fated venture modeled after *The National Enquirer*, although on an even less sophisticated level. Amidst the garbage about extraterrestrial werewolves and cyborgs was this ludicrous piece that claimed a chemical agent had been added to the paint that went onto the wall of the Oval Office, and the result had wrought havoc on the minds of the presidents. Quite a catalog:

(1) Truman had been lured into a land war in Asia.

(2) Eisenhower managed to abort the planned summit with Khrushchev over a meaningless U-2 spy mission, even going so far as to deny everything, only to learn that the pilot (Francis Gary Powers) had been captured alive and had already told the Soviets everything.

(3) Kennedy appeared to have engaged in "flings with Marilyn Monroe and Mafia broads."

(4) Johnson, like Truman, got himself mired in a land war in Asia.

(5) Nixon was forced to resign because of an apparently meaningless burglary, when he could easily have burned the tapes in question and survived the storm.

(6) Ford pardoned Nixon, after promising not to do so.

(7) Carter let the Shah of Iran into the country, precipitating the Iranian hostage crisis that sank his presidency.

(8) Reagan became so obsessed with the idea of overthrowing the Sandinista government in Nicaragua that he sold arms to Iran after Congress had refused to fund his subversion.

(9) Bush 41 proudly told the nation, "Read my lips. No new taxes." Then he raised taxes.

The article was published in 1992, a few years after the *Dynasty* episodes, so it stopped there. Of course, it requires no great leap of the imagination to see how the argument might continue, through Clinton, Bush 43, Obama, and Trump. However, it also seems reasonable to guess that every president will almost inevitably commit at least one epic blunder at some point or another, and I could find no evidence that an airborne neurotoxin had been deployed (in paint, yet!) to achieve that purpose.

Sherlock, who was suddenly showing his years, appeared almost depressed when he knocked on my door the next morning. I feared that he had hardly slept. Trying to cheer him up, I told him about the article and attempted to show him the text on my laptop at breakfast. He stared at the computer for a few seconds and slid it back across the table with a single, all-too familiar word. "Rubbish!" he declared, although I could have sworn I saw a slight smile on his face.

The hospital called shortly after 8:00 a.m. and told us that Dr. Moriarty would be well enough to receive visitors after lunch. The impatient Holmes, who by now seemed almost despondent, suggested that we play some Fischer's Random Chess if only for diversion, and thus I had my first opportunity to try a few of the many starting positions.

"What can I say, Sherlock?" I asked after we had blitzed through a few games. For the record, I lost the first, won the second, drew the third, and then lost the next four. "I can understand why this might have appealed to Bobby. He had not followed the game for many years and would have been handicapped by the advances in opening theory. Perhaps he imagined that he was still sharper than anyone in the world tactically and had a greater knowledge of strategy, so if he could deprive the top players of their theoretical advantages, he might prevail against them."

Holmes shrugged. "You may be right, but kindly tell me how that information brings us any closer to refuting Moriarty's confession."

I had to admit that it did not. The old man suggested we go our separate ways until lunch, claiming that he wanted to rest a while if he could. I do not know precisely how he kept himself occupied during the ensuing time, yet it was clear that he did not sleep. He ate sparingly at lunch, after which we took a cab back to the prison hospital.

Moriarty looked rather pale when we saw him next, yet he smiled as we entered the room and took our seats. "Ah, Sherlock, can you prove my innocence, or are you still looking for more clues?"

Holmes studied him for a moment. "As of right now, I must confess that your assertion cannot be disproven. However, the burden of proof is on you, given that you have made the claim. To draw an analogy, I might declare that there is in fact subterranean life on Mars and require that you disprove *my* assertion."

An obnoxious grin worked its way onto Moriarty's features. "My, my!" he declared. "I had completely forgotten that you passed a course on logic while you were in college. That is brilliant, Holmes, but you forget the obvious."

"Oh? And what, pray tell, is that?"

"My confession will be picked up in just two more days!"

This alarmed me. "By *whom*?" I inquired.

Without so much turning toward me, Moriarty replied. "By all the major media. *BBC News* will get the exclusive first rights, of course, but from there it will spread across the world. I have already made arrangements with *Le Monde* in France, *Frankfurter Allgemeine Zeitung* in Germany, *Izvestia* in Russia, *The People's Daily* in China, *Al-Ahram* and *Al-Jazeera* for the benefit of Muslim readers, the sacred and holy *New York Times* for the English readers on the other side of the Atlantic, and *El Nuevo Dia* for Spanish readers south of the border. And once these papers publish, my coverage by the electronic media will be even more extensive, I assure you.

"The whole world will hear my claim. The whole world will know that even the great Sherlock Holmes—admittedly in his dotage—could not disprove my assertions. The whole world will judge, and many will believe me. And that, Sherlock, will be my revenge on you."

Sherlock appeared to sag a little as he sat in his chair, saying nothing. I couldn't tell whether he was despondent or merely bored. I thought it best to continue. "Your story has two apparent weaknesses, Dr. Moriarty," I began.

Moriarty finally acknowledged my existence. He slowly turned toward me, and then nodded his head, as though to say I should continue. He seemed to hold me in complete contempt, and this fact emboldened me.

"First, what possible motive could you have had? You surely had no great love lost for the Soviets, who had thwarted your schemes on at least two occasions. You had no quarrel with Bobby Fischer, and you once indicated a great respect for his brilliance and determination. Why would you destroy him?"

Moriarty turned back to Sherlock. "You've really fallen pathetically, Holmes. Is this the best you can do for a sidekick?"

And still Holmes just sat there, saying nothing!

I felt myself becoming annoyed. "Even assuming that such a neurotoxin existed as far back as 1972—to say nothing of its primitive fore-runner, which your grandfather had presumably used to such devastating effect on poor Akiba Rubinstein six decades earlier—and even assuming that you had somehow disguised yourself, perhaps as a hotel maid, and applied it to the underside of Fischer's bed, two irrefutable facts remain: (1) Bobby Fischer won the match rather handily, and (2) despite my immense professional involvement in the fields of neurology and psychiatry, I have never found any credible reference to such an agent, and—"

Moriarty cut me off. "Please stop! You weren't even born when the match was played, but I should have assumed that you would at least have done some research about it before your pathetic attempt to engage in such polemic."

Moriarty stared at me and then Holmes. Suddenly he asked, "Did you ever see how Fischer lost the first game?"

"Yes! He grabbed a pawn and—"

"Oh, please try to be a little more precise, Doctor! Black's 29th move, Bxh2, was a blunder that a club player rated one thousand points lower should not have made. Was this move worthy of a man considered one of the greatest players of all time, if not *the* greatest ever?"

"Many grandmasters have committed blunders, and the pressure of a world championship match, particularly against someone whom he had never beaten to that point, may have blinded him somewhat."

"So badly blinded that he felt obliged to forfeit the next game?" asked Moriarty with a chuckle—and a side-glance at the still-immobile Holmes.

I stood my ground. "Bobby always insisted on what he considered 'optimal conditions for the players,' which explains why he often refused to play or even walked out of a given match or tournament."

"Oh, very good, very good, Dr. Watson. And that is why in Game 11 he brilliantly chose to repeat the "poisoned pawn" try, from which he struggled to a draw in Game 7. Two questions for you, Doctor: why assume Spassky's team would not contrive to find an improvement, and why not resign against the world champion having lost his Queen?"

I refused to be intimidated. "Bobby got the better of the opening and certainly had winning chances in Game 7. Moreover, after a string of five wins and three draws, covering Games 3 through 10, perhaps Bobby was a little overconfident. And perhaps he simply sought some psychological advantage by delaying his resignation. Of course, I have no way to be certain, but I wouldn't be surprised if it briefly crossed the minds of a number of Soviet players—and perhaps Spassky himself—that the brilliant Fischer had something up his sleeve, even though he seemed hopelessly crushed on the board."

Moriarty seemed to snort. "I suppose one might say that, and I suppose one might say something charitable about seven listless draws, Games 14 to 20. I know you will explain that with a four-point lead, he was simply 'grinding it out' toward the twelve and one-half points he needed, but he never really seemed as brilliant as he had in Games 6 and 13.

"One of the early symptoms of the agent I developed is that it induces inconsistent, if not erratic behavior and performance. Wouldn't you agree that even as early as the 1972 match the victim appeared somewhat inconsistent?"

I looked at Holmes, who said nothing.

"And how would you explain his bizarre behavior, beginning within mere weeks of his epic triumph? He had once spoken of 'breaking' FIDE, playing matches against whomever he pleased. He could surely have found backers for matches against any number of possible challengers, notably Korchnoi, Mecking, or even the 60-plus-year-old Reshevsky. Instead, he meekly gave away his title to another detested Soviet. Give Gary Kasparov credit. He successfully broke away from FIDE for a while, defending against Short and Anand, and later losing to Kramnik. Fischer waited twenty years before 'defending' against Spassky, who was no longer even among the top hundred players in the world!"

"True," I replied, "but Bobby was also losing interest in chess. Moreover, he was by this time quite paranoid, and I think I am qualified to offer that as a clinical evaluation."

"Ah, and the next stage of my drug is that it exacerbates any negative behavioral tendencies. True, Fischer was paranoid, but he was also terrified by the prospect of losing. The loss of his physical fitness might have cost him his edge in and of itself. The paranoia made it virtually impossible for him to consider a defense of his title.

"The sad thing is that his paranoia was probably justified, although it was directed at the wrong targets. No intelligence agencies were out to destroy Fischer. His threat came from one person, and one only. However, he would never have suspected me, and I doubt he even knew of my existence."

This last statement seemed to garner a reaction from Sherlock, who suddenly stirred in his seat. "But why?" he demanded. "You had no dealings whatsoever with Fischer, Spassky, or international chess."

Moriarty laughed, began to cough, and struggled to contain his mirth. "Chess, my dear Holmes, is considered one of the quintessential intellectual pursuits. It is at once a game, a sport, and an art, and the possibilities over the board seem nearly endless. Fischer was considered a genius, perhaps the greatest chess genius ever. Thus, I was resolved to destroy him, simply for the perverse pleasure of reducing one of the world's superstars to something hideous and ugly. You cannot imagine what joy it gave me!"

Holmes frowned. "You are despicable, James. I can merely express disgust for this preposterous tale. If it were true, I would cheerfully concede that you are the most loathsome excuse for a human being yet known to me."

"But it is true," Moriarty insisted.

"An assertion you cannot prove."

"And one even the great Sherlock Holmes cannot discredit. At worst we have a Mexican standoff, but one that will be tried in the Court of Public

Opinion. Knowing the mentality of the masses as well as we both do, I think we can safely guess that the majority will believe me, rather than you, even though I hold them in the vilest contempt. I shall carry this triumph to the grave."

I shook my head, prompting Moriarty to question me. "Does something bother you, Dr. Watson?"

"Such a toxin, assuming it exists, would either kill off its victim or else tend to lose power after a time. You claim to have poisoned Fischer in 1972, yet he lived until 2008. Yes, he spiraled downhill, but his first game in the 1992 match against Spassky was certainly impressive and hardly indicative of a man who was cerebrally compromised."

"Dr. Watson, Dr. Watson! Do I need to remind you that Fischer was playing the shell of Spassky, a man rated outside the top-100, and that he nevertheless contrived to fall behind by losing Games 4 and 5? And look what followed:

"He went to Hungary, where he spent time as a guest of the Polgars. It was widely reported that he would play a blitz match against Judit Polgar, and such a man vs. woman contest would truly have been a fantastic event, particularly given the recent accomplishments of Polgar. However, Fischer pulled out of the match, offering the explanation that the Polgars were Jewish.

"He went to Japan, his passport expired, and the next thing we knew he was in prison. Bobby asserted that he had been 'kidnapped' and imprisoned 'near a leaky nuclear power plant'—probably alluding to the facility in Tokaimura. He also said he was being poisoned. He didn't seem to realize that he had already been poisoned—by me!

"Okay. So he married in Japan, but we also know he was involved with someone in the Philippines and presumably even had a child with her."

At this point Holmes interrupted. "I suppose you will next tell me that no man has ever been led to believe a child was his, or that no other man ever married one woman after having impregnated another."

After his 1992 match with Spassky, Fischer spent some time with the Polgars at their home in Budapest. In this photo, Bobby and Susan Polgar are playing Chess960, a/k/a FischerRandom Chess.

"I merely remind you, Sherlock, that Fischer's behavior grew steadily worse as he aged, because the neurotoxin continued to affect him adversely. In fact, speaking of the two women and what followed, how do you explain the fact that a presumably brilliant man—with an I.Q. of a reported 181 or higher—knowing that he was in very poor health, never even bothered to write a will?"

"But your proof, James!" replied the detective. "All you need to do is provide that chemical agent. Where is it? What is it? How did you discover and produce it? With answers to these questions, even I might take you seriously. After all, notwithstanding your narcissism, bitterness, and elephantiasis of the ego, you are certainly a brilliant fellow."

Already the electrocardiogram had begun to register the patient's distress. "True, I am brilliant," he rasped. "However, a man of your limited intellect simply couldn't even begin to fathom my discovery. Neuroscience and neurophysiology are simply quite beyond you. And now, if you will excuse me," he panted, "I must rest."

A nurse and a resident had already rushed into the room. "I'm sorry," said the latter, "but you will have to leave."

The last sounds I heard as we departed were the beeping of the electrocardiogram, which seemed somehow just slightly faster still.

Chapter 7

Moriarty's Fantasies Exposed

Holmes, who had at times seemed almost asleep during our last interview with Moriarty, was quite chipper as we left the hospital. "Thank you so much, Joan! You have been an enormous help to me, in more ways than one," he stated warmly.

I was puzzled. "Really?" I asked. "I don't see how I contributed anything at all."

Sherlock put his index finger on his lips, indicating that we would have to remain silent until we were back at the hotel. Fortunately, the taxi brought us to that destination in short order, and we were soon safely ensconced therein.

"You were brilliant, Joan, absolutely brilliant!" cried the old man, giving me an awkward hug.

"Please tell me what I did, other than ask the obvious questions. And how closely did you follow the conversation, anyway? You seemed half-asleep during most of it."

A wry chuckle answered me. "Once you had gotten the names of the papers, there was no need for me to stay awake at all," Sherlock replied. "Come, now. You surely remember the list, don't you?"

I blanched. "Uh, I think so. There was *BBC News*, *Le Monde* –"

In an impressive display of memory, Holmes rattled off the rest. "Now, all I have to do is present my refutation even before his ridiculous fantasy can be printed."

"Your refutation?"

"Of course. It wasn't hard, since the poor man left so many clues. However, it was you who truly cracked the case for me."

Needless to say, this assertion caught me totally by surprise. "Really? What on earth did I do?"

Holmes smiled. "Do you remember how my grandfather worked on the case of Paul Morphy?"

I nodded. I was, of course, quite familiar with that famous story.

"Well," he continued, "I also recently solved the murder of Alexander Alekhine."

Confusion surely registered on my face. "But I thought he died when a piece of meat got stuck in his throat," I exclaimed.

"Not quite, Joan," replied Holmes, his eyes twinkling. "I'll tell you about that one in a few minutes, but first back to the neurotoxins.

"You have stated pretty much conclusively that such chemicals do not exist now, and surely could not have been used so adroitly in 1972, when Moriarty IV claims he poisoned Bobby Fischer. Would you not agree with me that it is vastly less likely that his grandfather, the second James Moriarty, could possibly have used the forerunner of such a toxin to the detriment of Akiba Rubinstein?"

"I would say there was no chance whatsoever!" I declared.

"Excellent! Now, the next piece of the puzzle comes from the mind of Moriarty. I have studied him far more closely than he seems to appreciate, and I might add that I understand him far better than he does himself. As is not uncommon amongst men with prodigious memories, he has a weakness for numbers. He seeks coincidences, and when he finds them, he is driven by some mysterious, internal urgency to draw an inference. If there is no such inference to be found, then he must create one, even if it exposes him and leads to his eventual defeat.

"Let us see how quickly you catch on, Joan. Do you recall what year Paul Morphy died?"

I hesitated. "I believe it was fifteen to twenty years after the Civil War, but I don't quite remember."

"Try 1884. Remarkably enough, that was just two years before Steinitz defeated Zukertort to claim what we now consider the 'official' world chess championship. Hold that number: two.

Though still at a complete loss as to where Holmes was going, I nodded meekly, and he continued:

"Next, do you remember the year when Alekhine died?"

"Why, yes! That was 1946."

"Excellent. And what happened in 1948?"

"That was the year of the tournament through which Botvinnik became world champion," I said. "And that brings up the number two again, doesn't it?"

"Very good, Joan. Now, when did Bobby Fischer die?"

"2008, as you know perfectly well," I answered.

"The pattern is now abundantly obvious, isn't it?" asked Sherlock.

I frowned and shook my head. Nothing made sense.

"Joan, Joan. It's simple math. How many years were there between 2008 and 1946?"

I had no clue where he was going with this, but I blurted out, "Sixty-two."

"And how many between 1946 and 1884?"

"Sixty-two again!" I exclaimed, adding, "What an amazing coincidence!" Then I paused, still baffled. "But how does that help us?"

"Well, Joan. You surely heard your father explain that in many ways Dr. Moriarty was my mirror image, in that he applied his brilliant mind and talents toward criminal pursuits, while I applied mine toward the prevention of the same. Does that help you?"

I could only shake my head helplessly.

"OK. Let me ask you another question. How old was Bobby Fischer when he died?"

"Sixty-four," I replied.

"And how many squares are there on the chessboard?"

"Sixty-four."

"Excellent. Now, we already have the deaths of two reigning champions—Morphy, who must be considered an unofficial world champion, and Alekhine, who was still the undisputed titleholder—and add to the above Fischer, whose claim was surely quite weak, but who nonetheless had never lost his crown. The deaths of these men are sixty-two years apart, and new champions are crowned two years after Morphy's death and again two years after Alekhine's. So, if we add two to the sixty-two, we return to our sixty-four.

"This is all well and good, but Moriarty had pounced on another numerical coincidence. Bobby won the crown in 1972, and this year, 2018, is now forty-six years after the fact. He could laugh all the way to the grave, knowing that those forty-six years were the reverse—or in some way a warped mirror image—of that same sixty-four. And thus, forty-six years later, as he approached death, he wanted to taunt me with his fraudulent confession."

I desperately tried to absorb everything Holmes was telling me. "OK. I see that the deaths of these chess champions are loaded with coincidences, but for those who are neither numerologists or Kabbalists, the numbers are little more than that: coincidences. Besides, you still haven't told me how you can be so certain that everyone will believe you rather than Moriarty."

At this Holmes let out a belly laugh. "Elementary, my dear Watson!" he cried, almost convulsed with laughter. "The article you showed me gave away the whole plot!"

I could not believe what I had just heard, and for a moment I feared the old man had taken leave of his senses. "What are you talking about?" I asked.

"It was you who told me about 'The Curse of the Oval Office.' Do you remember what year the fatal painting occurred?"

"Why, yes! That was presumably in 1950."

"And when did Bobby win the title?"

"In 1972. Oh—" The lights were beginning to come on. "I see. Twenty-two years, which would give us a pair of twos to add to each sixty-two, bringing the total up to sixty-four. Is that what you're suggesting?"

Sherlock beamed with joy! "Well, you're half-way home, Doctor. That was the calling card. Here's the last piece, and it was Moriarty's crowning blunder. What was the name of the author?"

"Mary Jo Maestri," I answered. "I remember her clearly, since I recently had a patient with the same name."

Once more Holmes began to laugh. "Didn't you catch the anagram? Scramble the letters, and you'll soon find the author's real name."

It took me only a matter of seconds. "James Moriarty!" I gasped.

"Of course," replied Holmes, beaming. "Having enjoyed his pseudonymous fiction, he wanted to reprise the concept in real life. Ah, the colossal arrogance! He even had the effrontery to ask whether I was still 'looking for clues.' Well, he overplayed his hand!"

We enjoyed a good laugh and ordered a celebratory bottle of champagne. As we sipped it, I felt compelled to ask the obvious question.

"Do you plan to shatter the dying man's illusions, or will you let him slip away, convinced that he has outwitted you?"

I shall never know whether Holmes had made up his mind, one way or the other. At that very moment we got a call from the hospital. Dr. James Moriarty had died just a few minutes earlier.

Chapter 8

Afterword

Holmes placed a call to a highly ranked editor within the BBC and shared all the details. As we both suspected, James Moriarty had not yet sent any "exclusive" to the broadcast, digital, or printed editions of the news service. Nevertheless, as a prophylactic measure, Holmes's contact fired off emails to his counterparts at all of the other papers, assuring them that if they ever received communication about the murder of Bobby Fischer by Dr. Moriarty, they could safely dismiss it, since its refutation by the redoubtable Sherlock Holmes would soon hit the newsstands.

Sherlock continued to heap praises upon me and assured everyone that he would never have solved the case without my assistance. I am rather certain he exaggerated, but I could never convince him of that.

At the end of the week, I flew back to Boston. While I had enjoyed working with Holmes, I found it painfully difficult to get the experience down on the printed page—or, in this case, on the computer screen. Given Sherlock's age and my great love of my chosen profession, I think it will be better if I just stick with medicine.

Part II

Sherlock Holmes Interprets Four More Chess Mysteries

Notes to Part II

Grandmaster Soltis has already suggested other mysterious deaths for Sherlock to explore. However, I was anxious to put the detective's talents to problems of different sorts, none of which could possibly have involved murder (or even speculative murder). Thus, I selected the last four, which present totally different challenges.

(1) The Lasker-Schlechter match has puzzled chess aficionados for over a century and surely warrants Holmes's attention. (2) Some people still believe that the death of Harry Nelson Pillsbury was hastened by the mental strain of his memory stunts. (3) Because of my association with Viktor Korchnoi, I had followed the Korchnoi-Maróczy game carefully, and I have spoken with people who genuinely believe the contest proved "the survival of consciousness after death." (4) Finally, I was anxious to attempt at least one story that had no connection whatsoever to an actual chess player, and since I have also begun sketching a novel involving an *ibbur*, the last "mystery" fell almost naturally into place.

As with Part One, I must again suggest that anyone who takes the author too seriously should report for an immediate mental health evaluation. Notwithstanding this admonition, I devoutly hope the mysteries that follow will provide readers with harmless entertainment.

Sherlock Holmes and the Mystery of the Title Tiff

The 1910 Lasker-Schlechter Match

Notes on the Lasker-Schlechter Encounter

Four recent matches for the world chess championship ended in 6-6 standoffs. All four outcomes were ultimately decided by "rapid chess" tiebreaks, and the world champion prevailed on each occasion. In 2012 Viswanathan Anand defeated Boris Gelfand by a score of 2½-1½. Magnus Carlsen topped Sergey Karjakin by a more convincing 3-1 in 2016, and two years later he clobbered Fabiano Caruana by 3-0. In the 2006 "reunification" match, Vladimir Kramnik and FIDE champion Veselin Topalov also went to a tiebreaker, and Kramnik prevailed, 2½-1½.

One way or the other, tied matches have occurred before, and they will doubtless arise in the future. Meanwhile, many purists have expressed disappointment with these outcomes. Some insist that the champion should simply retain the title if the match ends with a tied score—an argument perhaps more reasonable when matches were longer (e.g., twenty-four games). Others would like to see the contest continue, but under "classic chess" time controls, as was indeed the case in the last successful defense by the first official world champion. In 1892 William Steinitz and Mikhail Chigorin locked horns for a twenty-game match, with draws counting as one-half point. The rules stated that if the contest stood at 10-10, the players would continue until one of them had ten wins, with the proviso that if both had notched nine victories, the match would be declared a draw, and Steinitz would retain the title. After twenty games the champion and challenger had eight wins each, with four draws, but Steinitz closed out the match with a draw and a pair of wins (thanks to two horrific blunders by Chigorin).

Sometimes the outcome simply remained a tie. Of course, the chess world has never had "co-champions," so in these cases the defending titleholder kept the crown.

David Bronstein faced Mikhail Botvinnik in 1951, and after twenty-two games he led 11½-10½. However, he lost Game 23 with Black and could only draw Game 24 for a 12-12 tie.

Peter Leko challenged Vladimir Kramnik for the title in 2004. The fourteen-game match stood 7-6 in favor of Leko, but Kramnik pulled out a victory with White in Game 14 to hold the title with a 7-7 tie.

Vasily Smyslov (1954) experienced this disappointment in his first match against Botvinnik, which he tied 12-12. However, he won the title three years later, only to lose the rematch in 1958.

Leading 12-11, Anatoly Karpov lost the twenty-fourth game against Kasparov in their 1987 match. However, he had held the title previously and would later claim the FIDE "world championship."

One other challenger suffered the disappointment of a tied match. Here, however, the tale remains shrouded in mystery. In 1910 Carl Schlechter lost the tenth and final game of his match with Emanuel Lasker, and pundits have weighed in on the "real" story ever since. Indeed, it has proven an enigma worthy of Sherlock Holmes!

[Note: The narrator is Dr. John James Watson, son of the "original," and the detective in question is Sherlock Holmes Jr.]

Chapter 1

The Champion Keeps the Title!

It was always great to see my son, of course, but as the years passed, his own medical education had often kept us apart. By 1951, however, things were far more settled, and we were usually able to get together at least briefly over the weekend. Most fortunately, we were both practicing in the Greater Boston area.

I was sixty-five, still seeing patients, and my wife and I were both in good health. John Michael Watson was thirty-one and had completed his residency in dermatology. His days as an eligible bachelor were also drawing to a close, as he was now formally engaged and would tie the knot the following month.

John's visit that Saturday afternoon coincided with publication of Hermann Helms' last report on the title match. Indeed, back in 1951, the best chess news one could find came from those updates, which were a fixture in *The New York Times*. From the Ides of March until the eleventh of May, two Soviet grandmasters locked horns over the course of twenty-four games. At stake was the world chess championship; challenger David Bronstein sought to wrest the crown from titleholder Mikhail Botvinnik.

After twenty-two games Bronstein held the lead, 11½-10½, but Botvinnik won a complicated endgame in the penultimate encounter, and Bronstein could only draw in the finale. The result was a tie: 12-12.

Although he had practically abandoned chess during medical school, my son still shared my enthusiasm for the game. He played only a little more during his residency, but he was once again pushing wood from time to time, though admittedly not as well as he once did. Nevertheless, it was a pleasure to review the score with John Michael and pretend I actually understood the game at that level!

"Pawn to Q4," I began, and my son dutifully moved the White Queen-pawn up two squares.*

Well, the two giants made one move after another, but by ten moves into the game, Bronstein was already a pawn behind, and I didn't like White's position. On Move 19, the champion seemed to give up a Rook for a Bishop, but two moves later he gained back a Rook at the cost of a Bishop, and Bronstein agreed to a draw on the 22nd move. We both felt that Black stood somewhat better, since Botvinnik was still a pawn ahead.

"It's all over," I declared, returning the pieces to their starting positions.

John Michael shook his head. "Yes, but it's a little unsatisfying, since that leaves the score knotted at 12-12. Don't you think they should have some sort of 'overtime' or 'extra innings'? After all, when Bronstein and Boleslavsky tied in their playoff last year, the match was extended for two more games."

"True," I explained. "That was for the right to challenge, but in a title match it's more like boxing, The champion keeps the title in the event of a tie."

"Oh? Has this happened before?"

I smiled. "Just once, John. The match was only ten games, and it ended 5-5. World champion Emanuel Lasker won the final game of his match against Carl Schlechter back in 1910."

---

* In 1951 and for some years thereafter *The New York Times* and most chess periodicals in the United States used descriptive notation rather than algebraic.

My son frowned. "Ten games seems a little short for a match, doesn't it?"

"...and therein hangs a tale! Indeed, rumors began almost immediately, and some people believe we shall never know the whole story."

My hand hovered over the Queen's pawn and the King's pawn, as though deciding which one to move first.

"Of course, one man was able to sift through all the details, reject the speculation, and resolve the mystery. You know who he was, don't you?" I asked, pushing the King's pawn up two spaces.

He nodded. "Of course. Sherlock Holmes Jr.—who else?" he replied, moving his King's pawn up two squares.

I now advanced the Queen's pawn two squares, and Black captured it. I then moved the Queen's Bishop's pawn one square, and he snatched that as well. My King's Bishop came out three squares next, and my son greedily pounced on my Queen's Knight's pawn. I recaptured with my other Bishop, and he began trying to figure out how to stop the onslaught that would inevitably follow.

I sensed that he wasn't really in the mood to match wits over the chessboard. On the other hand, I had never known him to turn down an entry from my Sherlock Holmes log. Rather than squander a short visit on a slow game, I proposed an alternative.

"Well, we could complete this game, but if you prefer, I shall gladly tell you all about the 1910 match, and how Sherlock did what Sherlock always does."

One look at John's face assured me of his interest. "By all means, please do!" he declared, with genuine enthusiasm.

I took a quick glance at the board. "Shall we call it a draw?"

"Gladly!" he replied.

We adjourned to the living room. "Of course, I don't have nearly as many stories to convey about the two Holmeses as your grandfather shared about the original Sherlock. Nevertheless, I helped both of those geniuses on a few occasions, and I was with Holmes Jr. when we ran into Franz Wiedermeyer back in 1934."

John took a seat on the couch while I dashed off to my library to retrieve my "Sherlock Holmes Notebook." I returned clutching that precious volume, sat down on the armchair opposite my son, and began to read.

I must append one quick note: Like my father, I have faithfully chronicled those occasions on which I assisted either Sherlock Holmes, save only that I worked more often with Holmes *fils,* while he worked exclusively with Holmes *père.* I also decided to adopt a writing style reasonably similar to my father's, simply because it seemed the right way to continue the symbiotic tradition. I was by no means surprised when John Michael later followed my example.

Chapter 2

An Intriguing Letter

In 1934, the world economy was still in turmoil, and while there were signs of recovery in the USA, many nations were struggling. As a general practitioner (a so-called "family doctor"), I sometimes got as little as one dollar for a house call, yet I realized that for some of my patients a medical visit was a luxury not to be indulged unless absolutely needed.

Overall, though, I was doing relatively well, and I was grateful for the security my profession provided. Needless to say, I was also paid better by most of my patients. I had purchased a modest two-family house and used the first floor as a medical office while my wife, children, and I lived upstairs.

My friend across the ocean—"the pond," as he and his fellow-Brits used to call it—was doing extremely well. As though blessed with some sort of "sixth sense," he had abruptly liquidated his stock holdings in 1928 and put his cash to good use during the ensuing years, acquiring various properties, art works, and a Stradivarius violin.

I was delighted when Holmes announced that he intended to come to the United States during that summer. His wife and son (whom he called "Third") planned to visit the grandparents (hers; his parents were deceased by this time) in Scotland, while Sherlock Jr. had been invited to present lectures on deductive reasoning at the Boston Division of the Federal Bureau of Investigation. This gave us the opportunity to enjoy a week together, before he took the train back to New York and then the ship back to Liverpool.

During the third morning of Sherlock's visit—a Monday—we received a letter addressed to Holmes at my residence. Even I could sense that the missive was remarkable for its clearly European handwriting. My address was 17 Main Street, and both the "one" (with an extended serif) and "seven" (with a crossbar through the middle) were certainly unusual. My guest opened the envelop and began to read:

> *Dear Mr. Sherlock Holmes,*
>
> *I have been told that you have considerable interest in the chess—*[Note that he writes, "the chess." He's probably German.]*—so perhaps you will be able to help me. Nearly twenty-five years ago a relative of mine played in a match, and while I know the outcome, I have not been able to learn the story behind the results.*
>
> *I would not wish to ask you to investigate, but perhaps you would be so kind as to meet with me, so that I might share such information as I have been able to accumulate. I would be anxious to learn your thoughts about the match in question.*
>
> *Like so many other people, I have suffered severe losses during the past several years. Nevertheless, I have been able to keep myself occupied, and I believe I can pay for an hour or so of your time.*
>
> *I thank you very much for your reply. I am,*
>
> *Yours truly,*
>
> *Franz Wiedermeyer*

Holmes studied the paper carefully, returned it to its envelop, and slid it across the table to me. "What do you think, Watson?"

I shrugged my shoulders. "Somebody lost a game a quarter of a century ago, and now some relative wants to know how he lost? Or what? I don't understand."

With a wry smile Sherlock shook his head. "Not a game, John; a match! Not a quarter of a century ago, but slightly less. What important matches were played in late 1909 and early 1910?"

I paused. "I'm afraid I don't have chess history at my fingertips, Holmes."

"No matter! I can tell you in a heartbeat. After drawing a short exhibition match 2-2, Emanuel Lasker clobbered David Janowski by 8-2, with seven wins and two draws in ten games, between 19 October and 9 November of 1909.* They met again almost a year later, commencing on 8 November of 1910 and concluding one month thereafter. The result was even more lop-sided; Lasker won eight games out of eleven with three draws."

I was duly impressed by my friend's prodigious memory. Of course, he could retain information effortlessly, and having read something once, he "owned" that information in its entirety.

"So you think this involves Janowski?" I asked.

"Absolutely…not! You forget that Lasker had another championship match in between."

I frowned. "Was that against Dr. Tarrasch?"

"That one," said Holmes with a sigh, "was against Carl Schlechter from 7 January to 10 February 1910. They played only ten games, finishing with one win apiece and eight draws."

"And you think this one, short match is more likely than either of the two with Janowski to have troubled your prospective client?"

Holmes shook his head again. "Just look at the name on the letter, John. 'Wiedermeyer'—Germanic, for sure. Janowski was from a Polish-Jewish family, but Schlechter was born in Vienna and is thus more likely to have been related to *Herr* Wiedermeyer.

---

* Holmes, like most Europeans, conveyed the date before the month—i.e., 19 October, rather than October 19.

"Moreover, the author of this letter expresses an interest in 'the story behind the results.' Given the lopsided scores of both Lasker-Janowski encounters, I doubt there is a mystery worthy of anyone's attentions, let alone mine. The Schlechter match, on the other hand, was a strange one. Carl Schlechter was known as something of a 'drawing master,' so why could he not draw the last game, when he was leading the match by 5-4?"

I shrugged, while Holmes smiled.

"I am interested, John! Kindly give me a pen and a sheet of paper, and I should like to invite this Wiedermeyer to spend an evening with us—with your permission, of course!"

"Oh, definitely!" I declared.

Since we planned to attend a violin recital by Fritz Kreisler on Tuesday night, Holmes invited the gentleman to visit Wednesday evening. Wednesday morning's post brought in a short note of confirmation, and we awaited his arrival.

Chapter 3

Wiedermeyer's Narrative

Franz Wiedermeyer arrived promptly at 8 p.m., and we showed him into my living room. He declined the offer of an aperitif but accepted a cup of tea with gratitude.

Wiedermeyer was a thin man of relatively fair complexion, whose studious face—accented by wire-rimmed spectacles—conveyed intelligence, but whose attire reflected financial duress. He wore a rather inexpensive bracelet of some sort on his right wrist and one of those low-priced Elgin watches on his left. He seemed somewhat in awe of my guest—who wouldn't be?—but Sherlock, in his own unique way, soon put our visitor at ease.

"Well, Mr. Wiedermeyer," he began. "You are doubtless far more comfortable in your present place of employment than your last. Born under the Emperor Franz Joseph—you were named for him, weren't you?—you emigrated with your parents at some point before the Great War. You have a gift for languages, or certainly learned English rather quickly, and you are a voracious reader. Unfortunately, you lost almost everything when the market collapsed, and the company that employed you also went under. These circumstances necessitated a dramatic change in your lifestyle, and you accepted a rather demeaning position at a frightfully low salary. Happily, your circumstances changed fairly recently, and you now work indoors."

The poor man's jaw dropped. Holmes turned to me and asked, "Are not all these things blatantly obvious, Watson?"

I swallowed nervously and sighed. "My dear friend, I am afraid I lack your powers of deduction."

"Oh, come, Doctor! Our visitor has a Germanic name, does he not? To judge by facial appearance—the lack of wrinkles or grey hair—I would guess he is less than forty years of age. He speaks quite well, but with a tiny accent, which suggests that he arrived in this country as a teenager. Since travel was so severely restricted during the Great War, and that dreadful epidemic shut so many borders for most of the next two years, it is safe to assume, judging by his age and command of English, that he arrived not much later than 1910."

Holmes now gave Mr. Wiedermeyer one of his penetrating stares. "Shall I take a guess? 1909."

Our guest's countenance turned even more pale. "Why, that is true, Mr. Holmes, but how could you tell?"

"Ha! You practically gave it away with the make-shift bracelet you wear. It has a penny from that glorious year embedded into it, and I cannot find any other reason why you would carry a twenty-five-year-old coin so prominently."

To be perfectly candid, I had not even noticed the penny!

Wiedermeyer was astounded. "Why, yes, that is also correct. However, most people assume I am German, not Austrian."

Holmes smiled. "Because of another case a few years ago, I endured a brief exposure to the science of linguistics. At that time, I learned there were differences between the Austrian High German, Swiss German, and the Standard German. Of course, your accent is too slight for me to attribute it to any of these, but you contacted me through a handwritten letter, did you not?"

"I did, Sir!"

"Your numbers immediately gave away your European background; your name indicated Germanic origins, and your interest in a chess match less than twenty-five years ago led me to conclude that you alluded to the Lasker-Schlechter match. Am I correct in concluding that you are a distant relative of Carl Schlechter, who was from Vienna?"

Weidermeyer's eyes nearly popped out of his head. He could barely nod confirmation.

"The rest was easy. Of course, I do not wish to embarrass you, but you wear a blend of newer and older garments. Your shoes, for example, have seen better days—along with numerous repairs—whereas your trousers are relatively new. Like so many others around the world, you suffered a major reversal of fortune when the markets collapsed. One of your recent jobs involved work outdoors, while you are now more comfortably employed indoors. I note for my evidence a few fading signs of exposure to sunlight, which were doubtless somewhat darker against your skin when you worked under the solar rays."

As often as I had heard Holmes present his deductions, I still marveled each time a new one arose. I had missed those "few fading signs," which I should probably have noted, given that our visitor was rather fair. Mildly disappointed in myself, I now tried to make an observation of my own. "I suppose the spectacles are the dead give-away for a 'voracious reader,' aren't they Holmes?"

My friend pursed his lips with disapproval. "Eyeglasses alone do not a reader make, Doctor; surely you, of all people should know that! However, I point to the subtle signs of wear on the left elbow of our visitor's shirt. Like so many bookworms, he sometimes rests his head on one side and reads while he reclines."

I squinted, while Wiedermeyer cast a nervous glance at the back of his left sleeve. My friend had indeed spotted some nearly undetectable differences between that one and the right!

Wiedermeyer could not resist a smile. "Everything you say is true, Mr. Holmes. To put food on the table, I took whatever employment I could get, and for some time I picked up trash and debris at sports stadia. Fortunately, a friend enabled me to get a position as a secretary at the Federal Bureau of Investigation. I heard that you were presenting a lecture there, found out where you were staying, and here we are. And yes, like so many other children, I was given the name of Franz after our emperor!"

I clapped my hands, and Wiedermeyer joined me. I thought I detected the slightest flicker of a smile on Sherlock's face, but it was gone in an instant.

"But now, down to business," cried that gentleman. "Something about the 1910 match bothers you enough to seek my assistance. Dr. Watson is an intimate friend and long-time associate, and I might add that his father assisted mine on numerous occasions, so please start wherever you must."

Our visitor finished his tea and sat upright at the edge of the chair, and the mystery commenced.

Chapter 4

"Here's What We *Do* Know, Mr. Holmes."

"I suppose I should begin with the family connection. I'm not exactly sure, but it seems the late *Herr* Schlechter was some sort of very distant relative—fourth cousin, twice-removed, or maybe fifth cousin, once-removed. In our family the designations were simple: children of the same parents were brothers and sisters; their children were cousins, and after that one was simply *ein Verwandter*."

Holmes turned to me abruptly. "That's 'a kinsman,' Watson," he explained.

"I never met him, of course, and I heard about him only in December 1909, when my father mentioned that back in 'the Old Country' a distant relative of ours would play a match for the world chess championship the following month.

"I played a little chess, which is to say that I had learned how to move the pieces, though not very much more than that. Nevertheless, I felt the excitement, and I wanted him to win.

"We got news as it became available, and eventually we learned that the match had ended in a tie, 5-5. *Herr* Schlechter did not become champion, and he died shortly after the Great War ended.

"Meanwhile, we had already moved to the United States in May 1909. I was thirteen years old. I enrolled in the public school, and did quite well in English and history, though not so well with the mathematics.

Emanuel Lasker, the second world chess champion, held the title longer than any other player, 27 years.

"I never enjoyed the American sports, but I did become more interested in the chess, at which I improved. My real passion was reading, and after the War I learned much more about the match my kinsman had contested."

"Schlechter was still a young man, only in his mid-forties when he died in 1918. Did he succumb to the influenza?" I asked.

"The official cause was given as pneumonia," replied Holmes, "but from what I have heard, either the influenza or tuberculosis might instead have been to blame, and outright starvation may have been a factor, also. He was in abysmal financial straits toward the end of his short life." Turning to Wiedermeyer, he continued, "Please resume!"

"Well, I don't really know where to begin, but perhaps the first question is whether this was in fact a match for the championship at all. It seems that conditions changed notably before the first move could be played.

"Lasker had prevailed in some matches that required either ten victories or eight, with draws not counting. However, my distant relative apparently had a well-deserved reputation as 'King of the Draws,' and it was quite likely such a contest might have gone on for eighty to one hundred games. It was therefore decided that the match would run for thirty games, with draws counting as half a point for each side. It was also agreed that the challenger—Schlechter—would need to win by two points in order to become the next champion. In other words, if he prevailed by 15½-14½, he might claim the victor's share of the purse, but Lasker would retain the title.

"Then something very strange happened. Despite the great reputations of both men, they were unable to obtain adequate funds for thirty-games.

151

They settled for a ten-game match.

"Thus, the first question that arises is the most obvious. Was this truly a match for the world chess championship at all, or was it merely an exhibition?

Wiedermeyer paused, glanced over in my direction, and then turned back toward Holmes.

"The next question is where the mystery deepens. We know the original terms governing a thirty-game contest, but

Carl Schlechter

no one seems to have a copy of the documents—signed by both—governing the ten games they ultimately played."

"Forgive the interruption," said Sherlock, "but why does that matter?"

"Because, Mr. Holmes, the original match required Schlechter to win by two points, or by at least 16-14. The question is whether he was required to win this abbreviated match by the same margin."

"It would seem an insufferable handicap," said Sherlock, "but pray continue."

"Some claim Lasker's title was at stake, but others say it was not, because the match was too short."

I shook my head. "Boxing championships have been contested over the course of twenty-six rounds, but they have also been scheduled for only six. We should assume that a title match is a title match, regardless of its duration."

"That is probably true, Watson," replied my friend. "However, a champion may agree to a shorter match in which his title is not at stake. You may remember that Chigorin defeated Lasker in a "Rice Gambit" match in 1903, winning two, losing one, and drawing the other three. The loser remained champion, since the title was not at stake."

Holmes now turned to our visitor. "Please resume. You have more, I am certain."

Weidermeyer frowned and bit his upper lip nervously. "Have you played through that last game, Mr. Holmes?" he asked.

"Of course! In fact, if the doctor will bring us his set and board, I can go through it for you from memory."

The other man let out a gasp of surprise, but then shook his head. "Oh, that won't be necessary, Mr. Holmes. I don't really play well enough to understand chess at that level. However, many people have said that Schlechter played uncharacteristically. He seemed far more aggressive and played as though *he* was the one who needed the win. Is that not true?"

Holmes nodded. "One might question such a strategy, given his one-game lead."

"And what about the mistakes? I was told Schlechter made some similarly uncharacteristic blunders toward the end, overlooking a possible win and later a probable draw."

Now, I should mention that while Sherlock's father used cocaine and tobacco, and was a connoisseur of French wines, his son had a much lesser "addiction," if we may call it that. The younger Holmes positively loved to pick his teeth, particularly when he needed to think clearly. "Kindly get out your board, Watson," he directed, "and let us review the tenth game for clues."

While I set up the pieces, Holmes began staring out the window, even as he picked food particles out from between his teeth. "We are ready, Sherlock," I said, as Mr. Wiedermeyer pulled up closer to the board.

"Excellent! Move the two Queens's pawns out two squares," he instructed. "Then push the Queen's Bishop pawn ahead two squares for White, but only one for Black."

Picking away yet more vigorously—he was on his third toothpick by this point—Holmes brought us up to the critical thirty-fifth move. "It would seem he had far more promising prospects by moving his Rook to the half-open Queen's file, wouldn't you say?"

He then led us to the position after White's 39th move.

"Suppose he checked on the diagonal instead?" Sherlock asked. "Study that alternative, while I seek solace from this thin stick of wood."

Wiedermeyer and I tried a few lines, and in each of them White either allowed a threefold repetition or else lost his Rook on the eighth rank. If we could see this, surely Schlechter should have seen it!

Our visitor soon became rather defensive. "Now see here, Mr. Holmes," he protested. "You aren't suggesting that my kinsman lost the game deliberately, are you?"

There was no reply, whatsoever, from the other. In fact, he seemed to have frozen in place. Wiedermeyer was baffled, of course, while I knew exactly what was coming next.

Some three minutes later Holmes snapped back to life. "Ah! Now it all comes to light!" he declared. "Watson, let me indulge in some of your excellent port—a celebratory glass on the occasion of solving this case almost before my client could articulate it."

I more or less knew what to expect from my old friend by this time, but Wiedermeyer was positively overwhelmed. "You, you, you…you mean that you know what actually happened?" he stammered.

"Of course!" replied the detective.

"Then I shall be very much in your debt, sir!"

Holmes put up his hands. "On the contrary, Mr. Wiedermeyer. It is I who am in your debt, for had you not brought this strange case to my attention, I should surely never have had the opportunity to find the solution."

I now took the bull by the horns. "Enough of these mutual expressions of gratitude, Holmes. Tell us what really happened in 1910!"

Chapter 6

"Elementary, My Dear Watson!"

Sherlock and I clicked glasses. Mr. Wiedermeyer, who was evidently a teetotaler, declined to join in this celebration, but accepted a little more tea.

"I must confess," Holmes began, "that I was already well acquainted with this match. I played through all ten games, of course, and I was somewhat intrigued by the tenth—albeit more fascinated by the fifth, though more on that anon. However, I have followed my father's advice and vowed not to allow myself to become consumed by what is, at the end of the day, a mere pastime. There are too many important things to learn about the world, gentlemen, and chess is a luxury in which I simply cannot overly indulge.

He turned toward our visitor. "That said, I asked myself some of the same questions you have raised. Was it truly a championship match? Was there a 'plus-two' clause? Why did Schlechter play so uncharacteristically in the last game, and why did he make such errors? These are surely reasonable questions for any reasonable man, would you not agree?"

"Indeed, Mr. Holmes, and that is why I sought your assistance."

Sherlock gave him one of those wry smiles of his and glanced at me. "Ironically, my dear Mr. Wiedermeyer, it was you who helped me resolve the last of the mysteries. But allow me to begin with the others.

"First and foremost, it was indeed a match for the world chess championship. Second, there was no 'plus-two' clause. These facts are irrefutable."

"How so, Holmes?" I asked.

"Elementary, my dear Watson: the answers on both fronts come directly from the pen of the best witness available, Emanuel Lasker. You see, when the score stood 5-4 in Schlechter's favor, Lasker had braced himself for the seemingly inevitable loss of his title. A few days before the final game—which, by the way, was adjourned twice—Lasker sent a dispatch to *The New York Evening Post* in which he not only acknowledged his likely defeat in the match but added the following key passage, which I believe I cite more or less correctly: 'If that should happen, a good man will have won the world championship,' or words to that effect. From that one sentence alone, we can see at once both that the title *was* at stake and that the 'plus-two' clause was, as my father used to say, rubbish."

We were both stunned to learn of this development. "Are you certain, Sherlock?" I ventured timidly.

"Absolutely, John; I have read it myself."

"Why, so all my kinsman needed to do was make a draw in that last game!" Wiedermeyer interjected excitedly. Then his face dropped. "But how do you explain the errors he made, Mr. Holmes?"

Sherlock took another sip of port. "One of the reasons I never pursued the game seriously—not that I wouldn't have excelled, of course—is that I prefer the logical to the inexplicable. At the highest levels, we encounter many cases of what is called chess blindness. Even the greatest players are occasionally unable to find their ways through relatively simple positions, and some of the blunders by the top competitors are as frightful as those that any pathetic wood-pusher might commit.

"Yes, to be sure, Schlechter miscalculated in the tenth game, yet I must ask whether you have seen the fifth game, in which the world champion played aggressively with the Black pieces, obtained a clear advantage,

Emanuel Lasker (left) playing Carl Schlecter in the famous Cambridge Springs tournament of 1904.

blundered away a win, and then later squandered even the opportunity to secure a draw. Does that game not, in fact, almost mirror the tenth?"

Even before we could reply, Holmes answered the question for us. "Of course, it does!" he snapped. "The reason is simple: at this level, with a world title at stake, the psychological stress is enormous. One player's nerves slipped in the fifth game; the other player's failed him in the last."

Sherlock now turned to me and added, "If you worked in a different medical field, Doctor, you might now offer a diagnosis of simple chess blindness, true? In fact, Dr. Tarrasch—a practicing physician as well as a competitor of Steinitz and Lasker—went so far as to coin the humorous expression, *amaurosis scacchistica*, to describe such phenomena."

I grinned, but our visitor was still not satisfied. "All of this is well and good, Mr. Holmes, but you still do not explain why my kinsman chose to play as he did. Would he not have had a far better chance for a draw had he played in his normal manner?"

My friend smiled broadly. "You are correct, of course, Mr. Wiedermeyer, but you overlook something. My father had a saying, and I think it applies here. 'Once we eliminate the impossible, whatever remains, no matter how improbable, must be the truth.' I trust you both follow me perfectly."

We did not, but Sherlock soon explained.

"The last remaining question is why Schlechter played so aggressively, a decision that has doubtless spawned the entire 'plus-two' speculation which, as I have explained, is total rubbish. Why would he play for a win when he needed only a draw? It is impossible that he lost the game deliberately. It is also impossible that he needed to win such a dreadfully short match by two games, since Lasker was far too much of a gentleman to insist on such a preposterous handicap.

"On the other hand, we also know that Lasker was an astute businessman at the time, even though during the Great War he invested heavily in German war bonds and squandered most of his resources. Now, this is what I realized just moments ago, when our guest's questions directed me to the only logical explanation.

"Lasker had agreed to risk his title on the outcome of a thirty-game match, in which the challenger would be required to score at least 'plus-two,' or 16-14, to wrest the crown from him. As a matter of fact, Lasker sought the same sort of advantage during the abortive efforts to arrange a match with Capablanca in 1911.

"Alas, neither Schlechter nor Lasker could raise adequate funding, and in the end, they were unwilling to engage for longer than ten games, a duration far too short to demand a victory by two points. Lasker was reluctant to risk loss of his title by a mere one-game margin, but what could he do?"

Holmes paused for dramatic effect and continued only after I prompted him.

"Again, gentlemen, 'whatever remains, no matter how improbable, must be the truth'! He would surely have interpolated a sort of hybrid clause. A one-point victory by Schlechter would suffice to claim the championship, but the new titleholder *would be obliged to play a rematch under the financial terms of the original thirty-game agreement unless he could win the truncated match by a minimum of two points*!

"Schlechter was confident though by no means certain of victory before the match began. He was unafraid of Lasker, despite the champion's great reputation, particularly in matches. Moreover, he had not lost once during the first nine games, and he had good reason to believe he could garner one more draw with careful play.

"At the same time, he was a practical man. His style produced a high number of draws, and most financial backers of chess contests preferred the more swashbuckling play of the romantic era. He and Lasker had failed abysmally in their attempts to raise funds for thirty games. With eight draws in nine games already and a probable ninth draw in the tenth, he feared that he could not hope to raise the resources the original match required, if we assume the most probable contingency: *that Lasker had thrown in a clause that would have required Schlechter to do so, nevertheless*! However improbable, gentlemen, this is the only logical explanation.

"Now let us return to the tenth and final game. Schlechter's defensive resources had proven adequate for the challenges through the first nine games. Even in the fifth game, he had defended solidly in the face of a powerful attack. Perhaps for the first time in the match, he felt truly confident that he could hold Lasker to a draw and win the title, no matter what. Thus emboldened, he decided to play more aggressively, certain that if necessary, he could always pull back into a defensive shell and weather whatever storm might come his way. If he won, he would be the champion by a clear margin, unencumbered by any sort of ruinous rematch clause. If he drew, he would at least have won the title, although he would need to start trying to raise money almost immediately.

"Remember: at that time Schlechter had won nearly three times as many games as he had lost, and he had drawn roughly 50% of his games! The possibility of a loss seemed sufficiently remote that he was willing to risk everything.

"This explanation, however improbable it may seem, is the most reasonable we can hope to find. Lasker, for his part, was doubtless unwilling to publicize the rather unsporting pressures he had put on the challenger, and Schlechter was not the type of person to make excuses for what happened. In the end, he lost his nerve and succumbed to 'chess blindness.' Case closed, don't you think?"

I burst into applause, and even the reserved Franz Wiedermeyer could not resist joining me. "Your explanation does make sense, Mr. Holmes. I thank you so much!"

"As I thank you, Mr. Wiedermeyer, and I am sure the entire chess-playing world owes you a debt of profound gratitude for your contribution to solving this mystery."

The rest of the visit passed uneventfully, and Sherlock returned to England the following weekend.

Sherlock Holmes and the Mystery of the Memory Maven

The 1906 Death of Harry Pillsbury

Notes on Harry Nelson Pillsbury

Harry Nelson Pillsbury (1872-1906) was one of the most gifted chess players of all time, although his career was disrupted by a serious health problem as early as January 1896. While his accomplishments on and off the chessboard were in many ways remarkable, he never achieved a triumph quite as extraordinary as his first place in the Hastings chess tournament of 1895. That epic round robin was arguably the strongest event in chess history up to that point, and the field included the past and present world champions (Wilhelm Steinitz and Emanuel Lasker), two challengers whom Steinitz had narrowly defeated (Mikhail Chigorin and Isidore Gunsberg), and three men who would later challenge Lasker for the title (David Janowski, Carl Schlechter, and Dr. Siegbert Tarrasch).

When the smoke cleared, Pillsbury had triumphed with 16½ (out of 21). Chigorin, with 16, took second prize, while Lasker (15½), Tarrasch (14), and Steinitz (13) rounded out the top five. Interestingly, Pillsbury had lost to Chigorin and Lasker (and also to Schlechter, who finished with a more modest 11-10, in 9th place). Chigorin had dropped a game to Steinitz (and two other opponents); Lasker had lost to Chigorin and Tarrasch (and two others); Tarrasch had lost to Pillsbury and Chigorin (and two others). Steinitz had suffered six losses in all, including games to Lasker, Pillsbury, and Tarrasch, but defeated Chigorin and also won the brilliancy prize.

The top five were invited to compete in a multiple round robin in St. Petersburg, which ran from December 13, 1895, through January 27, 1896. Tarrasch, citing the demands of his medical practice, declined to participate, but the others contested a sextuple round robin. After three full cycles had been played, Pillsbury sat atop the cross-table with 6½ points, one ahead of Lasker, two ahead of Steinitz, and five ahead of Chigorin (who had a dreadful result). In three games against the world champion, Pillsbury had scored two wins and a draw, and had his good form continued, he might have found adequate financial backing for a title match.

Alas, it was not to be. Over the next nine rounds the American managed three draws (two against Lasker, one against Chigorin) and six losses. He finished third with 8-10, a point and one-half behind Steinitz and far behind Lasker (11½).

We do not know precisely what happened to cause such a collapse, but Pillsbury reportedly suffered from severe headaches. His health continued to decline, and he expired on June 17, 1906. The official death certificate attributed his demise to "general paresis," which was a more delicate designation for syphilis, and both his symptoms and later behavior were consistent with the final stages of that dreadful disease.

There does not seem to be much of a mystery here. However, events in the worlds of Sherlock Holmes Jr. and Dr. John Michael Watson are rarely as open-and-shut as the account above presents them. In fact, things become even more complicated when Watson's wife, Martha Watson, a clinical psychologist, offers assistance to the famous detective.

[Note: The narrator is the son of Dr. John James Watson and grandson of the "original" character. He is the father of Dr. John Simon Watson and the uncle of Rabbi Solomon Rosenbaum, who solve the final two mysteries of this volume. He will later become the grandfather of Dr. Joan Watson, who will help solve the Bobby Fischer "mystery" some fifty-six years later.]

Chapter 1

A Pleasant Surprise

I always kept my waiting room well stocked with popular magazines, although I rarely bothered to give any of them so much as a cursory glance. A rare exception arose with the August 20th, 1962, edition of *Sports Illustrated*, which included a blistering article by Bobby Fischer, who claimed "The Russians Have Fixed World Chess." I promptly removed the entire issue from office circulation, so that I could share the piece with my father when we picked up our children from my parents' summer place the following weekend.

Martha and I lived in Cambridge. We both worked in the Greater Boston area: I as a dermatologist and she as a psychologist.

Dad was now seventy-six and had retired from practice. He and my mother still lived in Brookline, but during August they rented a cottage on Nahant, a small island connected by causeway to Lynn. It was a great place for the children (John Simon, going on ten, and Deborah, eight) to visit, and they enjoyed day trips to nearby Salem and Marblehead, and—of course—excellent swimming at Canoe Beach.

We soon learned Dad would have some additional company. On Saturday, August 20th, we received a call from London. Sherlock Holmes Jr., a spry seventy years old, explained that he would be coming into Boston on the following Wednesday. "I have an interesting case involving someone practically in your neighborhood, and I could truly use your assistance—

and your wife's, by the way, and perhaps even your father's, though I understand he is retired."

I was delighted by the prospect, of course. While Dad had worked several cases with Sherlock over the decades, I had never had the opportunity. "You are most welcome to stay with us," I assured our mutual friend, "but who is this neighbor?"

"Isn't Somerville rather close to Cambridge?" Holmes asked.

"Depending upon the precise location, it's probably only two to three miles, or ten to fifteen minutes. Why?"

"More when I see you, Doctor, but I suspect you will recognize the name at once."

Hints like that exasperated me. Holmes and my father used to play games of this sort when I was a child, but I was now a licensed physician in his forties and the father of two. "Oh, come on, Sherlock. Spill the beans!" I cried.

I heard that familiar chuckle over the phone. Then, to my relief, he explained. "Does a Pillsbury from Somerville ring any bells?"

I felt a chill down my spine. "You don't mean Harry Nelson Pillsbury, do you? Why, he's been dead for over half a century!"

"Dead, but not forgotten, John Michael. I shall see you Wednesday. Good-bye!"

I called my father immediately, and he was thrilled by the prospect of seeing his old friend again. However, he surprised me by what he said next.

"I've had quite a few opportunities to watch Holmes in action, and as you know, I have provided considerable assistance on more than one occasion. Now, however, it's time for the Old Guard to step aside. This one is for you, John Michael. Unless you suddenly find you require the assistance of an old, retired family doctor, I would rather let you have the fun on this occasion. Just call me if you need me, or once the case has been solved. Meanwhile, if this involves Pillsbury, I recommend you do a little homework. Refresh yourself on the subject of syphilis!"

Well, that was that. Martha and I would be left to our own devices.

Chapter 2

Dangerous Distractions

We picked up Holmes at South Station. He had flown into New York and taken the train to Boston. I had not seen him in close to six years, but he looked almost exactly as he had the last time. At seventy years of age, he still boasted a full head of hair with scarcely any grey. He had the same, excellent posture and seemed extremely fit.

"It's all in the genes, John," he explained. "Most of the Holmes men invariably look years younger than their ages. Then again, the women don't fare so well, and my own mother looked eighty when she was in her late fifties!"

Be that as it may, Sherlock the septuagenarian could easily have passed for early fifties!

As soon as Holmes had gotten settled—if we dare imply that such a man can ever be truly "settled" when he is just starting a case!—he asked whether he might telephone one Svetlana Patel. That woman was not at home but was expected shortly, and Holmes left my number with her mother, who had taken the call.

"Who is Svetlana Patel?" I asked.

"Ah, an excellent question, Watson. She is a third cousin, thrice-removed of the late Harry Nelson Pillsbury."

"Third cousin, thrice-removed?"

"Precisely. We'll make a genealogist out of you yet, John! You see, her great-grandmother and the chess player in question were third cousins.

Her grandmother was thus a third cousin, once-removed; her mother was twice-removed, and I'm sure you can figure out the rest!"

Dad always said there were times when it was best simply to take Holmes at his word, and this was one topic sufficiently far afield that I wanted no part of it. Nevertheless, I was somewhat taken aback by the name of this distant kinsman. "Isn't Pillsbury an old English name?" I inquired.

Holmes smiled. "You are quite correct. In fact, the root-surname, Spellsbury, appears as early as the twelfth century. Nevertheless, people do marry out of their tribes, clans, ethnicities, races, and religions, and we may safely infer that this woman has both Russian and Indian ancestry in addition to the British-American. Now, we know that one William Pillsbury settled in the Boston area during the middle of the seventeenth century, and if you would like more historical background about the name…"

To my immense consternation, Martha was truly fascinated by this superfluous information, and Holmes was never one to squander the opportunity to entertain an appreciative audience.

We were interrupted (and in my own case, rescued) by a telephone call. Miss Patel asked whether she might drop by early the next afternoon. This plan seemed amenable to all, and while we awaited her arrival, I shared the *Sport Illustrated* piece with Sherlock, who read through it very quickly and handed it back.

"Well, what do you think of it?" I asked him.

"Pure…rubbish!" exclaimed our guest. "Your American champion has apparently not learned how to lose."

"Well, those quick draws are a matter of record, Sherlock," Martha interjected. "Petrosian, Keres, and Geller seem to have made pre-arranged draws, giving them an effective 'rest day,' while the rest of the field had to do battle."

"Rubbish!" repeated Holmes. "How could draws possibly have damaged Fischer? If he had obtained a winning score against the three

Soviet players, he would have positioned himself splendidly. Instead, he managed two victories, four losses, and six draws. That is hardly the way to win a tournament!"

Martha glanced at me and then ventured a reply. "Yes, but after his slow start, Bobby was under dreadful psychological pressure. He did so much better in the big qualifying tournament before that."

"Ah, the Interzonal: thirteen wins, nine draws, no losses, and first place, two and one-half points ahead of Geller and Petrosian," recited Holmes. "Now contrast that with his showing in Curaçao, where he had eight wins, seven losses, and twelve draws, which made a first-place finish virtually impossible. Those three opponents did him the greatest possible service by drawing their games, but he was unable to exploit the opportunity."

"Well and good, Holmes," I interrupted, "but what about Fischer's claim that Viktor Korchnoi may have thrown games to the other three Soviets."

"A charge Korchnoi will vigorously deny. Oh, I suppose it looked a little strange when he lost to all three of them and also to Tal—four games in a row!—and then sat down and clobbered Fischer the very next round. Nevertheless, the burden of proof is on Bobby."

"Ah," I cried, "but aren't you the one who always says, 'Once we eliminate the impossible, whatever remains, no matter how improbable, must be the truth'?"

"Indeed, John Michael. The problem, alas, is that you are putting the cart before the horse. We have by no means eliminated the impossible, Mr. Fischer to the contrary notwithstanding. Still, the young lad is quite gifted, and I have no doubt he will challenge for the title someday."

"Well, he is certainly head and shoulders above everyone in the USA," Martha ventured.

"Quite true, even if Sammy Reshevsky thinks otherwise," I added, "While Bobby couldn't really establish superiority over the old man in their match, he has certainly enjoyed vastly superior results in tournaments."

"With one notable exception," Holmes retorted, "although he was clearly in bad form for that event."

My wife looked confused, so I explained. "It was in Mar del Plata, Argentina, a couple of years ago, Martha. Fischer finished with 8½-10½, way behind Reshevsky and Korchnoi, who tied for first with 13-6. In fact, rumor has it that the seventeen-year-old had his first sexual experiences during the tournament, and these distracted him from what was going on over the board!"

Our guest burst out in laughter and clapped his hands. "That is one I had not heard!" he declared. "It's almost as good as the Capablanca story."

Now it was our turn to plead ignorance. "Do you have a set handy?" Holmes asked.

Fortunately, I had a chessboard set up in the library, so we adjourned to that room while Holmes rifled off the first few moves from memory.

"This was from a tournament in 1929, two years after the great Cuban had lost his world title. The game began simply enough—an opening called the Nimzo-Indian Defense." Holmes rifled through the opening moves:

1.d4 Nf6 2.c4 e6 3.Nc3 Bb4 4.a3 Bxc3+ 5.bxc3 d6 6.f3 e5 7.e4 Nc6 8.Be3 b6, 9.Bd3.*

---

* By the 1970s algebraic notation was much more widely accepted than it had been even a decade earlier in the USA. Within a few years, books and magazines would make the switch, and the older descriptive version would go the way of the dinosaur.

"And here," he continued, "Capablanca played the absolutely dreadful 9…Ba6. His opponent, Fritz Sämisch, answered with the obvious 10.Qa4, and after Bb7 11.d5, the former champion had a vastly inferior position."

Even my wife, admittedly a weak player, could see that Black's position was rather bad. However, she was also confused. "But what does this have to do with Bobby Fischer?" she asked.

Holmes could not suppress his grin. "Well, my dear, Capablanca was more than a little distracted when he sat down to play. He had been seen earlier in the tournament—this game was from Round 16, by the way—with a most attractive mistress. Unfortunately for him, at precisely this point he was startled by the unexpected arrival of his wife."

"Oh, my Lord!" gasped Martha.

"And the end result?" I asked.

"Capa lost this game and ultimately finished half a point behind Aron Nimzovitch, who won the tournament with 15-6. I guess we can conclude that women may be dangerous to chess players, one way or the other."

Far more sadly, this was precisely what we would discuss with our visitor.

Chapter 3

The Distant Cousin

Miss Patel was an attractive woman with both European and Indian features. She wore some sort of ring, but it was definitely not a wedding band. She was probably in her mid-to-late-twenties, but that was as much information as I could glean. Holmes, I was certain, would instantly see far more.

Sherlock studied our visitor intensely as we took our seats at the dining room table and waited for Martha to bring in a pot of tea. At one point he twitched his nose and moistened his lips. Then he began:

"Thank you for dropping by, Miss Patel. I see this is a very busy time for you, so let me begin with congratulations!"

Our guest's face registered mild surprise, but she smiled politely. "And I thank *you*, Mr. Holmes."

Sherlock turned to me, grinning. "You see, Doctor? In addition to the Russian and Indian lines we cited, the Pillsbury clan can soon welcome the scion of an Irish family."

I threw up my hands in despair. "All right, Sherlock. You are many steps ahead of me, just as always you were with my father. Please explain everything."

The old detective gave me the same sort of look he must have given my father, as though to convey the idea that everything was right in front of us. I half-expected him to say, "You look, but you do not see," or words to that effect. Instead, he began at the beginning, and with the utmost patience.

"Miss Patel has recently accepted a marriage proposal from a gentleman either from Ireland or of Irish descent—fairly recent Irish descent at that. This information I could glean at once from the Claddagh ring. You will note that she wears it on her left hand, with the crown turned outward and away from the body. That is a dead give-away that the lady is engaged!

Miss Patel nodded and smiled.

"We can readily see that this status is quite new by looking at her other hand. The faint traces of that very same ring may be perceived by one who looks carefully at the ring finger and contrasts its details with those of the index and middle fingers. She wore it there while she was merely 'being courted,' so to speak."

I squinted, and Miss Patel graciously moved the back of her hand closer. As my father would have noted, Holmes was correct, as usual.

"Fair enough, Holmes. Your vision is remarkable."

"…and that's not the only sense involved, John. For example, we can readily discern that our visitor has come to us after meeting her fiancé for lunch—is that not so, Miss Patel?"

The young woman could scarcely suppress her surprise. "Why, yes, but how can you tell, Mr. Holmes."

"He uses a marvelous cologne called English leather. Although the name suggests British roots, the scent was actually developed in Austria during the 1930s. Obviously Miss Patel and her fiancé exchanged a warm hug, and sufficient traces of the scent remained so that a well-trained nose can detect them."

The young woman showed not the least embarrassment and in fact seemed positively delighted. "You glean so much of my personal information, and you do so with such ease!" she remarked.

"You are much too kind," replied the other. "I merely draw upon what limited knowledge I have gained over the years. For example, I know your father's family came from Gujarat or some area nearby, is that not so?"

Martha and I exchanged glances, while Miss Patel merely smiled once again. Holmes turned toward us.

"That was simple! One need only study the names and learn whence they originate. It is really no different than explaining how an Italian with the surname of Calabrese probably comes from Reggio Calabria or environs, whereas one named Romano probably hails from the area around and including Rome. The overwhelming majority of the Patels are from Gujarat, which is a region quite familiar to me, because its Gir Forest National Park hosts the last of the Asiatic lions, which have otherwise been hunted to extinction in the wild."

Our visitor smiled. "Yours is truly an encyclopedic knowledge, Mr. Holmes. That is why I have some hopes that you will be able to shed a little light on the story of poor Harry Nelson Pillsbury. I am encouraged yet further by your esteemed colleagues, who are trained in medicine and psychology. Surely, with a team of this sort, I shall be in good hands.

"First, however, I must discuss your fee. I am a schoolteacher, and my fiancé…"

"My dear Miss Patel," Holmes began. "I have always felt that chess was no way to make a living. I shall accordingly not endeavor to supplement my own by investigating a mystery involving that game. Moreover, I am a man of independent means, and I rarely charge a fee for my services. I wanted an excuse to see John's father, and your letter provided it for me, so I am already in your debt."

He turned to me and Martha, and my wife continued. "John and I have no financial concerns, either, so let us call this a wedding present!"

The poor woman was beside herself with gratitude, and after a brief, feeble protest she was ready to begin.

Chapter 4

Is Chess Dangerous?

"I learned how to play chess, but I am not at all good, and none of my friends is anywhere near the level of a professional player. Because of my interest in the late Mr. Pillsbury, I studied the history of the game and learned a few things about the greatest players. I am not altogether comforted by what I have read."

Martha, ever sensitive to a client's discomfort, leaned forward. "Are you able to explain why you feel uneasy about the game?" she asked softly.

"Yes, I am. Of course, many great players appear to have been quite stable, yet a number should probably have been put in hospitals for their own protection, as indeed a fair number, including Mr. Pillsbury, were."

"My husband and Mr. Holmes are surely more acquainted with these details," explained Martha, "but I am afraid I lack their historical knowledge."

Miss Patel glanced up at Sherlock, who dutifully obliged her with information at his fingertips. "The first American champion, Paul Morphy, became a tragic case in point," he began. "He vanquished the greatest players in the United States and then traveled to Europe, where he overwhelmed everyone he encountered. Shortly afterward, he returned to the United States, insisted that chess was not a profession, and squandered away what might have been a career in law. Thereafter things went truly bleak. In fact, John's grandfather and my father investigated the poor fellow's death. He was constantly challenging people to duels, talking to himself, and suffering from delusions of various sorts. He played no chess whatsoever for the last fifteen wretched years of his life.

"Wilhelm Steinitz, who later became an American citizen, lost touch with reality after losing his matches to Lasker. Among his rumored symptoms: he could make a telephone call without a telephone, and he was on intimate terms with God—to whom he could give odds of pawn-and-move!"

"Oh, dear," Martha interjected. "That doesn't sound any better than Morphy!"

"I must respectfully decline to discuss Pillsbury, but we see signs of instability in others. Poor Akiba Rubinstein suffered from what your father-in-law has already explained to me was schizophrenia. He experienced full-blown hallucinations, as when he reported that an enchanted princess was keeping him awake during the night by scratching on the walls of his hotel room. He sometimes changed his room, lodging on a different floor altogether, and on occasion he even moved to a different hotel, but apparently the "princess" followed him everywhere. Does that suffice, or shall I add some more?"

My wife nodded. "I get the overall picture. Hallucinations are consistent with schizophrenia."

"Even when the behavior was not so psychotic, it was frequently destructive. We shall be kind and suggest that Capablanca was merely a philanderer, and Alekhine was merely an alcoholic. Still, such excess by the one and substance abuse by the other can scarcely be deemed wholesome."

Martha smiled. "Yes, you shared a Capablanca anecdote earlier. What happened with Alekhine?"

"He lost his title to Euwe, and alcohol must undoubtedly share some of the blame for the disappointing outcome. But did you know it is even said that he once came to a tournament hall so inebriated that he proceeded to urinate on the floor?"

"Merciful Heavens!" I interjected. "That's a new one for me, too."

Holmes paused and then resumed somewhat more tentatively. "We can but hope that young Bobby Fischer is truly in his right mind, since I must confess that at age nineteen, he already shows some troubling signs on that score. But time will

Harry Nelson Pillsbury

tell. Meanwhile, let us return to Harry Nelson Pillsbury," he concluded, turning once again toward our visitor.

"I have read what I could," she began, "traveling to the hospital in Philadelphia—where he died—and to the libraries in that city, New York, and Boston. By the way, he is buried in the Laurel Hill Cemetery in nearby Reading."

"How old was he when he expired?" Martha asked.

"Thirty-three. Well, technically half a year closer to thirty-four, but still quite young."

"Bear in mind," Holmes interrupted, that he had twice attempted suicide roughly fifteen months earlier."

"That is true," agreed Miss Patel, "but perhaps I can discuss that somewhat later. My primary concern is the cause of death, because I see inconsistencies in what has been reported. Officially, it seems he died from syphilis, but I am not so sure, and—if I may be totally honest—I certainly hope that was not the cause of his demise."

My ears must have perked up with this information. "I thought the death certificate answered the question rather unequivocally. The cause of his death—forgive me for being blunt—was indeed tertiary syphilis."

Miss Patel let out a sigh and may have blushed slightly; I could not tell. "Oh, I have read that document, but I have also read other reports relating to a different cause of death. Perhaps that is where we should begin."

Sherlock, Martha, and I all encouraged her, and Miss Patel proceeded.

"Various experts point to the enormous mental strain that chess creates at the highest levels of play. Obviously, Mr. Pillsbury, who had met and defeated so many of the world's top players, including two world champions, competed at such levels. In addition, he was prodigious at checkers, and then there were his blindfold exhibitions and other memory stunts."

"Blindfold?" asked Martha.

"That refers to simultaneous exhibitions without sight of the board. For example, suppose I tell Sherlock, "e4.""

The latter replied, "c5."

"Nf3."

"Nc6."

"d4."

"c5xd4."

"Nxd4—and now both of us can run off to the chessboard and show you the exact position. However, we have played only to the fourth move of a standard line. It would be far more difficult for us to show you the position thirty or forty moves further along into the game—and now try to imagine what it must have been like playing fifteen, twenty, or even more games without sight of the board or score sheets, but merely holding them in one's memory. Why, I'll bet even Sherlock would find that rather challenging."

The old man frowned. "I have no doubt I could have handled six to ten games had I been willing to put in the effort, John. However, I would have needed to abandon so many more promising pursuits that I decided to follow my father's verdict on chess, which was essentially not to take it seriously."

Martha nodded. "I suspect that was good advice."

"If I may continue," said Miss Patel, "the biggest problem—and perhaps my sincerest hope—is that various reports I have read attributed Mr. Pillsbury's deterioration not to syphilis, but rather to the extraordinary pressures of the game itself, exacerbated by these exhibitions. May I trouble you for a medical opinion?"

My wife and I readily agreed.

Chapter 5

Not *That* Dangerous

"The official cause of death was given as general paresis, as you mentioned." She paused and looked right at me, as though waiting for the less sanitized terms.

"Of course, this is not my field, but I am certainly familiar with that diagnosis. General paresis usually refers to syphilis," I explained. "More specifically, in the last stage of untreated syphilis, the victim suffers brain atrophy, caused by chronic inflammation of the cerebrospinal fluid."

"And the symptoms, John?" asked Sherlock.

"The most immediate are the headaches, which are often so severe as to cause nausea and vomiting. It gets worse from there: loss of muscular control, spastic movements, numbness, and sometimes even paralysis, among others. In plain English, it's extremely unpleasant."|

Holmes turned to Miss Patel. "Pray continue."

She swallowed nervously and then took a sip of tea. "As you can probably imagine, it was initially somewhat distasteful for me to accept that disease as the cause of death. Of course, I did not know Mr. Pillsbury at all; he died more than thirty years before I was born. Moreover, he was only a very distant relative. Nevertheless, I grasped for straws and sought some other possible explanation, if only to attribute the dreadful symptoms to an alternative cause.

"I found one hope. Mr. Holmes has already discussed the instability of several prominent chess players, and it seems many people believe—or at least believed—that chess may put too much strain on the nervous system and in turn cause cerebral deterioration. My question is whether all of those tournaments, blindfold games, checker games, and stray memory feats merely exacerbated the symptoms, or whether they might in fact have prompted his decline."

Miss Patel stared at Sherlock, who turned to me. However, before he could say anything, Martha asked a relevant question: "What memory feats did he perform?"

Our visitor reached into her pocketbook and pulled out a slip of paper. "I don't know enough about chess to judge how brilliant he was in tournaments, but this list tells me he must have had an incredible memory.

"The story is that he was doing one of his blindfold chess exhibitions, but before he started, someone gave him the following list." She read as follows:

antiphlogistine, periosteum, takadiastase, plasmon, ambrosia, Threlkeld, streptococcus, staphylococcus, micrococcus, plasmodium, Mississippi, Freiheit, Philadelphia, Cincinnati, athletics, no war, Etchenberg, American, Russian, philosophy, Piet Potgelter's Rost, Salamagundi, Oomisillecootsi, Bangmanvate, Schlechter's Nek, Manzinyama, theosophy, catechism, [and] *Madjesoomalops.*

"Mr. Pillsbury looked at the list for a few minutes, played his chess games, and recited the list forward and backward. And in case you think this was just a 'short-term' stunt, he apparently repeated the same set of terms the next day."

"Remarkable!" I murmured with sincerity, while Holmes was inscrutable. I wondered whether he perhaps felt the slightest pang of envy, since I doubt that even *his* prodigious memory could have withstood such a brutal challenge.

Miss Patel's eyes darted from Sherlock to Martha, and then to me. "This is a serious question. Could the strain of highly competitive chess, checkers, blindfold games, and memory stunts have caused damage to his brains? Don't forget that he also played whist, and could memorize each card played, down to the last. So, his memory was always burning. After all, when could it get any rest? This is what some people have written, and it's—"

"Rubbish!" declared Holmes. "It's utter rubbish. It makes an illogical assumption, and then extrapolates to draw conclusions."

"How so, Holmes?" I challenged.

"This hypothesis—assuming we must grace such an absurd notion with that designation—assumes that the human brain is similar to an elastic. Elasticity always seems quite strong initially, but over time, an object like a large elastic band reaches its limits and begins to lose this property. These ignoramuses would have us believe that the brain collapses from overexertion, even as a muscle might suffer trauma from overuse.

"In fact, I must return to the earlier question about the mental instability of chess players. Here, too, the argument is poorly framed. Is it chess that drives people to insanity, or is it instead that many unstable people are attracted to the game? Once again, John, we have that problem with the cart and the horse."

He paused just long enough to let his words sink in. Then he resumed.

"I should append that no less a figure than Emanuel Lasker wrote about this issue shortly after Pillsbury's demise, and his conclusions are no different than my own. In fact, he noted that Morphy seemed almost perfectly healthy while he was playing chess, and that the symptoms of his madness manifested only *after* he had given up the game."

We all sat in silence for perhaps half a minute. Eventually Martha asked, "You argue passionately, Sherlock, but can you name any feats of memory even remotely comparable to the one Pillsbury accomplished by reciting that incredible list of terms?"

Holmes burst into laughter. "I can tell you about a very stable gentleman who regularly performs stunts that beggar the parlor trick in question."

"Really, Mr. Holmes?" our visitor gasped.

"Absolutely!" replied the other. "First off, let's look at blindfold chess itself. Pillsbury's record was twenty-two games, a fair accomplishment to be sure, but George Koltankowski—better known as 'Kolty'—played thirty-four games without sight of the board. Moreover, Miguel Najdorf played forty-five such games in 1947, and just a couple of years ago, and Janos Flesch played fifty-two, although both of these records are disputed, because of claims they consulted with scoresheets during the exhibitions.

"But back to George Koltanowski. Do you know what a Knight's tour is?"

I nodded, but Martha and Miss Patel shook their heads, so I explained. "The Knight has that rather peculiar way of moving, and unlike the Queen, Rook, and Bishop, it cannot readily get from one side of the board to the other. Nevertheless, it is possible for a Knight to jump from one square to another, until it has covered all sixty-four squares of the board without landing on the same square twice, until it returns to the starting square. This sixty-four-move sequence is called the Knight's tour, and there are actually a number of different ways to accomplish it."

"Precisely!" cried Holmes. "And Mr. Koltanowski can perform this stunt blindfolded, but that is not enough of a challenge. Let me tell you what he does.

"In his exhibitions he sits with his back to a large blackboard that has an eight-by-eight grid that represents a chessboard. Members of the audience now come up and write words or numbers in the squares. For example, one person might write his telephone number, while another might write his address. A woman might provide the name of her first-grade teacher; another might write her mother's maiden name. A less imaginative person might give the mailing address of his accountant or lawyer, and the list will go on, including the names of movie stars and sports figures, the titles of books, and other such bizarre information.

George Koltanowski

"When all sixty-four squares are covered, Koltanowski studies the board for perhaps four or five minutes. Then he turns around—so that he is facing the audience—and asks someone to call out a starting square: something like e4, or King's file, fourth rank, if you still use descriptive notation. Well, he proceeds to do a Knight's tour with his back to the cluttered blackboard, while an assistant crosses out each square as the Knight lands on it.*

"Try to imagine it! 'Willie Mays goes to 1315 Bellevue Terrace, and then we jump over to Humphrey Bogart, thence to 203-777-2985, and once we get there we move to *A Midsummer Night's Dream*, and so on, until he gets back to Willie Mays on the sixty-fourth move. How's that for memory?"

"Unbelievable!" Martha murmured.

"Pillsbury's twenty-nine terms are certainly not any more remarkable than Kolti's sixty-four, are they? And yet he is almost fifty-nine years of age and has never shown signs of even the slightest psychological imbalance."

While we processed this information, Holmes assailed us with yet more. "Perhaps you need something equally impressive from a different field of

---

* "Kolty" performed this stunt on two or even three boards on occasion, although the author is uncertain as to whether he had done so prior to 1962. If he had, we may safely pretend that Holmes was unaware of these feats!

endeavor. Have you heard of the great conductor, Arturo Toscanini?"

Martha told us she had heard him with the NBC Orchestra on numerous occasions and had also seen him conduct during their celebrated tour in 1950.

Holmes raised an eyebrow. "Toscanini, like a number of other musicians, had a nearly photographic memory. He was once challenged by the wife of a friend to write the score of a given page of a symphonic work. He immediately requested paper lined for musical notation, on which he began to enter everything—first and second violins, viola, cello, bass, all ten of the wind parts, a dozen brass parts, the tympani, and several percussion parts. When all the notes were written, he asked the woman if he could borrow a hat pin, so that he might prick his finger and add a stain to the margin. 'There is a small ink smudge to the left of the second violin part,' he explained."

"Wow!" Miss Patel sighed, and I can assure you that Martha and I echoed the sentiment.

"Like Capablanca, Toscanini was evidently none too shy with the ladies, but he conducted until he was eighty-seven and lived to the age of eighty-nine.

"Ladies…Doctor…Blindfold chess is probably more exhausting than sighted chess, but I think we may safely dismiss the hysterical ramblings Miss Patel read and the dire warnings of various experts about the 'dangers' of blindfold chess as nonsense. We must therefore return to the actual cause of death, unpleasant though the prospect may seem. Is that not so, Miss Patel?"

The latter emptied her teacup—which Martha promptly refilled—and continued.

Chapter 6

Flaws in the Narrative

"Before he turned twenty-three years of age, my distant relative won a great tournament in Hastings, England in 1895. This led to an invitation to play in another event in Russia that December."

"St. Petersburg," Holmes interjected.

"Yes, that is right," Miss Patel replied. "He was winning half-way through, but then he did very badly at the end and finished with a losing score. The world champion and former champion finished first and second."

"Quite correct," I noted. "Lasker and Steinitz."

"He complained about bad headaches, and from what I understand, these may have come from syphilis," our visitor concluded.

All eyes now turned toward me. "Well, if you would like a quick overview—and I beg you to remember that this is not my medical specialty—"

"Please, Doctor," cried Holmes. "Let us have all the information at your fingertips."

I drained my cup of tea and declined Martha's offer of more. "The disease generally begins around three weeks after infection, although the first symptoms may appear as early as ten days thereafter or as late as three months. The symptom takes the form of a sore called a chancre. Initially there is but one, though multiple sores are not uncommon. The chancre itself is relatively small and painless, and it will go away on its own within three to six weeks.

"Unfortunately for people like Pillsbury, the disease will invariably proceed to its secondary stage if the victim does not get immediate treatment."

"How soon does this secondary level commence?" Holmes asked.

"Again, we find a fairly large time span, which can sometimes overlap with the primary stage," I explained. "It may manifest within two weeks of infection, although it is more likely to appear within five to eight weeks."

"And the symptoms?" Martha inquired.

I described them as more rash-like but noted that the rash does not cause itching. "Sometimes it is pronounced," I added, "while in other cases it may go almost undetected. Remember that the secondary stage can occur even while the chancre is healing, so sometimes the symptoms are overlooked, simply because the patient is more focused on the chancre. Other symptoms may also arise, though: sore throat, swollen glands, fever, and—yes—headaches, to name a few. In addition, the patient sometimes suffers from a sort of dissociative confusion, dizziness, and even numbness. However, it would be impossible to quantify the severity of a headache caused by secondary syphilis, and I must append that the pain the same person suffers during the tertiary stage is far worse."

I paused just long enough to make certain everyone was following me. Then I resumed.

"After this comes a latent period, usually without symptoms. The disease seems to have halted, and it may not manifest again for years, perhaps as long as two decades. Alas, sooner or later it reaches the tertiary stage, which damages the nervous system, most notably the brain. It can also wreak havoc on the heart, blood vessels, and liver."

Martha inquired as to the symptoms, and I listed dementia, blindness, and paralysis, which came to mind immediately. "The headaches experienced during this stage can be extremely painful, as I'm sure poor Pillsbury could have told us."

"Was there no treatment, Dr. Watson," Miss Patel inquired.

"Penicillin will do the trick during the early stages today," I explained. "In fact, it can halt the disease even in the final stage, although the damage done to the body is by that time irreversible. However, there were no such antibiotics in the 1890s and early 1900s. The only treatment during Pillsbury's lifetime was mercury, which was not without its own dreadful side effects. Shortly after his death German scientists developed Salvarsan, a drug based on the use of arsenic instead of mercury. Less than a decade later—during the Great War—an Austrian physician developed a sort of 'fever therapy,' which involved infecting the patient with malaria and then treating that malaise with quinine. Apparently, this caused the syphilis to diminish as well."

Holmes burst into applause. "Bravo, Watson! Your father always said you had a flare for the history of medicine, and I can see why. However, Miss Patel has explained that she had problems with the syphilis narrative, even if it was indeed the cause of her kinsman's decline and eventual demise."

We all turned to that young woman, who took another sip of tea, put down the cup, and stared at me. "My lingering problem, Doctor Watson, is with the chronology."

"The chronology?"

"Yes. You see, from what I have read, Mr. Pillsbury presumably contracted syphilis before or at the very beginning of the tournament in St. Petersburg. However, headaches as severe as the ones he described would be more consistent with the later stages of syphilis, would they not?"

I hesitated. "Yes, presumably."

"And it might take years to reach that third stage?"

I shook my head. "There are no clear timelines. To the best of my knowledge, at least one year, but as many as twenty may be involved. Somewhere in the five- to ten-year range is not at all unreasonable."

Holmes twitched noticeably. He was onto something.

"John Michael," he mumbled softly. "Pillsbury had just turned twenty-three earlier that December, scarcely a week before the tournament began. That the young man might have contracted the fatal disease the year before is not inconceivable. Five years prior to the tournament? Unlikely. Ten years? Virtually impossible for a thirteen-year-old in those Victorian times, don't you think?"

I shrugged. "Nevertheless, Holmes, tertiary syphilis may and indeed has manifested as quickly as one or two years following infection. However, headaches are also a potential symptom of the secondary stage of the disease, although whether they would be severe enough to disturb a chess player is something I do not know."

At these words Sherlock jolted upright in his chair. "The headaches are also a symptom of the secondary stage, which you said might occur within two weeks, and certainly within five to eight weeks?"

I nodded. "Yes, that is correct."

"Interesting!" Holmes replied. "Well, Miss Patel. We cannot confirm that your kinsman's collapse over the second half of the tournament was entirely due to his infection, but we can certainly present it as a plausible explanation, and one that might have manifested as either secondary or tertiary. As we have already ruled out the asinine notion that tournaments, simultaneous exhibitions, and memory stunts precipitated his decline, I am afraid syphilis is all that remains."

"But he continued to play tournaments and sometimes did very well," the young woman protested. "Moreover, he got married, yet he never infected his wife!"

Six eyes now stared at Sherlock, who blinked twice and nodded his head excitedly. "Very good points, Miss Patel, and they do help us unravel yet more of the history. Shall I begin?"

We all encouraged him.

"It is safe to assume that your distant relative experienced secondary symptoms, not tertiary, in St. Petersburg during January 1896. He would thus have entered the tertiary stages of the disease *after* a latent period, which might have lasted for several years. The headaches he experienced were by no means as excruciating as those he surely suffered later in life, but any nagging headache, particularly when accompanied by other uncomfortable symptoms, might have proven sufficient to disrupt his concentration. Remember also that his opponents in that event were world champion Lasker, former champion Steinitz, and two-time challenger Chigorin, who had come quite close to capturing the title less than four years earlier.

"Pillsbury died in June 1906, and a ten-year life span after untreated syphilis had reached the secondary stage is consistent with what Doctor Watson has told us. During the last fifteen months of his life, he suffered three strokes, again consistent with the neurological damage caused by the disease.

"Moreover, he continued to play in tournaments until 1904, when he finished a mere ninth at Cambridge Springs, even though he defeated Lasker in their individual encounter. That would give us a latent stage of more than eight years. His results were admittedly more modest than those at Hastings in 1895, but he garnered a number of top prizes nevertheless."

Miss Patel appeared to stop Holmes in his tracks with her next question: "But what about the marriage?"

From where I sat, Holmes seemed stumped, unable to respond. However, my wife came to the rescue. "That was something I researched on Monday. I learned that they had no children, and it is quite possible they never consummated the union. Mary Ellen Bush may have been as much his private nurse as his wife."

I felt obliged to contribute some medical information at this point. "Moreover, while the victim is indeed contagious at the beginning of the latent stage, sometimes syphilis lies dormant later within that stretch, before the final phase begins."

Holmes could not suppress a grin. "Thank you so much, Martha and John! Now permit me to add one last piece of information."

He moistened his lips for dramatic effect, smiled briefly, and mentioned that overwork, a questionable diet, irregular sleep, and heavy smoking all contributed to Pillsbury's demise. "He was surely in rather dreadful physical condition, and this made his struggle against syphilis even more problematic."

"But might not those very factors—overwork, a poor diet, insomnia, and tobacco—have caused the death?" ventured Miss Patel, still grasping at straws.

Holmes shook his head. "I think not. Remember that on two occasions during March 1905, he attempted to commit suicide by jumping out of the hospital window. Such suicidal impulses and other signs of irrational behavior are far more likely consistent with tertiary syphilis than tobacco."

For a moment we all sat in silence, until Holmes resumed.

"With that, Miss Patel, I think we can recapitulate. Harry Nelson Pillsbury probably contracted syphilis at some point in late 1895, although we shall never know from whom or precisely when and where. The disease reached secondary stage during January 1896, and it undoubtedly had an adverse effect on his second half results at St. Petersburg. The latent stage of Pillsbury's syphilis may have lasted for as many as eight years; it is impossible to say. He evidently did not infect his wife, although it is unclear whether they were ever intimate. His lifestyle was not at all healthful and may have hastened his demise, but the suicide attempts and other erratic behavior strongly suggest the onset of the tertiary stage, which was invariably fatal in the early 1900s."

The young woman pursed her lips but then gave a smile of resignation. "Well, I wish you could offer a different conclusion, but if nothing else, you have put my uneasiness to rest. Mr. Holmes, you are truly as logical and deductive as they told me you were. Doctor Watson, I thank you for all the medical information you have shared, and Mrs. Watson, I thank you for both your own input and a splendid wedding present—one I shall always remember and cherish!"

We showed her to the door and wished her the best.

Chapter 7

The Reunion

It would be the Devil's folly to leave Holmes and Dad separated at this point. After all, they were scarcely sixteen miles apart. With our business concluded, I called Nahant, and Dad immediately suggested that we come up for a celebratory dinner.

The children were immediately quite in love with Sherlock, who amused them with a couple of bizarre tales (including one I had never heard) as well as some card tricks he had picked up over the years. Later they spent some time with my wife, and while she helped them get ready for bed, we shared details of the Pillsbury case with my parents.

Dad was in complete agreement—of course! Nevertheless, he was glad that I had had the opportunity to assist the great detective.

"Don't sell yourself short, Dad. I'm sure you would have done an even better job, since the medical information is right at your fingertips. I needed to do a lot of 'refresher' work on syphilis."

My father shook his head. "I'm a retired physician, John Michael. You are the doctor of the family now," he insisted.

"Yes, but you have actually treated patients with syphilis. I am a dermatologist, and I have never even seen one!" I protested.

Dad and I both looked over at our mutual friend, who smiled as only Sherlock Holmes Jr. could smile. "You place me in an intriguing situation.

To agree with one of you is to say that I would have fared better working with the other!"

"You have worked with Dad before, Sherlock, and you would surely have benefited from his greater experience," I protested.

"True, but you needed a practicing physician, Sherlock, not an old, retired family doctor," retorted my father.

Holmes chuckled. "John James and John Michael. It would have been wonderful to have worked with both of you, but had I been forced to choose between you, the choice would have been clear, at least in hindsight. Your father is right, John Michael. I am most grateful to have had *you* to assist me."

"And why was that, Sherlock?" I asked.

"Explain, Holmes," added my mother and father in one voice.

"Why, elementary my dear Watsons! John Michael's services came with those of Martha, who contributed the missing detail of which I was unaware: that Harry Nelson Pillsbury and Mary Ellen Bush had no children."

…and with perfect timing, my wife walked into the room at that precise moment, positively beaming!

Sherlock Holmes and the Mystery of the Mystical Maróczy

The 1985-93 Korchnoi-Maróczy Game

Notes on the Korchnoi vs. Maróczy Event

Over the course of nearly eight years—1985-93—Viktor Korchnoi participated in one of the strangest chess games ever contested. His opponent was neither Anatoly Karpov nor Gary Kasparov, the world champions during that period. It was not former champion Fischer or either of the future champions, Anand or Kramnik. In fact, his opponent never held the title, although he and the world champion had agreed to terms and were scheduled to play such a match—nearly eight decades earlier!

The opponent was presumably Géza Maróczy (1870-1951), undeniably one of the top players of the early 1900s. Emanuel Lasker indeed accepted his title challenge in 1906, but plans fell through for one reason or another (probably funding).

As this author quipped in *Superstition and Sabotage: Viktor Korchnoi's Quest for Immortality,* "Korchnoi is [perhaps] also the world champion of the 'spiritual' domain, having won the bizarre contest against an opponent some believe was the spirit of Géza Maróczy in a game played and channeled through the late spiritual medium, Robert Rollans. Some are genuinely convinced the one-game contest was truly an example of life from beyond the grave. Others believe the entire event was just another chess 'fraud.'"

Sherlock Holmes III—whose father called him "Third"—takes a careful look at Korchnoi-Maróczy. On this occasion he works with Dr. John Simon Watson, great-grandson of the original and father of Dr. Joan Watson, who will assist this same Holmes twenty years later. At this time, however, Joan is only fifteen years old, and her forty-six-year-old father is better able to lend expertise to the seventy-two-year-old Holmes.

Chapter 1

Holmes Requests My Assistance!

I first remember Sherlock Holmes Jr. from the summer of 1962. I was almost ten years old, and my sister and I were staying at my grandparents' cottage on Nahant. My parents drove up with Sherlock, and we had a great time with him. I saw him intermittently and visited him in England while I was in college, taking a semester abroad.

I got to know Sherlock Holmes III—the grandson of the "original," about whom my great-grandfather wrote so copiously—considerably better. The younger Holmes—who, by the way, was still my senior by twenty-six years—flew to the States periodically to consult with various agencies, and invariably stayed with my grandfather, father, or me. He also sent a lavish wedding present when Carol and I tied the knot and promised that someday he would ask for my assistance on a case. "After all, John Simon, three generations of Watsons have assisted three generations of Holmeses, so it is surely time to bring the fourth generation into the picture!"

I suppose I should mention my background. Like my great-grandfather, grandfather, and father, I pursued medicine as a career. However, after graduation I entered and completed a unique residency in psychiatry: a five-year program (since discontinued) that added a master's degree in psychoanalysis to the psychiatric training.

My practice is devoted primarily to psychiatry, but I feel profoundly grateful that I have the background in psychoanalysis as well. Had it not been for our plans to start a family, I might indeed have pursued a Ph.D. in that field. However, my wife and I were blessed with the birth of our daughter, Joan, in 1983.

I should mention that both Sherlock Jr. and Sherlock the Third were highly amused to hear about my interest in psychoanalysis. They repeatedly mentioned Reuben Fine, and the older Holmes admonished that I would never become chess champion of the world. Given the rewards of my career, I am sure it was worth the sacrifice—particularly given how little talent I have for the game! However, notwithstanding my rather feeble skills, I follow chess avidly, enjoy "pushing wood," and even play an occasional one-day tournament. My rating, alas, remains mired in the 1600s, and the highlight of my career was a draw against an expert!

I followed football, at least superficially, and I remember the early 1990s, when the Buffalo Bills made it to the Super Bowl four consecutive years, only to lose each time. This reminded me somewhat of grandmaster Viktor Korchnoi, who played what ultimately served as three title matches against Karpov: 1974 (technically the Candidates finals), 1978, and 1981, only to fall short all three times. He also lost to Kasparov in the semifinals of the 1983 Candidates cycle (after earlier winning the match via forfeit), effectively ending his hopes for the world championship.

The next thing I saw about Korchnoi was an article that appeared on the front page of one or other tabloid someone had left in the waiting room. He was apparently playing a game against the great Hungarian, Géza Maróczy. Ordinarily, a single game would not have been particularly noteworthy, but Maróczy had died almost forty years earlier, and this encounter was presumably facilitated through the services of a medium, Robert Rollans. Oh, well…

Then, out of nowhere, came an email from Third:

My dear John Simon,

I was wondering whether I might request your assistance at some point over the stretch from 24 to 27 July, the middle two days of which are the weekend. I am also anxious to visit your parents, of course, but a woman has recently asked to meet with me about a rather bizarre matter, and I suspect I shall benefit from your professional expertise. I shall call you tomorrow, either way, but please let me know whether you will be free at that time. Yours, Third

I hit "reply" at once!

It's always great to hear from you, Sherlock! I shall indeed be available, and in fact may otherwise be rather lonely. Alas, I regret to inform you that Carol and Joan are off visiting relatives in northern California. They will be most disappointed to have missed you, unless you can linger until the following weekend. Thus, I must welcome you with mild regrets myself, since you have still not met my daughter, who is now fifteen. Knowing you as I do, I fear she will have to wait.

On the other hand, I am truly flattered that at long last I shall have the opportunity to lend you my skills, such as they may be! I had begun to despair of ever having that opportunity.

More when we talk. In haste, J.S.

Naturally, I called my father at once. He had already heard from Sherlock, who would stay with him and my mother most of his brief visit. Dad also gave me some much-needed encouragement, assuring me that I was ready for the challenge ahead.

"If Third has specifically asked for your assistance—as opposed to mine—it means that he requires the information and skills at your disposal. You will find it enjoyable to work with him, but be prepared for the almost inevitable. He will probably see some "elementary," obvious connections that will have sailed over your head. Don't be overwhelmed, though, and I'm sure you will provide a valuable contribution to whatever case is on his plate."

Easier said than done, since "overwhelmed" was an understatement. Nevertheless, I was cheered by my father's confidence in me, and I eagerly awaited the call from Third.

Chapter 2

A Reunion of the Holmes-Watson Team

Sherlock was even more abrupt than usual on the phone, but I was able to get a general idea of his itinerary. He planned to fly into Washington, D.C., on Thursday for some "consultation work" in Washington the following morning. As usual, he held his cards rather close to his vest, and I knew better than to expect any more information than he had provided. That business concluded, he planned to fly directly to Boston, where he would spend Friday night in Cambridge with my parents. The following morning, he would walk to my place ["I need the exercise, John Simon!"], and his client would call upon us during the afternoon. His updated itinerary now dictated that he would return to my parents' home that evening and fly to Chicago Sunday night, ostensibly for another consultation on Monday. Thereafter, the itinerary was direct: Chicago to New York, and thence back to Heathrow.

"You are incredible, Third!" I remarked. "That's a brutal pace for a man my age, let alone yours. At seventy-two, you really should begin to think in terms of slowing down a little."

The short silence on the other line of the telephone was eventually punctuated by a single word: "Rubbish!"

* * *

With his customary good luck, Holmes hit excellent weather. It had cooled down to sixty degrees during the evening, and it had reached only sixty-two when he set off on the walk to my home.

It was good to see the not-so-old fellow, who still looked mid-fifties at the most. We got caught up on our respective families, and he promised that someday he would contrive to drop by when Joan actually *was* around. Third also asked whether I had been keeping up with chess.

Garry Kasparov

"Oh, about as much as always," I replied. "I know that Shirov upset Kramnik in their Candidates final, but at last word, no one seems to want to pay for a Kasparov-Shirov match."

"Well," Third offered, "would you? Not counting the draws, it's 7-0 in the champion's favor!"

"I also read that Kasparov offered Anand another shot at the title, but Anand turned him down. And meanwhile, FIDE pretends that Karpov is champion. It's almost as bad as boxing, with three or four champions in each division," I noted.

Holmes grinned. "After all those matches against Kasparov, Karpov can still retain his pretensions. FIDE sanctioned a "title" match between him and Timman back in 1993, after Short—who had defeated both of them in the Candidates tournament—and Kasparov bolted to play for the real championship. I doubt anyone took the FIDE crown too seriously, but then came the Linares tournament the following year. Karpov's domination was extraordinary: nine wins, four draws, and two and one-half points ahead of Kasparov! In fact, Karpov registered the highest FIDE performance rating of all time. He then defended against Kamsky in 1996 and Anand early this year, while Kasparov had defended against Anand more convincingly in 1995. Still, I always like to cite the American expression, 'put your money where your mouth is,' and I doubt anyone wants to bet on Karpov against Kasparov right now!"

Sherlock then told me that he had recently discovered the joys of kriegspiel. "It's so much better than chess in many ways," he explained. "It requires us to make deductions, draw logical inferences, and see what is not so readily apparent—in other words, to become detectives of the chessboard. No wonder Lasker liked the game!"

Viswanathan Anand became the 15th world chess champion when he won the tournament for the title in Mexico City in 2007. It was the first time a player had won the title by winning a tournament since Botvinnik won at The Hague-Moscow 1948, after the death of Alekhine.

Kriegspiel? Not my cup of tea! However, I now felt prompted to ask the question that had been on my mind for some while. "Tell me, old friend. Does your present case—the one with which you want my assistance—involve chess or kriegspiel, and is it somehow related to the world championship?"

Third grinned from ear to ear. "The world championship? Not even close! Kriegspiel? Definitely not. Chess? Let us say that the issue certainly involves the game, but that it is only in the background."

I made a hand gesture to request more information, which Sherlock dutifully ignored. Mildly frustrated, I asked the obvious question: "And what is in the foreground?"

An engraving of Wolfgang von Kempelen's Automaton Chess Player ("The Turk"), with open cabinets displaying its inner workings.

All at once my friend became much more animated. "I thought you would never ask, John Simon," he declared. "We are either dealing with the most remarkable game ever played or what is perhaps the greatest hoax ever perpetrated in the history of chess!"

"Greater than even that so-called Turk device from the 18th century?" I asked.

"You mean the Automaton Chess Player, designed by Wolfgang von Kempelen," Holmes replied. "Of course, other inventors later devised comparable machines, including Mephisto and Ajeeb. The latter should be of great personal interest to both of us, because your parents helped my father solve a case involving Harry Nelson Pillsbury. You know about him, don't you?"

"Indeed! Of course, I was a child at the time. I remember that they brought your father over to visit my grandfather right after they finished."

"Did you know that Pillsbury was one of the masters responsible for the actual moves that Ajeeb made?"

I nodded in the affirmative.

"Ah, but did you also know that one of the humans 'Ajeeb' defeated was Eric Weisz, an escape artist far better known as Harry Houdini?"

This was news to me, I acknowledged, but then I asked the next question. "What does Harry Houdini have to do with this case and chess fraud? Only one chess machine has been in the news recently, and that is Deep Blue, which defeated Kasparov by 3½-2½ in a short match a couple of years ago."

Holmes smiled. "Deep Blue is a perfectly legitimate technology, and while I am not at all certain it is stronger than Kasparov, it is surely quite powerful over the board. No; that is not the possible fraud of which I speak. What do you know about Houdini?"

I hesitated. "He was a famous escape artist in the early 20th century, but I didn't even know that he played chess."

"His chess is of no importance. What is of consequence is that during the last years of his life he devoted himself to exposing many so-called spiritualists as frauds. *Now* do you see the connection?"

I shook my head.

"Okay, let's look at recent chess history. Whom did Karpov defeat to win Fischer's title? Against whom did he defend successfully twice? Whom did Kasparov defeat in the Candidates tournament en route to his title match with Karpov?"

My jaw dropped. "Of course! Viktor Korchnoi! And you must be referring to that game against 'Maróczy' that made its way to *The National Enquirer* or a periodical of comparable journalistic merit. I saw that piece, Third!"

The old man merely smiled. "I'm sure we'll hear a lot more about the game when my client arrives. Again, my sincerest gratitude for allowing me to meet with her here."

I grinned. "Not at all! By all means, be my guest, and please feel free to entertain as my co-host!"

Chapter 3

A Strange Visitor

Holmes called his client to confirm the appointment, which was set for 2 p.m. To kill some time while we waited, he asked whether I would care to see one of his kriegspiel games. I was surprised by how naturally he had played and how well he understood the variant. I even went so far as to suggest he consider writing a book about kriegspiel.

Sherlock would have none of it, of course. He explained that such a project would obligate him to spend far more time on the "useless diversion," while he collected and annotated games. "How can I possibly justify the countless hours I would squander, just to write a book about an amusing trifle?" he asked rhetorically.

While we were waiting, I also learned a little more about Holmes's involvement with chess. It seems he had inherited his father's natural ability, and he had once faced—and defeated!—Alexander Alekhine in one of the champion's simultaneous blindfold exhibitions, although he had also received odds of pawn-and-move. Nevertheless, it was a remarkable accomplishment, and he was only twelve years old at the time. However, like both his grandfather and father, Sherlock ultimately decided that chess simply wasn't worth the effort.

At 2:20 p.m. my doorbell rang, and Mrs. Anita Stone, clutching an attaché case, asked which of us was Sherlock Holmes.

"I am he," announced my guest, "and this is my good friend and associate, Dr. Watson, who will assist me on this fascinating case. Please come in."

I showed them both to my living room, offering coffee or tea, which our visitor declined, although she gratefully accepted my offer of water. I took a moment to study her: a woman who looked perhaps mid-to-late-thirties, rather lean, with reddish brown hair (that was clearly beginning to fade), blue eyes, and fair complexion. She was dressed simply, in attire appropriate for the summer. She appeared to wear no makeup, and she had both an attractive engagement ring and a wedding band on the fourth finger of her left hand. I wasn't sure how much more Third would be able to tell.

"My dear Mrs. Stone," said he. "Let me begin by extending my sincerest—albeit rather belated—condolences on your loss, which your correspondence all but articulated. Many people have been and remain curious about the strange exhibition, a few truly wanted to know more, but only one has ever felt compelled to ask me to investigate. I naturally deduce that your motivation relates to someone close to you and your hopes that he might yet communicate from the other side of mortality. Hence, your interest in the Korchnoi-Maróczy/Rollans contest."

The woman showed no surprise that Holmes had made the connection. "Yes," she replied, "but perhaps I should begin with some background information."

"Please do."

"I attended Chester Alan Arthur College in Vermont and fell head over heels in love with my English professor and faculty advisor, the late Robert Stone. He was—" she hesitated, but continued, "much older than I, of course. I was twenty-two when I graduated; he was fifty-nine. Nevertheless, the feelings were indeed reciprocated, and out of nowhere he proposed to me.

"I remember he called it, 'a moment of madness,' and it caught me completely by surprise. I immediately asked him if he was serious.

"Robert sighed and told me he would love to spend the rest of his life with me. 'However,' he admonished, 'you must look at our respective ages. I am thirty-seven years your senior, and my family cannot be cited for longevity.' He added that his father had died at sixty-four, and while his mother made only seventy-one, and none of his grandparents reached the biblical three-score and ten.

"I had no immediate plans to attend graduate school, and Robert had already helped me procure a position as a journalist for *The Herald-Gazette*, the regional weekly paper. The appointment delighted me, since it meant I would be able to see much more of Robert. Marriage wasn't really on my list of top priorities, but when he asked for my hand, I was the happiest woman in the world.

"Of course, we could not ignore the age gap. He reminded me that I would almost surely be a widow in my early thirties and also told me he did not want children, but none of it mattered to me. I was so much in love and felt so blessed to be with him.

"We married that summer and enjoyed ten wonderful years together. Robert continued to teach, and I worked my way up to associate editor. Then it all fell apart. The college precipitously announced that it was going to shut down, and two days later Robert suffered his first heart attack.

"Needless to say, this brush with mortality provoked an emotional tsunami. I know that many people could never understand the relationship between a woman in her early twenties and a man in his late fifties, but we had something rare and beautiful. We shared a love of literature, drama, and film that complemented our love for one another. Truly, the notion of 'soul mate' comes to mind. He was mine, and I was his, notwithstanding the chronological distance between us.

"Naturally, I was terrified about losing him, but Robert seemed remarkably at peace and kept telling me not to worry. 'Everything will be all right,' he assured me, 'and if I must "shake off this mortal coil," I shall reach out to you, even from beyond the grave. I swear it, Anita!'

"Robert seemed to rally, but shortly before he was scheduled to leave the hospital, he had a second heart attack, which triggered a sudden cardiac arrest. The prognosis was bleak, and he was weak and deathly pale when I visited him for the last time. Nevertheless, he seemed so happy to see me.

"His last words to me were the ones I have already shared: 'even from beyond the grave.' Just a few seconds later, he suffered a third heart attack, and this one proved fatal."

The widow now took a few sips of water. Holmes sat by impassively and waited for her to resume.

"Of course, Robert provided for me quite nicely. He had lived simply, saved as much as he could, and invested rather well. I requested a leave of absence from the paper, so that I could deal with the estate. After learning how relatively affluent I had become, I served notice and decided to move away from Vermont and the college that—in my mind—had ultimately precipitated my husband's death.

"For a while, I simply could not believe he had died. After that I felt anger more than grief. Robert had been fine at his last physical exam, and I still believe the sudden decision by the college to shut its doors delivered a mortal wound. Eventually, I…I grieved."

Once more she reached for her glass, but this time she seemed unable or unwilling to continue, so I ventured some thoughts gleaned from my own training.

"Elisabeth Kubler Ross developed what she called the 'Five Stages of Grief,' of which denial is the first and anger is the second," I explained.

Our client looked up. "I am familiar with her work," she responded. "I even fantasized about some sort of bargaining. I would gladly have sacrificed some of my allotted years if he could somehow have had a few more to share with me. Then came the so-called depression, which left me resigned to the reality, but still unable to accept it."

"And now?" I inquired.

"I keep focusing on his last words and what he had promised earlier—that he would reach out to me even from beyond the grave. But of course, nothing of the kind ever happened, and it is perhaps time for me to move on.

"As Robert had accurately predicted, I was a widow at thirty-two. That was five years ago; I am thirty-seven. I was finally getting ready to let him go, when a friend showed me an article about a chess game between a Swiss champion and a Hungarian who died in 1951. The article concluded that this strange encounter proved that consciousness could continue even after death.

"I do not play the game particularly well, but I could follow everything they were saying. At first I assumed it was a fraud, but I went to the library and did some additional research, and now I am not so sure. That is why I contacted you, Mr. Holmes," she added, looking directly at Sherlock, who continued to sit impassively.

My friend's face registered no emotion, but at length he spoke. "I think you would like me to play the Devil's Advocate—is that not so, Mrs. Stone?"

She nodded. "Indeed."

"And at the same time, you hope I shall conclude that the event may have been legitimate, thereby providing you reason to continue hoping."

Again Mrs. Stone nodded.

"Well, then. Let us begin at the beginning!"

Chapter 4

The Evidence

Mrs. Stone resumed. "The strange game, as some readers may recall, was the brainchild of Dr. Wolfgang Eisenbeiss, a Swiss stockbroker and financial analyst with a deep and very sincere interest in such paranormal topics as life after death and communication with the spiritual world. He, in turn, contacted Robert Rollans, a spiritual medium, who had reportedly developed the capacity to communicate with various deceased individuals through a process known as automatic writing."

Holmes shook his head. "Automatic writing? Please explain."

Our guest hesitated, so I answered on her behalf. "In clinical circles it is called psychography, and it refers to the presumably psychic ability to write without any conscious awareness."

A scowl from Sherlock led me to believe his skepticism was on high alert. "One may dream without conscious awareness, though some people claim to enter a state of 'lucid dreaming.' However, I do not see how one can write without involving the conscious faculties. How, for example, does one even know how to shape letters?"

I swallowed nervously. "As with any other paranormal reports, these cases have been greeted with skepticism. Nevertheless, I did witness a strange exhibition of clinical hypnosis in which the therapist presumably gave suggestions to facilitate the process. The subject was able to dissociate from his right arm, and because he was in trance, he could tap into his subconscious mind to access information. This, in turn, was transmitted to the subject's arm. Of course, I had no way to ascertain whether the subject conveyed repressed information or merely material of which he was completely aware."

"And this was all delivered on the page?" Holmes asked.

"The subject was obliged to write on an easel, since his letters were somewhat too large and juvenile for a lined sheet. However, I have read credible accounts asserting that some people can engage in psychography on regular lined paper. In answer to your question: Yes; he did not speak the entire time, but he wrote. Moreover, after the therapist had brought him back to full consciousness, the subject claimed he had no knowledge of what he had written and seemed genuinely surprised when he read it."

"And you believe this automatic writing is a legitimate technique?"

I paused. "I cannot say. I merely note that it has been reported, and it may be valid."

Third turned to our visitor. "Apologies for my digression. Pray continue."

Mrs. Stone now explained that Eisenbeiss asked Viktor Korchnoi for his top three choices of an opponent from the spiritual world. The grandmaster listed Capablanca, Keres, and Maróczy in that order. Eisenbeiss also asked Rollans to contact any of a dozen or so important figures from chess history to see whether one of them might be willing to participate in such a contest. Eventually the medium reached or got through to Géza Maróczy.

Holmes looked a trifle bored at this point. "Yes, I know of him. A Hungarian, he was certainly among the world's top players in the early 1900s, and he and Lasker agreed to terms for a title match in 1906. Unfortunately, the funds could not be raised, and it all fell through."

"He was awarded the title of grandmaster by the FIDE in 1950, when the first such titles were given out," Mrs. Stone noted, "and he died the following year, in May."

Sherlock grimaced ever so slightly. "Of course, an immediate question

Viktor Korchnoi

arises. Where were Steinitz, Tarrasch, Chigorin, Lasker, Rubinstein, Alekhine, and other notables? Did none of them even have the courtesy to decline the challenge?"

I could sense the tension this question created. Mrs. Stone explained that to the best of her limited knowledge, Rollans had been unable to create contact with them.

"This is not so implausible, Holmes," I noted. "After all, sometimes when we make a phone call, the person we are trying to reach is either unavailable or else disinclined to communicate with us. Why expect anything different from the deceased?"

Third looked at me and grinned. "Very logical, Watson! All right; let us proceed to another question. Why did Eisenbeiss select Korchnoi as his living grandmaster to play the dead one?"

The widow answered without hesitation. "That question should be far easier to answer, Mr. Holmes. Five of the top eight players in the world at the time came from the USSR, and the Soviet chess bosses would never have allowed any of them to participate in such a bizarre exhibition. Hungarian Lajos Portisch was ranked sixth in the world, and he might have been the ideal opponent for Maróczy. However, once again we encounter the restrictions of a Communist state, where the authorities would never have permitted him to proceed.

"The remaining players of the 'elite eight' were Jan Timman of the Netherlands and Viktor Korchnoi of Switzerland. Timman was on the way up; he would lose to Karpov in the Candidates tournament final in 1990 and again for the FIDE title in 1993. Korchnoi's stature was descending, and after the loss to Kasparov in the semifinals, his world championship dreams had effectively come to an end. Moreover, Korchnoi, who was living in Switzerland, may also have been a more comfortable choice for Eisenbeiss, since it was easier to approach a countryman.

Géza Maróczy

"Thus it was Korchnoi vs. Maróczy," concluded Mrs. Stone, "although as I mentioned, Viktor's first two choices were Capablanca and Keres. Several people have expressed skepticism about the opponent ultimately selected. After all, why would Maróczy have been on Korchnoi's list in the first place?"

Holmes sighed, and for a moment he looked tired, if not old. However, the sparkle returned to his eyes, and he sat up straight, as though springing to attention.

"Let us hold that question. So far, we have Korchnoi hand-picked to play against someone who had presumably been dead for thirty-four years. The moves were relayed through Rollans and materialized as automatic writing. What was the precise duration of the match?"

His client had that information at her fingertips. "Nearly eight years. It began on June 15, 1985, and it concluded on February 11, 1993."

"I read that Rollans did not play chess prior, and that Eisenbeiss taught him the game, so that he would be better able to communicate moves to and from Maróczy. How was the actual contest conducted?"

Mrs. Stone cast a nervous glance in my direction. "This is also something I find rather troubling, Mr. Holmes and Dr. Watson. You see, Maróczy was White and made the first move, communicating it by way of Rollans' automatic writing. Rollans forwarded the move to Eisenbeiss, who shared it with Korchnoi. The living grandmaster made his move as Black and relayed it to Eisenbeiss, who in turn shared it with Rollans. Rollans would then retreat to his home office, write the move on a piece of paper, make the move on a chessboard, and await the response from the deceased grandmaster. He was always alerted to the latter's presence by a tingling sensation."

Holmes frowned. "And how long did the sequence of a full move last?"

"If everyone was available, a single move might take around ten days. However, Rollans, who died shortly after the game concluded, was ill on numerous occasions. Similarly, Grandmaster Korchnoi was frequently obliged to absent himself for long periods of time, since he had a busy schedule of tournaments and matches, and he also needed time to prepare for those events."

Sherlock shrugged. "He was only fifty-four when the game began, and he certainly had to earn a living. He never mounted another challenge for the world championship, but he did win the Interzonal tournament in Zagreb in 1987—during the course of this game against Maróczy.

"But back to the matter at hand. From what you tell me, forty-seven moves by both men, plus the resignation: ninety-five communications in total over the span of almost 2,800 days, which brings us to an average of more than twenty-nine days per individual move. Think a fraction more than six full moves—one each for White and Black—per year, and we have an idea as to the slow pace of the contest, although presumably some stretches of time were considerably more productive than others."

I marveled at how this seventy-two-year-old man could make these mathematical calculations in his head so quickly and effortlessly! His penetrating stare now focused on the poor woman, who seemed uncertain how to respond. To my relief—and surely to hers!—Holmes made his point. "We see one immediate problem here. While we would like to believe that Eisenbeiss and the late Mr. Rollans conducted themselves honorably, we must surely acknowledge the possibility that *someone else* was selecting the moves for White. This, however, is mere speculation, so let us merely hold the thought."

Mrs. Stone resumed. "I shared your reservation, Mr. Holmes, and I felt that the best thing to do was to learn what people thought of both the quality and the style of the play. May I tell you what I have learned?"

"Please do!"

She pulled out a notebook from her attaché case and read aloud. "Korchnoi stated that his opponent mishandled the opening but played quite well in the endgame. A commentator explained that this apparently makes sense, since Maróczy would have had no way to keep up with all the new opening theory, but the endgame theory hasn't really changed much."

Holmes's face remained inscrutable, and he said nothing, so I ventured an observation. "The fact that someone plays an opening poorly and does better in the endgame does not necessarily confirm anything about the identity of the player. I'm sure there are people even today who stopped playing chess during college and graduate or professional school, began their careers, and perhaps a dozen years later resumed play again. They, too, would doubtless be weaker in the opening and stronger thereafter."

"Irrelevant, Watson!" Sherlock snapped. Turning to Mrs. Stone, he smiled briefly and said, "Do continue!"

"All right," she replied. "Here is where things get more interesting. Dr. Eisenbeiss prepared a set of questions about Maróczy, so that Rollans could test the entity he had contacted. He then asked László Sebestyén—a man who was fluent in Hungarian but presumably unaware that this strange game was in progress—to glean as much information as he could and prepare responses to the questions. The researcher confirmed a very high percentage of the answers, among which were some tricky details and at least a pair that could be neither confirmed nor corrected."

Holmes frowned. "A high percentage, but not all of them?"

At this point, I thought it best to volunteer more information. "This is quite consistent with the memories of even highly functional people in their forties, fifties, and sixties, Sherlock. I suspect that if someone had asked similar questions about Korchnoi's life, he might have missed one or two details, or else given responses that were equivocal at best."

"Fascinating to be sure," my friend agreed, "but insufficient to 'prove' spiritual contact with the late Géza Maróczy."

Our visitor hesitated but then resumed. "All right. Here is something considerably more convincing, at least in my opinion.

"Eisenbeiss presented a question about a famous game between Maróczy and Massimiliano Romi from the tournament in San Remo during 1930. Through Rollans, the spiritual contact stated that he had never played anyone named 'R-O-M-I,' but that he won a game from someone named 'R-O-M-I-H' at that event.

"This correction prompted a flurry of research, and Eisenbeiss soon uncovered the truth. Max Romih was born in Istria, which was part of the Austro-Hungarian Empire at the time. After World War One it became part of Italy, and shortly after the San Remo tournament the chess player changed the name and spelling to Massimiliano Romi. This was probably a good move politically, since Italy was controlled by Mussolini's fascists, who had a clear preference for names that looked and sounded Italian.

"Moreover, after 'Maróczy' made this correction, someone found an official document from the tournament, and it confirmed that one of the competitors was indeed R-O-M-I-H."

Holmes raised an eyebrow. "And surely any competent chess historian could have uncovered that information earlier," he insisted.

"That may be, Sherlock," I noted, "but you have not proven anything by noting the possibility."

"Ah, but you forget something, John Simon. The burden of proof is on the person who makes the assertion—to wit, that a man who died in 1951 played a chess game between 1985 and 1993."

"I was intrigued by this part of the story," Mrs. Stone declared. "However, I looked into it a little further and caught a blatant error. When asked about R-O-M-I, the presumed spirit of Maróczy responded, "I had a friend in my youth, who beat me when I was young, but he was called Romih." However, Maróczy was born in 1870, while Romih was born in 1893."

"Undeniably wrong!" exclaimed Third. "But let us turn to another question. What were those involved in the game paid for their participation?"

"I can answer that easily enough, Mr. Holmes," our visitor assured him. "Neither Rollans nor Korchnoi received any fee whatsoever."

"This I did not know," Sherlock conceded. "It is rather strange, though, since Korchnoi is a professional chess player and normally expects to be paid."

"What about the quality of the game?" I inquired.

Mrs. Stone had that information at her fingertips, also. "It is unclear. At this time, we do not have a computer technology that can evaluate the level of a single game with mathematical precision. Thus, we must confine ourselves to subjective appraisals. Almost everyone agrees that Maróczy did not do well in the opening, and he stumbled into an inferior position very quickly. However, some experts believe Korchnoi probably played somewhat below his own level, and at one point he claimed he was uncertain that he could score a victory, even with a one-pawn advantage. One analyst declared that Maróczy—transmitting moves through Rollans—was playing at perhaps international master level, which was not quite enough to hold off a top-ten grandmaster. However, another commentator felt that the deceased grandmaster played at a mediocre level, and one even went so far as to claim Korchnoi was deliberately finding inferior moves in order to create the illusion of a real struggle."

I was by now feeling a little less certain about where I stood on this matter. "It sounds preposterous on the surface, Sherlock, but look at the big picture and pretend for a moment that this medium did in fact conjure up the late Géza Maróczy. The spirit fielded the most obscure questions about his life with apparent ease, and I am quite sure most chess players—grandmasters and wood-pushers alike—have forgotten some of the details about various personal trivia, to say nothing of specific tournaments and opponents. I find it remarkable that the presumed Maróczy spelled the name of an obscure chess player, a relative unknown, the way it was actually presented at the time of their encounter. He—or it—battled reasonably well against a top grandmaster, and no one thinks the style was inconsistent with that of Maróczy. Permit me to parody your grandfather, father, and you yourself: "Once you have eliminated the impossible, whatever remains, however improbable, *may perhaps* be the truth!"

Holmes merely smiled. "Mrs. Stone…Doctor…I think it is time to look at the big picture."

Chapter 5

What We Knew All the Time

He turned first to our visitor. "Once again, tell us why you became so interested in this strange game."

"I want to believe in it," she replied. "If, as Dr. Eisenbeiss maintains, this event proved 'the survival of consciousness after death,' then perhaps Robert may yet be able to reach out to me from the Other Side. However, if this is simply a fraud, I fear I must let go of even these vain hopes."

Holmes now motioned to me, while maintaining eye contact with his client. "Your thoughts, John Simon?"

I hesitated. "It is clear that Mrs. Stone's desire is not unique. We all lose loved ones, and many people would like to believe their losses are not permanent. This psychological imperative may have spawned the concept of an afterlife of some sort, and at that a happier one.

"Much has also been written about the notion of ghosts and other spectral beings. Some people sincerely believe that their appearance manifests either when the ghost is not ready to move on, or when someone in the ghost's life is unwilling to let go.

"Of course, in this case we deal with a chess grandmaster with no ties to any of the other participants. However, the need to believe in a spiritual world in which the deceased retains his or her earthly personality may be stronger than most would acknowledge."

Holmes drummed his long fingers on the table, one at a time, like a pianist playing an abbreviated scale. "That would explain the motivation of Eisenbeiss, and arguably also our client. What about the other people involved?"

Anita Stone began tentatively, "As I began my research, I tried to find some information on Robert Rollans independent of this particular event. Eisenbeiss maintains that he was a gifted medium, yet I could not find any information about him. This does not mean he did not accomplish remarkable communications with the spiritual world, but it raises the question as to how famous he truly was."

Sherlock nodded and thanked her for this information. "Let us look at related reports of communication with the deceased. Seances have long been discredited, and any number of frauds have been exposed. Nevertheless, people continue to cling to hopes of some word from the spiritual realm."

"Quite naturally so, Holmes," I interjected. "Consider, for example, the tragic case of parents whose adult child committed suicide. They would surely be comforted if a psychic told them that their son or daughter was finally at peace and advised them not to feel sorrow about what had happened. In fact, one might almost argue that such a session could be therapeutic in cases where the parents suffered from feelings of guilt."

Holmes suddenly sat upright again. "Have you ever consulted with a psychic, Mrs. Stone?" he inquired.

She shook her head.

"And you certainly feel no guilt whatsoever."

"No. Robert never expected a long life, and if anything hastened his demise, it was the decision of the college to shut its doors. There was absolutely nothing I could have done to save him."

"So, Doctor—this is apparently a common occurrence?"

I scowled. "I am not sure about the frequency with which it is seen, but it is certainly not unheard of. Some people—particularly creative artists—may even want to believe they can continue their work after death."

Sherlock now grew animated. "Precisely!" he declared, pointing his finger at me. "Many believe that at its highest levels, chess is an art, and various grandmasters, notably David Bronstein, have been applauded for their creativity. Now, what can you tell us about Viktor Korchnoi?"

"He was surely the ideal candidate for such a contest for many reasons. To begin with, he has long believed in bizarre phenomena—parapsychology, witchcraft, and the like. In fact, the Soviets exploited this weakness ruthlessly, convincing poor Viktor that he was battling inexplicable forces. He referred to Spassky's bizarre swaying motions as 'witchcraft' amidst the 1977 Candidates final, during which he lost four consecutive times, including one dreadful game in which he blundered away his Queen. The following year Korchnoi was terrified by Dr. Zukhar's apparent hypnotic control over Karpov during their championship match. In fact, he went so far as to appeal the last game (which he had lost) on the grounds that the Soviets had broken an agreement that Zukhar would not sit any closer than the seventh row in the audience."

"An ill-fated litigation that went against him," noted Sherlock. "He had never even noticed that Zukhar was in the fourth row of seats, and his second, Raymond Keene, did not object while the game was in progress."

I acknowledged what my friend had reported and continued. "In Merano, Italy, he faced Karpov for the third time, and this time he claimed the Soviets were disrupting his brain waves and clouding his mind with some sort of 'psi-weapon.'

"Given all the above, if I had to choose someone for such an experiment, I would surely have gone with Korchnoi, and for yet another reason. It was clear that he had slipped during the three years after the 1978 contest. Until that time, he and Karpov were almost evenly matched, but by 1981 the younger man's superiority was no longer in doubt.

"Now, what had Korchnoi wanted more than anything else? The world championship! This, however, was beyond reach; Karpov and Kasparov were out of his league. However, if consciousness could remain, even after death, perhaps he could claim a championship of some sort in the afterlife."

Holmes and Mrs. Stone exchanged glances, and she murmured a single word softly: "Fascinating!"

"Bravo, John Simon!" added Holmes enthusiastically. "His desire for the title provided the psychological imperative that prompted him to play, even without a fee. Now, what about the choice of opponents?"

I shook my head. "It's a strange one, to say the least, Holmes. Korchnoi defeated all the post-World War Two champions: Botvinnik, Smyslov, Tal,

The eighth world champion, Mikhail Tal, was extremely popular with chess players worldwide.

Petrosian, Spassky, Fischer, Karpov, and Kasparov. One would think he would turn to the giants of the pre-War period: Lasker, Capablanca, and Alekhine. Capablanca topped his list, but the other two are conspicuously absent."

"I believe he was on reasonably civil terms with Keres," Holmes replied. "He also had a losing record against the great Estonian, for whatever that might be worth. However, he certainly never played Maróczy, so that choice is very strange and seems almost contrived."

To my surprise, Mrs. Stone brought up some additional information. "I did a little research on Dr. Eisenbeiss and learned that he had been fascinated by the musical compositions of Rosemary Brown. You have heard of her?"

I shook my head, but Sherlock responded immediately. "Of course! She is a spiritual medium who writes musical compositions in the styles of the deceased geniuses we all know—Bach, Beethoven, Brahms, Chopin, Schubert, and others. Some, like Dr. Eisenbeiss, believe she truly channels the works of these composers, but others claim the music emerges from Mrs. Brown's subconscious mind. Several musicologists applaud her work, but others dismiss it as mere pastiche and note that composition students are routinely assigned the task of writing in the style of one of the great giants from the past."

I pounced on this information. "Precisely, Holmes! You or I might dismiss her as a different sort of 'fraud,' while Eisenbeiss—for his own personal and psychological reasons—asserts that she channels those composers. He is doubtless sincere in his convictions and devoutly believes that consciousness continues after death. Thus, a deceased person might compose music or just as easily play chess."

Holmes now grinned like the Cheshire Cat. "Well, then. I think our conclusions should be obvious."

Chapter 6

It Doesn't Matter What I Think!

Mrs. Stone and I turned to Holmes and eagerly awaited his verdict. When none was forthcoming, I took the bull by the horns and prodded him.

"Well, come on, Sherlock. Out with it! What do you think?"

An enigmatic smile should have alerted me to what he would say next. "Honestly, John Simon? It doesn't matter what I think—or what you and Mrs. Stone think. The only issues of consequence are what we can prove. Permit me to recapitulate:

"First, this strange game was indeed contested over the span of nearly eight years. This is a fact, unless everyone involved lied about it.

"One of the participants was Viktor Korchnoi. The evidence is overwhelming: his own testimony.

"The opponent has been presented as the spirit of Géza Maróczy, who had died some thirty-four years before the start of the game. He was presumably channeled by the spiritual medium, Robert Rollans.

"Our first objection arises from the dearth of information about Mr. Rollans. This, however, does not preclude the possibility that he operated within a small occult circle, without fanfare or publicity. He had somehow come to the attention of Eisenbeiss, a man who clearly believes in consciousness after death.

"We all agree that Viktor Korchnoi was the best choice for a contemporary grandmaster. At the start of the game, he was still among the elite players in the world, but clearly past his prime. His life experiences make him altogether open to the possibility that a match of this sort is possible, and he may even entertain some personal motivation to learn more about chess after death.

"The choice of Maróczy gives rise to a second objection. However, the great Hungarian may have been the only deceased grandmaster Rollans would 'reach.' Perhaps he had shared this information with Eisenbeiss, who then drew up a short list and asked Korchnoi to make his first, second, and third choices *from a restricted sample of names.* He might have left Capablanca and Keres on the menu but filled up the others with less desirable opponents. Korchnoi then made Maróczy his third choice, and the rest of the tale fell into place. We have no way to prove that Eisenbeiss lied, and even if he withheld some information, that omission has no bearing whatsoever on the validity of the chess game that ensued.

"The quality of the game may or may not prompt a third question. Maróczy did not play the opening well. However, grandmasters have fallen into traps on numerous occasions. Who can forget how Fischer snared Reshevsky's Queen in twelve moves, effectively springing the mortal blow after his opponent's blunder on move 9? Surely, no one has ever suggested that Fischer merely defeated a 'Reshevsky' whom some medium had channeled! I respectfully submit that 'Maróczy' handled the opening far better than Reshevsky did during the 1958 encounter in question.

"At the very least Maróczy (or whomever/whatever Rollans contacted) handled the list of questions the medium presented quite adequately. In the case of Romih vs. Romi, the spirit appears to have made an interesting correction, although he was clearly wrong in suggesting that he and his opponent had played during the Hungarian's youth.

"It is interesting that Eisenbeiss took such great pains to validate Maróczy's identity, yet the net effect has been to create two more questions. The first is whether the small errors and inconsistencies in Maróczy's testimony make the contact unreliable. However, Dr. Watson assures us that long before age eighty-one most people have forgotten numerous details of their lives. The other question is whether Eisenbeiss gave Rollans these questions in advance as part of a deceptive fraud. Here, we can find no evidence one way or the other, and it seems unlikely we ever shall.

"To recapitulate, then: We cannot refute the claims of Eisenbeiss (and presumably Korchnoi). A game was played, and Korchnoi's opponent may perhaps have been Géza Maróczy.

"At the same time, we must also acknowledge that an exhibition of this sort cannot possibly match the standards necessary for scientific proof. We cannot quantify the extent to which the presumed spirit of Maróczy played in a style consistent with the way he played when he was alive. While the answers to various questions are impressive, they did not present any information that was unknown at the time. Rollans died a few weeks after the game concluded, so there is no way to get additional information from the one person who might be able to provide it."

My friend's eyes skirted from our client to me, and then back to her. "My dear Mrs. Stone. I regret that I cannot answer your question. Consciousness may continue after death; it may not. Rollans may have accessed the spirit of Géza Maróczy; he may not. The entire exhibition may have been legitimate; it may not.

"I believe the person better able to help you from this point is my inestimable colleague, Dr. Watson, who is a psychiatrist trained in psychoanalysis. What are *your* thoughts, Doctor?"

I drew a deep breath, reflected for a moment, and offered the only reasonable advice I could:

"I would never presume to tell someone what she should or should not believe. If you wish to believe—or at least hope—that your late husband will someday reach out to you from beyond the grave, by all means do so. However, I also think it is time for you to move on with the rest of your life. If Professor Stone is truly able to contact you from the Great Beyond, it is reasonable to assume that he eventually will, no matter what you are doing with your life, or even if you have remarried. After all these years, you need to complete the grieving process."

Handing her a business card, I added, "When you feel ready to speak with a grief counselor, you may certainly contact me, and I shall be very happy to make a referral. Meanwhile, I must thank you for providing me with the opportunity to work with Sherlock Holmes."

"The reciprocal of which sentiment I must echo!" added my friend.

Our visitor smiled for the first time since she crossed the threshold. "Thank you so very much—both of you!" she exclaimed. "I truly do feel better, and I shall definitely call you next week, Dr. Watson."

The lady departed, and Third turned to me, grinning. "You were marvelous, Watson!" he exclaimed. "You provided just enough psychological insight to guide me to the best possible answer for our client."

"And your own opinion?" I had to know!

Once again, I got that enigmatic grin. "You would like me either to declare it rubbish or to identify myself as a True Believer. Alas, John Simon, I cannot accommodate you. I remain a skeptic and completely unconvinced, yet I am unable to disprove anything. Perhaps I have been in error all these years."

"Oh?" I asked, incredulous. "How so?"

"I am afraid that in certain situations we must also consider the corollary to the Holmesian adage: 'When you are unable to prove it impossible, your fundamental assertion, improbable though it may be, may nevertheless also be the truth'!"

* * *

This proved the only occasion on which I worked with Sherlock Holmes. Nevertheless, I was instrumental in facilitating two other cases. My daughter helped Holmes solve a bizarre mystery involving Bobby Fischer, and my cousin helped him with what was perhaps the strangest case of all!

Sherlock Holmes and the Mystery of the Ingenious Ibbur

The Narrative of Nascent Nesanel

Notes on the "Ibbur"

Fortunately for the great detective, the Watson family tree includes a great-grandson who became a rabbi, and it is he who assists Sherlock Holmes III with a most perplexing chess problem. Rabbi Solomon Rosenbaum will also explain the term (*ibbur*) to his colleague.

Unlike the other tales, the final adventure of our volume is not even loosely based on any historical event or chess personality. Instead, Holmes is asked to investigate an absolutely baffling mystery. A man in his twenties has picked up a pair of grandmaster norms. This would not be at all unusual, except that he was a hapless "wood-pusher" rated below 1300 less than a year earlier. An improvement of this sort is presumably impossible. Has he been cheating? Is he somehow getting help from a computer?

The chess authorities have been completely frustrated by their inability to figure out what is going on. Will Sherlock Holmes and the rabbi be able to help them put it to rest?

Obituary Notice, July 19, 2002

The chess world mourns the death of three-time United States champion and challenger for the women's world championship, Zehava Rosen, who died in an automobile accident yesterday afternoon. She was 22 years old and seemed destined to win the title. Sadly, she will not.

Rosen was only 19 years old when her accomplishments first became headline news. She captured the U.S. Women's title and qualified for tournaments in Europe. The following year, she defended her crown and dominated with a performance reminiscent of Bobby Fischer. She scored nine wins and two draws in eleven rounds, easily outdistancing the second-place finisher by three points. Last year, she won the championship for the third consecutive time, scoring eight wins and five draws against a larger field. More significantly, she won a series of qualifying matches and became the official challenger for women's world champion, Lotte Beekhof. The match was slated to begin in Amsterdam in October.

International Grandmaster Semyon Kuznetsov, who had served as Rosen's coach for the past five years, expressed sorrow upon learning of the tragedy. "She was phenomenal talent," he declared. "Zehava was true professional and beautiful kid. Yeah, officially I was her coach, but she was really more like daughter to me. It was always great pleasure to work with her, and I never saw more dedicated student of chess game. She was already rated thirty-one Elo points above Beekhof, and most people considered her favorite to win championship match. We'll never know how good she might have become."

Ms. Rosen was an only child. Her mother died when she was two, and her father died shortly after she captured her first United States championship. She was engaged to marry Nesanel Rabinowitz, a graduate student in literature at Samuel Clemens University.

Chapter 1

A Call from Sherlock Holmes (2003)

It was almost 6 p.m., and the *yahrzeit* candle I had lit in memory of my father was beginning to flicker. The telephone rang; it was John Simon, son of my mother's brother, whom I rarely saw these days but very much loved.

"How is my cousin, the rabbi, this afternoon?" he inquired.

"I am in excellent health, thank G-d," I replied. "How is my cousin, the doctor?"

This was a ritual in which we had indulged since shortly after I completed rabbinical studies twenty-two years earlier. He had evidently run across the old joke about the Jewish mother and "her son, the doctor," and readily adapted it to our own interpersonal relationship.

"Well, my dear rabbi," he continued, after we had briefly caught up with family affairs, "I am afraid I have ulterior motives for calling on you. I should like to ask you for a favor, although I must confess that I am totally in the dark as to precisely what I request."

"Do tell, John."

There was a pause at the other end of the phone line. "You surely remember the famous Sherlock Holmes, about whom our great-grandfather wrote so extensively."

"Of course. I also understand that my grandfather, uncle, and you all helped Sherlock Holmes Jr. and the Third on occasion."

My cousin chuckled. "Ah, I see the *Torah* and *Talmud* are not the only books you read. Now, let me ask you something a little more direct. How would you feel about assisting the last-named Holmes yourself?"

I gasped. "What would Sherlock Holmes III want with a rabbi, and how could I possibly help him? Surely, if he needs advice on Jewish customs and traditions, he can find people far better qualified than I."

"Ah, but you forget something, Solly. The Holmes and Watson families share a long history."

I hesitated. "That's true, John, but more often than not the Watsons provided a few medical details of which Holmes was unaware. I am a rabbi, not a physician. What is this case about?"

"Honestly, Coz, I don't know. The old man called me this morning, and I could tell he was agitated. "I think I require the services of a man of the cloth, John Simon," he began. 'This might perhaps beg the obvious question: priest, rabbi, minister, or perhaps an imam or swami, since I would not normally have a preference. However, on this occasion I must turn to the Jewish faith. I know you have a cousin who is an ordained rabbi, and while I never met the fellow, I have a feeling it is time for another Holmes-Watson collaboration."

"I told him that your surname was Rosenbaum, but he reminded me that you are my aunt's son, 'and thus as close to Watson *Primus* as you are, John Simon.' That's as much as I know. Now, are you willing?"

I still didn't follow. "Willing? Yes. Able? I...I don't know. Why don't you give me his number and let me get some details?"

"It will be easier if he calls you. He's in New York at the moment, and I'm sure he's busier than a one-armed paperhanger," John replied.

Well, who could turn down the chance to talk with Sherlock Holmes? "Sure," I said. "Give him all three of my numbers: home, synagogue, and cell."

* * *

My landline phone rang later that evening. "This is Sherlock Holmes, calling. Do I have the honor of addressing Rabbi Solomon Rosenbaum?"

"Sherlock Holmes!" I cried. "Yes; yes, indeed! Please call me Solly."

"Fair enough, then, Solly. Please call me Holmes, Sherlock, or Third, just as your cousin John Simon routinely does."

"With great pleasure, Third. Now, how can a humble rabbi be of assistance to a great detective?"

"It is a long story, my friend, and it involves the mystery with which I have been struggling for a full week. Perhaps we can discuss it in person. Are you free tomorrow?"

"More or less. We have morning and evening prayers, but nothing more, and I can easily have a colleague cover for me if necessary."

"Fair enough. You live in Westport, do you not?"

"Indeed."

"Can you pick me up at the train station on or around 10:47 tomorrow morning?"

"Of course."

"Excellent. I look forward to making your acquaintance, Solly."

"Likewise, Sherlock."

He hung up abruptly and left me scratching my head, trying to figure out what I had gotten myself into.

Chapter 2

A Baffling Mystery

The train from Manhattan arrived on time, and almost immediately my cell phone rang. Thanks to our dependable gadgets, we were able to locate one another quite quickly.

John had told me that Holmes was seventy-seven, although he didn't look a day over sixty, and but for the stubble of unshaven beard, he could probably have passed for mid-fifties. His eyes were remarkably clear; his gaze, penetrating.

"Have you had breakfast?" I inquired.

"Of course. We Brits can't get started without a hearty meal in the morning. I could use a cup of tea, though."

I smiled. "My wife keeps a marvelous collection on hand: black, green, or herbal. I'll brew up a pot as soon as we get home."

All the ride back I kept hoping Sherlock would start to discuss the case, but he seemed singularly disinclined to do so, and I felt it would be rude to ask. He did inquire about John, Carol, and their daughter, Joan, as well as my own family. Devorah and I have twin sons, Jacob and Mark, who were working as counsellors at a Jewish camp for four weeks.

Once the tea had been poured, Holmes was ready to get down to business. His first question, however, caught me by surprise.

"Do you play chess, Solly?" he inquired.

"Only occasionally, and not very well. However, my father, *alav hashalom*—excuse me, that means 'peace be upon him'—followed the game with great interest. He also played in tournaments and boasted that at one time he had an astronomer's rating of 2001."

Holmes looked puzzled for all of about two seconds. "Ah, yes; the Arthur C. Clarke novel, later a movie. So, you understand a little about ratings, then?"

I smiled. "I know that once his rating went down a couple of points, he was back in Class A, but that while it was over 2000, he was considered an expert. If I remember correctly, there are various classes below A, and master is above expert. The numbers relate to some sort of system that suggests the statistical likelihood that Player A will defeat Player B."

My visitor nodded. "Excellent, and you are correct. If the two players are a given number of points apart, the higher rated should win some given, higher percentage of the time. It's all mathematical, logical, and to at least some extent predictable, and that is why I am here."

I pulled gently on my beard. I had absolutely no idea what chess ratings, which had no practical meaning whatsoever in my life, had to do with Judaism.

"Perhaps I should begin at the beginning," Sherlock suggested, and I was in no position to disagree.

* * *

"Does the name, Yiorgos Papadopoulos, ring a bell? Do you know who he is?"

I nodded. "Of course. The leader of the Greek junta that overthrew the monarchy thirty-six years ago. He, in turn, was overthrown in 1973, and I believe he died two or three years ago."

An exasperated sigh from Sherlock assured me I was mistaken. "Both 'Yiorgos' and 'Papadopoulos' are common Greek names. The Yiorgos Papadopoulos who contacted me is Chairman of the Ethics Committee of FIDE."

The blank look on my face must have inspired Holmes to continue. "FIDE is the organization that organizes, monitors, and governs all aspects of chess at the international level. The acronym stands for *Fédération Internationale des Échecs*."

"I understand," I replied. "So, what do Mr. Papadopoulos and his committee actually do?"

"Their primary concern is sportsmanship, and of late they have become particularly concerned about cheating."

"Cheating?" I was skeptical. "How can anyone do that? Does a player walk into the tournament room with an extra Rook up his sleeve?"

Sherlock burst out laughing. "Would that it were that simple, Solly, but I'm afraid the game has a long and proud history of successful cheating, and now that we have computers and internet, I fear it can only get worse."

"Please explain," I said, and Sherlock began to tell me about various chess scandals over the centuries.

"If we agree that fraud and misrepresentation are forms of cheating, we can surely say that the various 'chess automatons' are prime examples. The Turk dates back to 1770, and the great Harry Nelson Pillsbury was among the masters who played the games for one of its successors, Ajeeb. However, the FIDE Ethics Committee has no interest in such ancient history.

"Collusion among players in tournaments is a far more legitimate problem. Some, including Bobby Fischer, have alleged that Soviet grandmasters often sat down to play games having agreed on the outcome ahead of time.

"Of course, players of all levels may be offered bribes. Take, for example, a situation in which one player will win a prize if he can draw his last-round game, while his opponent cannot possibly improve his standings, regardless of the outcome. A few dollars under the table may procure the half-point, but think how unfair that is to the player who would otherwise have garnered the laurels.

"Then there are the violations of the touch-move rule."

"What is 'touch-move'?" I asked.

"In tournaments, if a player touches a piece without first indicating he is 'adjusting' the piece on the square, he must move it; if he touches his opponent's piece, he must capture it, assuming it is legal to do so, and if he touches both one of his own and one of his opponent's, he must take the latter with the former if possible."

"Is that only in international tournaments?"

"No, Solly. It is the rule even in club events of the lowest level."

"But surely all the professionals know this rule, don't they?"

Holmes smiled. "Yes, but every once in a while, someone tries to evade it, particularly if his or her opponent is not looking."

"*Chas v'shalom*—excuse me again. You can translate that as 'G-d forbid,' if you like."

Sherlock blinked twice, nodded, and resumed. "Even more insidious, though, is the occasional incident in which a player may take his hand off a piece but then try to move it to another square instead. No less a figure than world champion Garry Kasparov would appear to have 'changed' his move in a game against then-17-year-old Judit Polar in a tournament in Linares, but he got away with it on some or other technicality."

"Wow! What about illegal moves, Holmes?"

"These are rare, but they certainly have arisen. In one tournament, a player had moved his King one square, then moved it back to the starting position, and later castled. His opponent somehow overlooked this clear violation of the rules. I also heard of a blitz tournament—that's five minutes for each player for the entire game—where both White and Black had just a few seconds remaining. Somehow, it seems the two opponents were in check at the same time. The tournament director noticed this, stopped the clock, and declared a draw.

"However, none of these has any relevance here. The real concern of Mr. Papadopoulos is that players may now be using technology to gain an unfair advantage. Have you heard of Deep Blue?"

"Indeed. That's the machine that beat the world champion a few years ago, isn't it?"

Holmes nodded. "Yes, and several chess engines have since been devised that can play at an extremely powerful level. As early as the 1993 World Open tournament in the United States, some unknown using the name of John von Neumann scored a remarkable 4½-4½ in the top section, drawing with a grandmaster and defeating a player rated 2350. Unfortunately for him, the device he carried in his pocket not only aroused suspicion but also made a buzzing sound. He was eventually disqualified.

"Now, bear in mind how much computers have improved in the past ten years, and how we also communicate more readily over the Internet. FIDE's concerns about potential problems escalate as cheaters become more and more refined in their craft."

It took me a while to process all of this. "But why has Mr. Papadopoulos contacted you?"

That mysterious "Holmes grin" flashed for just a second and disappeared. "Because," he said, "the gentleman is convinced that someone is cheating blatantly, yet he cannot establish any sort of proof whatsoever. However, something he said led me to believe that you, of all people, might be able to help me unravel the mystery. Are you interested?"

How could I decline? "Of course. But please tell me why you seek the assistance of a rabbi, rather than a physician. Such a preference is surely unprecedented."

Third gave me one of those penetrating stares before he spoke. "After nearly a week of deliberation, I have developed an absolutely bizarre suspicion, and if I am correct, you will surely be able to help me far more than John Simon possibly could. However, until I have more information, I must respectfully decline to offer anything further."

I reflected for a moment, nodded, and asked, "So, what do we do next, Sherlock?"

"If I may impose, perhaps you can drive us to Larchmont, New York, where Mr. Papadopoulos is staying with his cousin. I'm sure he can tell us more, and then we can drive back here."

Larchmont was only about forty-five minutes away. I asked for the address and directions, both of which Holmes had in his wallet, and we got into my car.

Chapter 3

"This Doesn't Smell Right, Sherlock!"

Westport, Connecticut, is an affluent town; Larchmont is probably even more so, perhaps simply because of the difference in population. I doubt Larchmont has much more than one-fifth the population of the community I now call home.

We made our way to the address provided, and Holmes telephoned as we were approaching. Mr. Papadopoulos and his cousin both came outdoors and waved to us as we pulled into the long driveway.

"My dear Mr. Papadopoulos," cried Holmes.

"My dear Mr. Holmes," responded the other. "Please call me Yiorgos, and if it's easier, feel free to call me George, since we shall converse in English."

"In that case," replied Holmes stiffly, "Sherlock or Third will do admirably. This gentleman," he added, pointing to me, "is my colleague and associate, Rabbi Solomon Rosenbaum."

I shook hands with George. "Please call me Solly," I said, smiling. "Everyone else does."

Papadopoulos introduced us to his cousin, Eleni, and we went inside. Eleni led us to the kitchen table, where we took seats while she brewed an enormous pot of some frightfully strong Greek coffee (the brand name of which eludes me).

"Well, then, George. Shall we begin?" Holmes asked, as we settled in.

"Indeed. You have both heard of Nesanel Rabinowitz?"

Sherlock had; I had not.

"He has become a sensation in the chess world these past few months. His rise has been meteoric. It is unprecedented, and it is also highly suspicious. Any rational observer would reach the same conclusion my committee reached almost immediately. Chess players can and do improve with study, experience, and coaching, but improvement on this scale can only be attributable to one thing. Nesanel must be cheating, and our task is to determine how."

Holmes stared at George without blinking, pursed his lips, and finally asked the obvious question. "Please share with Solly the reasons you assume he is cheating."

Papadopoulos slid a folder over to Third. "Less than a year ago, he was rated just under 1300 by the United States Chess Federation. Now he has two grandmaster norms and a FIDE rating of 2607. This doesn't smell right, Sherlock!"

"Explain."

"Okay. Nesanel has been working for a Ph.D. in literature at Samuel Clemens University. He rarely had time for chess, and had cracked the 1300s only once, dropping back down to 1295 the next tournament he played. But what happened thereafter?

"It was astonishing. He entered a couple of one-day tournaments, then a couple of others. He won every game he played. Then he entered the Cold Spring Open, and won that with a 5-0 score, defeating a master and two experts.

"Results of this sort defied logic, but what followed was stranger still. He entered the Western Hemisphere Open in Philadelphia. The top prize was $12,500, which is substantial, and the bonus was a place in the Western Hemisphere Invitational two weeks later. Do you both understand the system for grandmaster and international master norms?"

I shook my head, and the detective smiled. "Alas, no. My involvement with chess is rather minimal these days."

Papadopolous looked surprised. "Oh," he exclaimed. "I assumed...They told me you once defeated Alekhine, and by this time, you are probably the last man alive who can make that claim."

Holmes shook his head. "It was in a blindfold exhibition, and I received the added benefit of pawn-and move odds, so one can hardly say I defeated him one-on-one. That was before the War, and no; I rarely play these days."

The Greek swallowed and poured himself some more coffee. "Well, the normal route to the grandmaster title is as follows. One must enter a tournament with a sufficient number of titled players, an adequate average FIDE rating, and at least nine rounds of play. Depending upon the strength of the field, one must score some or other designated level to earn a norm. Three norms over at least twenty-seven rated games are required in all."

I wanted to contribute something, so I offered the only words that came to mind. "That sounds reasonable."

George shot me a quick glance. "Yes, it is, Rabbi. But how does someone who could hardly move a Knight sideways end up earning two such norms scarcely a year later? *That* is not reasonable."

"We must leave such judgments aside," admonished Sherlock. "Please provide the specific details."

Papadopolous took another sip of coffee. If you open up that folder, you will see the breakdown. Please read what you see."

Holmes took a moment to digest the information. "This was a fairly strong field. If I interpret the data you present here correctly, Rabinowitz played against nine players with an average rating of 2562. He required five points, and that is what he scored: a win, a loss, and four draws against the grandmasters, a win and two draws against the international masters: fourth place overall on tiebreak."

Even I could understand that this was an impressive accomplishment. As a rated expert, my late father never remotely approached this level—yet my father could also have given odds of a Rook to the Nesanel of just a few months earlier.

"The result was even better than it appears on paper," George continued. "The directors of the Merano Invitational in Italy had guaranteed that the top two finishers would be invited to their tournament. As it happened, the top two had committed to play in other tournaments, so the slots went to the players who finished third and fourth."

"And let me guess—Mr. Rabinowitz got another norm there?" I asked.

The FIDE chairman grimaced. "It was a similar field. Tell him what happened, Sherlock."

The old friend of my family scowled. "The average rating was lower—2530—and the event was eleven rounds, so a grandmaster norm was seven. Rabinowitz scored 8½-2½, with four wins, one loss, and two draws against the grandmasters, and three wins and a draw against the international masters. He also finished in clear first place by half a point. Extraordinary!"

We both looked back at Papadopolous, who stared into his coffee. At length he drained the cup and addressed Third. "You see my problem, don't you? That a child of ten years old might accomplish such prodigies within four years is unlikely but possible. That a man of twenty-seven could do this in little more than one year is impossible."

"Could he have been 'sandbagging' earlier?" inquired the detective. "Is it possible he was in fact quite strong, but preferred to 'lie low' and wait for the right moment?"

George shook his head. "To what end, Holmes? From what we have been told, he learned to play only a few years ago, when his girlfriend taught him."

Sherlock offered a wan smile. "You have checked him for electronic devices—cell phone, a microcomputer?"

"Of course. We found nothing."

"Ah, but perhaps he got some help when he was not in the tournament hall," suggested Holmes. "For example, when he went to the conveniences."

Papadopolous shook his head in confusion, so I explained. "The restroom."

"Impossible. Even if he could get help from a computer in one particular position, that would occur only once or twice per game without arousing suspicion. However, Nesanel walks into the hall a few minutes early, shakes hands with his opponent, sits down, and never once has anyone observed him leaving the room. He may occasionally stand up and walk around to observe other games, but he is always in the room. There seems to be no way for him to receive a signal, but perhaps you can see something I don't, Sherlock."

The old man drained his cup and frowned. "It is much too early for me to offer my thoughts," he said at last. "What can you tell us about the quality of the games and the style of play?"

George reached across the table and refilled his cup yet again, but then pushed it aside. "If I keep drinking Eleni's coffee like this, I'll be up all night," he declared. "I must confess I haven't studied the play that carefully, but there is someone who can tell us more."

"Of course, there is," replied Sherlock. "You told us that his girlfriend taught him how to play, but you neglected one minor detail, didn't you?"

Papadopolous smiled. "You are good, Mr. Holmes, and you do your homework. Yes, his girlfriend was the late Zehava Rosen."

My jaw dropped. If I live to one hundred twenty, I shall never forget the strange, eerie chills that ran down my spine. Somehow, this all sounded vaguely familiar, but I couldn't quite put my finger on what came to mind.

Third's voice snapped me out of my mild trance. "Let me guess again," he said. "We are going to place a call to Semyon Kuznetsov."

Chapter 4

A Coach's Evaluation

Fortune smiled on us, and Papadopolous was able to reach the grandmaster. Kuznetsov was at the Sonesta Hotel in White Plains, serving as coach for a team of high school players who had entered an interscholastic tournament. Later in the day he would give a simultaneous exhibition, but he assured us that within half an hour he would be free to speak with us for up to an hour. Since we were twenty-three minutes or so away, this would work perfectly for us, also. Kuznetsov knew George, of course, and he had certainly heard of Sherlock Holmes, although he did not realize he would be speaking with the grandson of *that* Sherlock Holmes.

We invited the FIDE official and his cousin to come with us, but they declined. "I think it will be best if I am out of the picture," he explained. "You are the detective, not I, and I don't want to get in your way. Nevertheless, I trust you will let me know what you learn—and please feel free to return if you have time."

The drive to White Plains was uneventful, and Semyon found us in the lobby less than five minutes after we arrived. He suggested that we adjourn to his room, where we might speak more freely. "It is old habit from Soviet Union," he explained. "We used to say, 'the walls have ears.' Here is not so bad, but I get uneasy when strange person walks by too close."

Kuznetsov had been given a large room with a table and chairs, and we made ourselves comfortable. As soon as we were settled and completed the customary formalities, Holmes began to ask our host about Nesanel Rabinowitz.

"Nice fellow," he began. "I met him twice when he accompanied Zehava. I offered to coach him, but she explained he does not really have much interest in chess."

He shook his head, sadly. "Then came horrible, horrible tragedy. She was such beautiful girl, always polite to everybody, her opponents, cab drivers…So talented, and she worked so hard, Mr. Holmes."

Third's face registered no emotion—of course—but he nodded sympathetically, which was perhaps the best he could do. "Have you had any contact with Mr. Rabinowitz since Miss Rosen's death?"

After a long sigh Semyon responded. "Yes. I actually went to funeral, but we didn't really talk there. Then, I came to house some few days later. Nesanel was sitting *shiva*—perhaps rabbi can tell you more about this," he added, motioning to me.

Holmes nodded. "I am familiar with the custom," he explained. "Now, what can you tell me about Zehava's relationship with Miss Beekhof?"

The grandmaster seemed to wince from the pain of an old wound. "They truly got along very well, Mr. Holmes. They played twice, you know?"

Sherlock shook his head. "I was unaware that they had ever faced off over the board."

"First time was two years ago, in Olympiad." He turned to me abruptly. "That is team event, and United Stated played Netherlands." Then he refocused on Third. "She was maybe little too excited about this game, in my opinion. She had even position, nothing more, but she tried too hard to make win out of draw. In end, she overextended and lost. We spent lots of time on that game afterward, and she learned from experience.

"Second time they played was in tournament one year later, where they tied for first. Both had chances, but Beekhof took game toward draw, and this time Zehava accepted half-point."

"There was no bitterness that she never defeated the champion?"

"No, no, no!" Kuznetsov insisted. "They were truly good friends. During tournament, they went over games together and played blitz for fun. After chess, they even enter big amateur badminton tournament and take bronze medal in doubles."

Holmes stared into space, his eyes almost glazed over. Then he looked up. "Did Miss Rosen ever speak to you about her goals and ambitions—things she wanted to do after she became champion? She was obviously a brilliant woman. Did she perhaps mention returning to the university and completing her degree?"

Semyon shook his head. "All she wanted was to become champion. In fact, she used to look me right in eye and say, 'I will defeat Lotte Beekhof for *you*, Semyon. I promise you!' She must have told me this twenty-five or thirty times, Mr. Holmes."

As far as I could tell, the grandmaster had given us absolutely nothing. I expected Third to thank him for his time, shake hands, wish him well, and depart. To my surprise, the old man pursued another line of thought.

"You surely knew your student's style quite well," he began. "Have you had the opportunity to review any of Nesanel's games?"

"Yes, I did. I never saw anything before invitational event in Philadelphia, but he sent me polite note and told me he had made first grandmaster norm. He also sent tournament cross-table and scores of all his games." Kuznetsov paused. "Now that you mention it, this is rather strange, because Zehava used to do that, also."

I suddenly found myself paying keen attention. "Fascinating," I mumbled.

"And the style of play?" Third asked.

"Was very similar style: not overly aggressive as White, much more so as Black. In fact, they both had better scores with Black. Here—let me show you on computer."

Semyon took out his laptop and opened the appropriate file. "Nesanel also sent scores and cross-table from second tournament. Now you will see."

He pointed to the screen, and I looked over Sherlock's shoulder as Kuznetsov continued. "In Philadelphia he has two wins as Black, one loss as White, the rest draws. In Merano he wins seven games, loses one, draws three. Four wins are with Black, while three wins and only loss are with White. Most players do better with White, and only other person I know who did better as Black—." He hesitated as though overcome by emotion. "Zehava!" he whispered.

"And the games themselves?" I asked, even before Sherlock could pose the same question.

"If I had coached Nesanel, I would perhaps be able to tell you more. I have seen only these twenty games, which is perhaps not enough. Still, many similarities are striking. The cautious style, waiting for slightest blunder and ready to punish opponent's mistake…the choice of openings. Sometimes those draws come from what looks like 'lost' position, but Mr. Rabinowitz is ferocious defender. I would need to see more, of course, but if I didn't know better, I would say that these twenty games were played by Zehava."

I thought I saw the slightest hints of a smile on my colleague's face. He nodded repeatedly and then he spoke. "Remarkable! I thank you very, very much. You have been immensely helpful, Mr. Kuznetsov."

We all stood up, and the grandmaster shook hands with us both. "It has been my great honor to assist famous Mr. Holmes," he assured us.

Third was in splendid humor as we got into my car. "You must permit me to take you to a tiny kosher restaurant I know in Scarsdale, Solly. It's a little dive, but they have some private alcoves, and at this bizarre hour—too late for lunch; too early for dinner—I am quite sure we can procure one. The food is delicious, and the service is marvelous. It's a tad in the wrong direction for Westport, but there is no need for us to return to Larchmont."

Who was I to decline such an invitation?

Holmes called Mr. Papadopolous and told him he was making excellent progress. "I shall call you again within a couple of hours," he promised. "I must first speak at length with my learned colleague, Rabbi Rosenbaum."

He hung up abruptly, looked directly at me, and asked, "Now, are you ready to tell me what needs to be done?"

Chapter 5

I Offer Holmes My Rabbinical Advice!

"How marvelous when things work out exactly as one has hoped," exclaimed my companion as we got into the car and worked our way down Route 22-South to Scarsdale. "I still find everything rather difficult to believe, of course. In fact, my first impulse was to dismiss my notion as rubbish. However, after our discussion with Mr. Kuznetsov, I am convinced that I do indeed have a viable hypothesis. If I am correct, you will surely be able to put this mystery to rest."

"Explain, Third."

"Without intending to do so, the grandmaster has confirmed my suspicions to at least some extent. Now it is up to you to verify them and tell me what to do about the situation at hand."

It was a short drive, and Holmes assured me he would fill in the gaps once we had been served. I knew better than to prod him.

Bloom's Restaurant in Scarsdale—not to be confused with the famous Bloom's of London—was one of those bizarre places that one would never expect to find in a town with a population of barely 15,000. Like its English counterpart, it was not destined for a long life, and I read (with sadness) that they closed their doors less than two years after Sherlock and I dined there. The food was excellent, and the service did not disappoint us, either. Moreover, we were indeed able to procure a small alcove, where we could speak freely in our near-isolation.

"Well, you have surely come to the only possible conclusion, haven't you?" Holmes asked.

I swallowed nervously. "If I catch your drift, I think you are saying that Semyon didn't tell the whole truth. They play in a similar style, because Semyon has been coaching Nesanel, probably for many years."

The old man gave me one of his polite smiles and said the word I was afraid he would use: "Rubbish!"

"Okay, Sherlock. What am I missing? Everyone agrees that Nesanel could not have made this type of improvement in so little time. However, if he practiced regularly with Zehava, and both of them were studying with Semyon, that would explain his meteoric rise and the similarities in their styles. Do you have a more plausible explanation?"

Another smile! "Of course, although as recently as earlier today I would have been embarrassed to articulate it. And I shall share it, though not before I remind you of an old adage that three generations of the Holmes family have shared with four generations of Watsons: Once you have eliminated the impossible, whatever remains, however improbable, must be the truth. You have heard this before?"

I nodded. "I have read all the accounts, from those of John Hamish through those of my cousin, John Simon."

"Excellent. And now let us agree that no player with a sub-1300 rating could possibly earn two grandmaster norms in just about a year. Let us also agree that two people, even a couple engaged to be married, could not possibly play the game in so similar a style. Had such improvement been even remotely possible, Yiorgos Papadopoulos would not have offered me a handsome fee plus expenses to investigate.

"Meanwhile, what were Semyon Kuznetsov's exact words? '...if I didn't know better, I would say that these twenty games were played by Zehava!' One player may mock the style of another in one or two games, but twenty in a row? Again: impossible."

"So, what 'remains, however improbable'?" I asked.

The great detective sighed. "As soon as I began to favor this improbable explanation, I knew I wanted you to assist me, Solly. Now we have reached the point at which I must put aside my rational cerebration and ask the obvious questions: Doesn't this entire mystery suggest a case of possession? More explicitly, since we are dealing with people of the Jewish faith, we must also consider whether Zehava has perhaps become a *dybbuk*—that is the right term, isn't it? If so, and if I remember correctly, a rabbi like you should be able to exorcise the spirit that possesses the young graduate student."

One could have knocked me over with a feather. "Uh…Sherlock. I'm afraid you have caught me off-guard. I am certainly not qualified to perform such an exorcism—"

"…but you can put me in touch with someone who can?"

"I—I think so."

Suddenly I remembered something. "No…wait! I'm afraid you have the terms confused, Third. What has entered Nesanel is not a *dybbuk*, but an *ibbur*."

And now it was Sherlock's turn to be surprised. He had never heard of an *ibbur*, so I first tried to explain the concept. "The *dybbuk* is essentially an evil spirit that has entered a living person. In its more popular form, the *dybbuk* is the spirit of a dead person that speaks through the mouth of the living person it inhabits."

"Ah," cried Holmes. "That is what we see in the play by Shloyme Zanvl Rappoport, better known as S. Ansky, is it not? I caught it on BBC Radio some years ago."

"Yes, that's the one, and as you surely remember, Rabbi Azriel ultimately performs the exorcism and expels the *dybbuk*."

The detective shrugged. "Khonen was not necessarily 'evil,' but he felt betrayed. Still, that did not give him the right to haunt the body of the woman he considered his betrothed. However, the play is clearly of no consequence with respect to the matter at hand. Please tell me a little more about the *ibbur.*"

I took a sip of the delicious tea we had been served. "An *ibbur* is decidedly *not* an evil entity. On the contrary, it may be a most righteous soul that does indeed meld with the soul of a living person, but only so that it can accomplish or finish some task or perhaps perform some *mitzvah.* Are you familiar with the term?"

"I believe it is a sort of righteous act or good deed of religious devotion, but that is also, irrelevant, Solly. What you just said provides our answer, does it not? You told me the *ibbur* seeks to complete a task, and I must assume you refer to something the soul could not accomplish in life. Is that not so?"

I hesitated. "Why...yes, I believe that is correct."

"And once the task or that *mitzvah* has been completed, it will presumably leave?"

"To the best of my knowledge, yes."

Holmes grinned from ear to ear. "Then it is blatantly obvious, Rabbi. Semyon Kuznetsov was kind enough to tell us what mission it—Zehava—must fulfill. She told him twenty-five to thirty times, 'I will defeat Lotte Beekhof for *you*, Semyon. I promise you!' It is almost too simple."

The confused look on my face must have alerted the perceptive Sherlock that his solution had sailed over my head. "We must convince Nesanel to play a match against Miss Beekhof. At the same time, I shall do everything in my power to encourage Mr. Papadopoulos to put aside what will surely be numerous misgivings and sanction the event. Now, let me ask you one final question. Is Nesanel even aware that the soul of Zehava has melded with his own, and that she is effectively 'inside' him?"

I assured Holmes that as far as I knew, the living person may have no idea of what is going on. "However," I added, "we cannot generalize, since sometimes the host may have given consent, and in the case of a man whose fiancée has perished, all bets are off."

* * *

When we returned to Wesport, Holmes called Papadopoulos from the landline, while I listened over the extension phone. "George," he began. "I would like you to arrange a short match—not a championship, but just an exhibition. Twist arms if you need to, but it is of the utmost importance that Lotte Beekhof and Nesanel Rabinowitz engage over the board."

The FIDE official did not sound particularly enthusiastic. "What? This is highly unusual, Sherlock. I do *not* like the idea at all, and I don't know how I can sell it."

"Bah!" exclaimed the other. "How can it *not* sell? Neither player will object to an extra payday. Miss Beekhof and her late challenger evidently got along quite well, and she will surely feel this is a token gesture for the benefit of her deceased friend. It is also a man vs. woman thing, and the man in question was engaged to Zehava Rosen. Their ratings are not too far apart.

"Look at the news coverage you will get. Corporate sponsors will be only too happy to raise a nice purse, and the champion does not even have to worry about possible loss of her title."

"But how will this resolve the issue of whether Rabinowitz is cheating?" George inquired, skeptical.

I could almost hear Sherlock's smile. "I can unequivocally guarantee you that once the match has concluded, you will not need to worry about that problem any longer," he promised.

Papadopoulos argued for a while longer, capitulated, and reluctantly agreed to sanction a four-game match. However, sponsors offered far more money for a contest of six games, which they felt would provide a more reliable result. Ms. Beekhof, who was a professional to the core, also expressed a preference for six, and the matter was settled.

Meanwhile, Holmes and I met with Nesanel, and as I suspected, he was completely unaware of the *ibbur* or any other manifestation of Zehava's presence. Nevertheless, he readily conceded that regardless of how improbable, this was surely the only possible way to explain his extraordinary success. He agreed to the match (of course) and specifically asked to have Semyon as his coach and chief second. The latter was only too happy to oblige.

* * *

Holmes had returned to London, while I resumed my rabbinical duties. However, we stayed in touch via Skype, and both of us followed the match.

Nesanel, with White, almost lost the first game in time pressure. However, he bounced back and took the second game with Black. A draw in the third gave him a 2-1 lead at the half-way point. The next two games were also drawn, and the score stood 3-2 in Nesanel's favor.

At the press conference Lotte promised to "go all out" in the finale, while Nesanel said he hoped he would fare a little better than Schlechter had against Lasker in the last game of their match.

So, what happened? Nesanel made it abundantly clear that he was playing for a win. He chose an aggressive opening, and the post-game press conference told the story.

"First off," began Lotte Beekhof, "I must congratulate my opponent. I am still a little stunned by the result, and particularly by this last game."

"You always open with e4. Why did you switch to the Queen's pawn for this decisive game?" a commentator inquired.

"I had lost to Nesanel's Sicilian defense in the second game, and I got nowhere when he switched to the Petroff in the fourth game. Since I always open with the King's pawn, my team and I thought he might be a little unprepared for the Queen's pawn. Moreover, we had also studied all of his games against that move, and we thought we saw several lines that might offer me some chances."

"But you never got the opportunity to try them. Nesanel, when your opponents have pushed their Queen's pawn, you have always answered with the same move or else by moving your King's Knight. This time you hesitated for almost three minutes and then moved your King's Bishop's pawn. What were you thinking?"

Rabinowitz smiled. "I should have played something quiet and safe, but instead I chose a truly aggressive idea. I wanted to gain a psychological advantage, and I could not think of anything more jarring than to play the Dutch Defense against this wonderful Dutch champion."

His defeated opponent laughed heartily. "It was definitely 'jarring,' I assure you."

And thus, the match ended, 4-2. Shortly afterward Nesanel withdrew from the next tournament he had committed to play, returned to Samuel Clemens, and resumed work on his dissertation. A few weeks later, he announced his retirement from chess and said he would never play again. I believe Sherlock Holmes and I—and perhaps Semyon—are the only people who understand why.

Having logged a total of twenty-six games—including the six-game match, which might not have counted—Nesanel Rabinowtiz fell at least one short of the number required for the title of international grandmaster. Somehow that didn't seem to bother him.

Semyon did not attend the final press conference, but we later heard the old grandmaster had been moved to tears when Lotte Beekhof resigned the last game of the match. He left the hall abruptly, and we never saw him thereafter.

The *ibbur*? As I had told the great Sherlock Holmes, she had one great mission to accomplish. Once she had fulfilled her promise to Semyon Kuznetsov, it was time to move on.